RUSSIAN TATTOOS: OBSESSION

A DARK MAFIA ROMANCE

K.M. SHEHATA

ANGEL BEA PUBLISHING

Cover design by Angel Bea Publishing

Eagle logo design by Jo Ellen

In loving memory of Jo.
Thanks for supporting my dream, Mom.

CONTENT NOTE

This story contains scenes of violence and emotional intensity that may be unsettling for some readers.

1

CROOKED

Dad steered the Camry down a narrow driveway and stopped in front of a wrought-iron security gate. He popped a handful of mints into his mouth, then pressed an intercom button to announce our arrival. A buzzer sounded, and the gate opened.

With barbed wire surrounding the compound and such elaborate security measures, it seemed more like a maximum-security prison than a private residence.

Dad rolled the car forward and eyed me in the rearview mirror. "Thanks for giving up your Friday night, Carter." He had one of those jolly faces that put people at ease, but since his layoff, it was rare to see him smile. "Vladimir is anxious to meet you."

"No problem." I had no clue why some Russian billionaire needed to meet *me* before he offered my dad a job, but with Dad unemployed since the spring, it was an offer I couldn't refuse.

"Fair warning, your dad's been bragging about you," my stepmom, Karen, said.

The tires crackled on the gravel as we inched toward a

humongous estate. It was hard to imagine a twenty-seven-year-old techie could afford this swanky mansion.

"Where did you meet this Russian genius?"

"Funny story. He was behind me in line at Starbucks and noticed a logo on my computer bag from an IT conference I'd attended last year. We got to talking, and it turns out he's hiring a CIO, so I gave him my business card. I know it's a big jump from my last job, but..."

I patted his shoulder assuredly. "It must be fate. He'd be crazy not to pick the greatest computer fixer guy ever, right?"

Karen put her hand on Dad's leg and squeezed his knee in support of my mini pep talk. Our financial situation had reached the tipping point. Dad had to get this job.

"There's a peacock." I tapped on the window.

I guess the bird heard me, or maybe it was afraid of the car, but it cawed and escaped to the safety of a low-hanging tree limb.

Beware. Turn around. Run for your lives...

At the top of a flight of marble stairs, a scowling butler opened the double mahogany doors and swept his arm forward but didn't utter a word. His invitation skills could use some work. The scent of burning firewood greeted us in the entryway, which was illuminated by an impressive crystal chandelier that hung above our heads.

The butler handed us house slippers in exchange for our street shoes, a Russian thing, I surmised. I changed out of my flats, and a domineering man with bushy eyebrows met us in the foyer.

"Good evening, Mr. and Mrs. Cook. I am Boris Chuchin, Vladimir Ivanov's personal assistant." His creepy Russian accent was so thick, I could barely understand him. Dad introduced Karen and presented Boris with a bottle of wine that I was certain cost more than our weekly grocery budget. Boris didn't smile or nod or even pretend to give a shit about the wine—or Karen.

"And this is my daughter, Carter." Dad put his hands on my shoulders and nudged me toward the big guy like he was serving up some tasty offering to appease the Village Giant.

Boris, who resembled a buffalo standing on his hind legs, let out a *humph* sound and glared at me like I was something nasty Dad had dragged into the master's house on the bottom of his shoe.

"Nice to meet you, Mr. Ch-ch-chuch—" I held out my hand.

"Boris." He stroked his bristly salt-and-pepper beard and eyed my hand like I had bird crap splattered across my palm. "I will let Vladimir know you have arrived." He narrowed his eyes at me and then left to fetch his boss.

Jeez. Are college girls germy plague carriers back in Russia?

As we waited, a black and white drawing of a woman with a lopsided face caught my attention. I squinted to see the signature: Picasso.

From across the room, Boris opened a set of French doors, and Vladimir breezed into the living room with the confidence of an expensive-suit-wearing Russian god.

"Ricky, my friend." He cruised over to Dad and greeted him with a smile and a handshake, like they had known each other for years. His perfectly tousled hair was slicked back, and the soft waves congregated above his crisp white collar.

Dad introduced Karen, and then Vladimir directed all his energy on me. His stare was intense, and his blue eyes lit up with adoration as though he *recognized* me. "*Privet*, Miss Cook." His words were laced with a delicious Russian accent. "Your papa speaks highly of you. It is a pleasure to meet you in the flesh."

Flesh. My cheeks warmed. "Nice to meet you." I offered my hand for a businesslike shake. A rush of nervous excitement tingled in my stomach when Vladimir took my hand, pressed his lips against my skin, and kissed me softly.

I inhaled a shaky breath and glanced away, embarrassed by my reaction to Dad's potential new employer. Vladimir placed his other hand on top of mine and patted it apologetically. "Pardon me for staring, but you have your sister's beautiful hazel eyes."

I blinked like a clubbed seal. "How do you know my sister? She's *dead*."

2

NEVERLAND

Vladimir straightened his back and relaxed his penetrating stare. "My apologies, Miss Cook. I should have been more sensitive. The accident—such a pity."

A pity? Sophia went up in flames.

"Sorry, I should've told you," Dad said to me. "Funny story. After we got to talking the other day, we discovered Vladimir knew your sister way back when. He lived in Brooklyn at the same time we did." Dad's forehead was as shiny as a greased pig. He dabbed off the sweat beads onto his sleeve and then draped his arm across my shoulder. "Some coincidence, huh?"

I shook off my bewilderment and gave Dad a reassuring smile. "Yeah, what're the odds?"

"Let's get some fresh air and enjoy our drinks outside." Vladimir extended his elbow to escort me to the patio. I shrugged off Dad's arm, placed my hand on Vladimir's ripped bicep, and strolled away with him out back to a tropical Ohio paradise.

Despite the early December weather, the patio felt

toasty and inviting. Heat lamps and potted palm trees lined the terrace, and a fireplace burned real wood next to the built-in stone bar. Vladimir handed Karen a glass of champagne and then offered one to me.

"Oh, I'm not old enough."

"One small glass for a toast. I insist." He had rings on all his fingers—some real, others tattoos.

I glanced over at Dad.

"One glass." Dad would've never agreed under different circumstances.

Vladimir lifted his glass and gave a toast in Russian. With a charming smile, he translated the toast, "To new beginnings."

We repeated the sentiment, clinked, and sipped.

Then Vladimir wrapped his arm around my shoulder and guided me to the chic seating area by the fireplace. "Your papa tells me you're a tennis player." When he lowered his arm, his hand swept over the long, bouncy, blonde waves I had curled into my hair. "You play for your college team?"

"Vladimir plays, too." Dad sounded relieved to move on to a subject more palatable than his dead daughter.

"I'm on two teams. My college team is finished with competitions for the year, so my teammates and I play in an interclub league to stay competitive."

"Carter is an incredible athlete," Dad said. "She's always on the court. The best part is, she practices at the tennis club next to our house, so she can live at home and commute to campus."

"Lucky me," I said, more sarcastically than I'd intended.

"You must be a talented athlete," Vladimir said, taking in my muscular biceps and shoulders. I bit my lip and fantasized about the cut of his body under his perfectly tailored suit. When his eyes finished making a lap around my body, he smiled, unashamed I had busted him checking me out.

"Just competitive." I smoothed down the fabric of the curve-hugging green velvet dress I'd borrowed from my best friend Kiki.

"Competitive is an understatement," Dad scoffed. "Last year, during a high school soccer game, she fell and broke her arm—"

"I didn't *fall*. The fullback tripped me."

"How awful," Vladimir said. "Did your team win the match?"

I pointed at Dad. "See? He gets it. What matters is the *outcome* of the game. Details about broken bones are just background noise."

Vladimir's eyes sparkled. He understood my win-or-die trying competitive spirit.

Dad tossed his hands up and laughed. "See these grays, Vladimir? I had a full head of thick dark hair—then, she hit high school."

There's his happy face.

"Finish the story, princess." Dad's cheeks were rosy, his complexion glowing.

"I stayed in the game, scored two goals, my team won. The end."

Vladimir licked his lips. "I admire your fire, Miss Cook." He lifted his champagne glass and rattled off something in Russian that sounded incredibly bold and supremely confident—and toe-curlingly sexy. He tried to clink my glass, but I held it back.

"Not until you tell me what it means." I challenged him with a wry smile.

He lifted an eyebrow, unaccustomed to being denied. "Something good." He flashed a wicked grin and raised his glass, not willing to reveal his secret. His teeth were crooked but dazzling white.

I sighed in mock defeat and raised my glass, momentarily giving him the impression he had won. Then I clinked his glass and replied, "*Za zdorov'ye.*" I was sure I'd butchered the *to your health* toast I'd picked up from Dad's Russian culture book that he'd been studying, but Vladimir seemed intrigued at my attempt to impress him.

"*Touché*, Miss Cook." Vladimir winked and downed his drink, amused either by the idea I had outplayed him or my horrid attempt to speak his language.

The staff laid out a spread of hors d'oeuvres on the table behind us. I'm a vegetarian, and it's tricky to find food at parties. Just the smell of cooked meat was enough to trigger a gag reflex. I decided to play it safe and steer clear of the buffet, so Dad wouldn't have to worry about my "overreaction" to rotting flesh.

"My personal chef has prepared this meal with my tastes in mind. I don't eat meat," Vladimir said. "I hope it's enough to sustain you."

No. Freaking. Way.

Boris brought out a bottle of vodka and set it down in front of his boss. Worried I had stolen the limelight from Dad, I made a plate and wandered off to sit at an outdoor couch at the edge of the patio that overlooked the pool. I didn't want to be a distraction as they imbibed and hopefully discussed the details of the job Dad so desperately needed.

I felt the searing heat of Boris's intimidating gaze and tossed him an obligatory grin. He narrowed his eyes at me like I was some troublemaking rodent that needed to be exterminated and disappeared into the house. Flipping through my phone, I saw my aunt had sent me a picture of my little sister cuddling a calico cat in her lap. Since we would be out way past her bedtime, Megan was spending the night with Karen's sister. I texted her back.

Sweet! Tell Chloe meow, meow, meow.

As I texted, I heard the tapping of toenails on the patterned concrete and set down my phone. Two big, poufy poodles pranced at my feet and whimpered for attention. "Hi, cuties." I held out my hands to greet them.

Boris towered over me, restraining them with long, leather leashes. "This one is Gustav," he pointed to the black one, "and gray bitch is Anastasia."

"Oh, they're so sweet. I used to carry twin poodles around with me when I was little, a black one and a white one—well, it started off white and then turned gray because I wouldn't let Dad drown her in the washing machine."

I picked up my phone and tapped the screen. "See?" I showed Boris a picture of my late sister Sophia, hugging me as I cuddled my favorite stuffed animals in my arms. It was taken in Brooklyn before Dad moved us here to a suburb of Cincinnati. It was a windy day, and our wild hair was flying all over the place. I laughed, remembering the fun we'd had at Coney Island. Our biological mother ditched our family when I was a baby, and Sophia was eight, leaving my big sister to fill her maternal shoes.

Boris glanced at the picture and managed a tiny smile that looked painful for him to conjure up. "You look like big sister."

"Dad said my resemblance to her is *haunting*."

He made a *humph* sound and handed me the dog's leads. "Take them out back to play. Be careful of construction." He picked up a remote from the bar and turned on the lights to illuminate the yard.

Across the patio, Karen and Dad cooed. I turned to see what they were gawking at, and then it was my turn to be wowed. The construction Boris was referring to was a nearly completed tennis court.

"Next time, bring your racket," Vladimir called out to me. His meat-free bachelor pad was too good to be true. Alcohol, playful poodles, and a tennis court: My own personal *Neverland.*

3

INFESTATION

The next morning, I went for a run and then headed to the tennis club to cover the early shift at the smoothie bar. I picked up all the hours I could get and saved every penny. Kiki and I were moving into our own apartment in June. I hadn't laid the news on Dad yet because he would come up with a thousand reasons why I shouldn't do it.

The dangers of two young ladies living alone... Dad's overprotective nature gave me a migraine. When he'd asked why I was working so much, I said I was saving for a car.

I jogged up the sidewalk and noticed a matte black G-Wagon with red leather seats parked in the lot. A small metal badge on the back of the truck read '*AMG*.' That must mean *extra expensive* in car speak. Maybe someone famous was there to visit the club owner, Mr. Cusimano, an Italian tennis god with powerful connections.

Rumors had been swirling that he associated with the mafia, but that seemed ridiculous.

I walked to the bar, tied on an apron, and yelped when I turned around and spotted Vladimir reading over the menu board. His muscular, sweaty body was covered in a black-and-blue Lacoste ensemble complete with coordinating shoes with little green gators on each side. In my shabby sweats and a craptastic t-shirt from Little Sibs Weekend, I felt like a mismatched athletic hobo compared to him.

"*Dobroye utro.* Good morning, Miss Cook." His soft, dirty-blond waves were curled up into sweaty ringlets above his shoulders.

Sexy. "What are you doing here? I mean, I've never seen you here before." I laughed at my awkwardness.

He dabbed his forehead with a gym towel. "I only play weekends. Just finished up a match with Anthony."

"Mr. Cusimano? You must be special. He usually only hits with pros."

He gave me an arrogant wink and asked me what to order. I told him I would make him something healthy. My stomach did flip-flops as the Vitamix annihilated the greens. I pushed the stop button and poured the thick sludge into a plastic cup.

When the veggie bile hit his taste buds, he winced.

Way to go. Give the guy who can have anything liquefied spinach. "You don't like it?"

"Tastes like sewage." He set it down and waved his hand over it.

I laughed and poured him a glass of water to chase down the slime. "I said it was healthy, not that it tasted good. By the way, the spread at your house was awesome last night."

My tennis coach, a stocky dude who carried himself like a badass, steely-eyed pit bull, stalked past the counter and flashed me "the look." He glanced up at Vladimir, then back to me.

Had I sounded flirty? Louder than necessary, I said, "So,

my dad had a lot of nice things to say about you after the party."

Perhaps also catching Coach's admonishing glare, Vladimir smiled. "Your papa is a smart man. With a beautiful family."

"Are you going to hire him?" As soon as I said it, I knew I'd crossed the line. "I'm sorry. It's none of my business."

He made a *tsk* sound to forgive my forwardness. "I called him this morning. He's going over the contract."

"That's great." The stress of him not having a job had weighed on all of us. "Oh, let me make you something else. Do you like peanut butter?"

"You have tortured me enough. Let me take you out to breakfast."

My mouth gaped. *Did he just ask me out?* It was fun to fantasize about him, but the invitation felt awkward. This was my dad's new boss. "I'm afraid I can't, Mr. Ivanov."

He paused like I had given him the wrong answer, and he was waiting patiently for me to correct my faux pas.

"I mean, not now. I just started my shift. Another time?"

He inhaled sharply and set a bill on the counter. "Keep the change." He headed to the locker room.

I picked up the money and stumbled to the register—it was a hundred-dollar bill. My stomach felt queasy. An important guy like Vladimir probably wasn't used to being turned down. Should I have been more receptive to his invitation?

Between customers, I kept myself busy restocking the grab-n-go items and sports drinks, and then a red-faced Mr. Cusimano appeared at my counter, rubbing the back of his neck like he had a termite infestation under his skin. The guy could be a crank, but the last time I'd seen him that stressed out, he'd lost a couple of stacks on a boxing match.

"Good morning, Mr. Cusimano. Can I make you something?"

He didn't answer. His body was tense, and his face so agitated, it appeared he was being burned alive from the inside out.

"Are you okay? Can I get you some water?" I reached for a cup.

He handed me a sheet of paper. "Go over these numbers and let me know where accounting has made an error."

I felt the blood drain from my face. It was a record of all my extra court time. Whenever I wasn't working, the pros let me join their group lessons. They loved it when I jumped in because I picked up all the balls in between drills so the members could keep playing. I hadn't realized the pros turned in the numbers upstairs. "There's no mistake, Mr. Cusimano."

He rubbed his hands together. "When I said you could have some extra lessons, I didn't mean this." He slapped the paper. "You're taking advantage of me. I can't have this happening. I'm running a business."

"But I just—"

"No, *I just*. It's unacceptable, Carter. I let one employee walk all over me, and then it's anarchy. You're fired. Effective immediately."

I steadied myself on the bar. "Please, I *need* this job. I'll never play outside of my team practice again, and I'll work every shift you'll give me. I can run the beginner clinics, help in the nursery, work the front desk—"

"My decision is final, *capisce*?"

"But you encouraged me to play. You said I'm good for the club's image."

He chuckled, but his eyes looked hard. "I meant you're an attractive young lady. Pretty girls are good for business."

"Are you kidding?"

"Listen, I'll be straight." He seemed less agitated now, like objectifying me was lowering his blood pressure. "You broke your winning streak last week. I was counting on you to go undefeated this season. Would've been great publicity for the interclub program." He lifted the comp sheet. "Worth all I pay to watch your tight little figure prance around in a miniskirt—"

"It's a tennis skirt, asshole." I clenched my fists at my side.

Mr. Cusimano's lips tightened.

My adrenaline was pumping bad ideas into my head. I snatched the paper out of his hand and shook it in front of his face. "I'm paying you back for every single *gratis* minute I spent on the court. I don't 'prance' for play, *capisce*?"

His nostrils flared. "You're through here. Never bring that disrespectful mouth inside my club again."

I snagged my tennis bag and stomped away before my hubris tipped over into self-destruct mode. The temperature had dropped since I'd been inside, and a steady stream of icy rain fell from the overcast sky. I lifted the hood of my windbreaker over my head and zipped it up to my chin, encasing myself in a mini body bag. My phone vibrated in my pocket. I had a couple of missed texts from Dad.

I got the job!

With a signing bonus!

Olive Garden tonight?

Finally, after months of uncertainty, Dad had a reason to celebrate, and predictably, I would torch his fifteen seconds of happiness. If I wasn't allowed back in the club, that meant

I was off the team. Dad bragged about my records and wins to anyone who would listen. Tennis and a straight A report card were the only two things I had to make him proud of me.

The aftershocks stemming from my big, disrespectful mouth were settling into my nervous system. I couldn't go home without a game plan. I changed course and headed toward the park where I could camp out and think in solitude. The wind whipped icy rain across my face, making my blustery commute almost unbearable. I trudged on and owned the biting winter air, as if enduring the conditions would somehow right my unremitting wrongs.

By the time I reached the park, I was shivering like a strung-out Chihuahua and sought refuge from the rain under a picnic shelter. While I marinated in self-hatred, I pulled out the invoice and stared at the long line of numbers. Even if I got another job, it would take months to pay off the balance. I could forget about moving out with Kiki in June.

The fancy G-Wagon I'd seen at the club earlier rolled onto the lot in front of my little sinner's sanctuary. I squinted to make out the driver: Vladimir. *Oh, God.* Before I could untangle my legs and scamper off into the woods like a spooked raccoon, the car door opened. "Carter." He rushed over to me. "What's wrong?"

"Nothing." I crammed the invoice in my pocket.

He removed his Burberry trench coat, wrapped it around my shoulders, and led me inside his warm, clean SUV. I sat there, inhaling the intoxicating scent of his cologne that lingered on his raincoat, and tried to come up with a non-humiliating reason for succumbing to the elements in a deserted park that was only a ten-minute walk from my house.

He turned on the seat warmer, cranked up the heat, and cruised out of the parking lot.

“Where are you taking me?” I stuttered, unable to keep my teeth from chattering.

“Home. You’ll catch the death.”

“Please, don’t.” I touched his arm. “I can’t face Dad right now.”

“As you wish, Carter.” He made a call, spoke in Russian, and drove down the winding road that led to his luxurious, secluded hideaway in the woods.

4

PROTÉGÉ

When we rolled up to the house, Vladimir slid the G-Wagon into the vacant spot next to a mouth-watering red Ferrari. We got out of the SUV, and he escorted me through a door that led to an immaculate kitchen with a long, granite bar lined with barstools, stainless steel appliances, and a breakfast nook by the window that overlooked a basketball court and a guesthouse.

Inside, Boris waited with a blanket in his arms and a contemptuous regard for me plastered across his face. Vladimir removed his coat from my shoulders and hung it up. Then he unzipped my inferior rain-drenched jacket and tossed it on the doormat, took the blanket from Boris, and wrapped it around my shoulders. He sat me down at a barstool and untied my shoes.

I stopped his hand with mine, the blanket slipping from my shoulders. "I can—"

"Hold the blanket in place. You're shivering, Carter."

I didn't argue. I wrapped the blanket tighter around me as he removed my soggy shoes and holey socks, which exposed my callused and blistered feet. I had worn out my tennis shoes months ago and didn't want to use my savings to buy another pair.

As if my situation could get any more humiliating, the rainwater had dissolved the grip of a Band-Aid around my big toe, and a flap of opaque skin dangled from the side of my foot. "Curse of the sporty," I said.

Vladimir shook his head, slipped a warm pair of fur-lined slippers onto my feet, and said something in Russian to Boris—probably warning him he was about to barf from the sight of my gnarly toes.

He guided me out of the kitchen, past a formal dining room, and into the living area, where he sat me down on a leather sofa in front of the fireplace. He tucked the blanket under me, which restrained my movement. With my arms restrained, swaddled inside the tightly wound blanket, I felt like a captive bird that just had her wings clipped.

Vladimir sat beside me and lifted a steaming teacup to my mouth. I hesitated, but he waited for me to change my mind. The aroma was pungent and too strong for my taste, but once I gave in, I found the flavor irresistible. "How are you feeling?"

My gaze drifted back to the tea. I wanted more of the hot, exotic refreshment. Vladimir loosened the blanket and placed the cup in my hands. I took another sip, licked my lips, and resisted the urge to gulp it down. "I'm fine. You don't have to go to any trouble for me. I'm so embarrassed."

"What has you so upset? Guy troubles?"

I snorted. "You could say that. Mr. Cusimano fired me."

"Why would he do that?"

"I play too much tennis. I took advantage of his generosity."

"That's your terrible crime?"

"One of them." I fiddled with the fringe on a silky throw pillow. "He said some things, I said some things, and then he banned me from the club. I'll have to quit my team."

Vladimir tapped the tips of his fingers together. "Anything else?"

I scoffed. "I'm just getting warmed up." I lifted the rain-dampened invoice out of my pocket. "As a matter of principle, I insisted on paying Mr. Cusimano back for the sixty hours of court time I'd amassed over the last three months. I shouldn't have to—it's a job perk, and he said I could—but hell if I'm going to owe that asshole anything." I winced at my language. Mr. Cusimano was Vladimir's friend.

"May I see it?" He plucked it out of my hand. Without looking at it, he spoke in Russian and passed it on to Boris, whom I hadn't realized was lurking over my shoulder.

Boris fired a nuclear death ray at me and tucked the soggy paper into his black suit jacket.

I held out my hands. "Whoa, whoa, whoa. You didn't tell him to pay it, did you? There's no way I can let you do that. Dad will kill me if he finds out I came crying to you about this."

Vladimir eyed my shaky hands.

I curled them up in a ball and tucked them under my legs.

"The amount is insignificant. I can make your financial problems disappear. Let me."

For a second, I considered it. "I appreciate your offer, but I'll find another job."

He sat back, eyeing me a moment. "What are you studying in college?"

"Double major in business and sports management. I'm going to be a sports agent."

He smiled like he was *proud* of me. "I have a business. You'll work for me. Problem solved."

My mouth gaped.

"Furthermore, I will personally speak to Anthony Cusimano and see to it that he welcomes you back to the club. Your membership will be restored, you will have unlimited court time and private lessons, and you will enjoy all the amenities the club has to offer—without limit. Consider it a *job perk.*" He winked. "Think of me as your mentor, Miss Cook. Anything else you need help with?" He stood and straightened his suit jacket.

"Wait. Work for you? What will I do?"

"Boris, you can assess her skills and assign jobs to keep my new protégé productive?"

Boris grinned sadistically like an overgrown housecat with a mouse tail dangling between his lips. "Of course, boss. I'll put her to work."

"It's settled then. Starting Monday, you will report to me every day after practice. Your homework will be completed, you will keep up with your athletic schedule, and you will stay out of trouble, understand?"

"What about Dad? He'll lose his mind when I tell him."

"Then maybe it's best you don't."

Wouldn't be the first time I lied and snuck around behind Dad's back.

During the car ride home, Vladimir stole glances at me, making me feel completely self-conscious. I broke the awkward silence. "How did you know my sister?"

Vladimir steered the car into the parking lot of the church by our house and turned off the car. I wondered if he knew Sophia was buried just over the hill in the cemetery behind the church. "I must be honest with you, Carter. Your sister and I were more than acquaintances. We were in love." His expression was like Dad's when he spoke of her—bright and wet.

"What are you talking about?" Sophia was in high school when we lived in Brooklyn. Did Dad know? He couldn't have, not the way he talked about Vladimir after they met at the coffee shop last week. I mean, Dad was clear that he'd just met Vladimir, and that meant it *wasn't* a coincidence that Vladimir bumped into Dad at Starbucks.

Vladimir studied my reaction as if he could hear the Tilt-a-Whirl inside my head. "Sophia was my world. You look so much like her, Carter. Her golden eyes, silky blonde hair. I never married, never started a family, never found another woman who could compare. She was younger than you when we met and equally beautiful."

I fidgeted with the zipper on my coat, unnerved by the comparison.

He lifted my chin. "She talked about you all the time. Her spunky little sister, Carter, always getting into trouble with her papa. Sophia would be proud of all your accomplishments. Helping you fulfill your dreams gives me great satisfaction."

Oh, God.

THAT NIGHT, I lay in bed and wrestled with a devil on my left shoulder and an angel on the right. The angel—whom I believed to be the spirit of Sophia—pleaded with me to tell Dad everything that had transpired between Vladimir and me. She'd always been my sensible voice of reason. Inside, I knew she was right, but over on the other side, the ornery little devil jabbed his pitchfork on my sense of duty.

If you tell your dad, you will incinerate his pride because you went behind his back and begged a stranger for money to cover up for your never-ending trail of bad judgment calls.

Sheesh. The devil was right, too, but Dad had finally landed his dream job. Last week, I'd seen an official-looking letter from the mortgage company on Dad's desk. If Vladimir hadn't hired him, we would've lost the house. Vladimir wouldn't take it well if I walked away, and I couldn't jeopardize Dad's new CIO position. I convinced myself to stick with the plan, and if things got *too* weird, I would tell Dad. Until that time, I'd been promoted from smoothie barista to Mr. Vladimir Ivanov's indentured servant.

5

KILL SHOT

On Monday, I had a package waiting for me when I got to the club. I opened it and found a pair of hot pink Asics and a dozen pairs of cushiony athletic socks. My cheeks warmed with embarrassment, but I was grateful yet slightly freaked out by the forwardness of my new boss.

I changed into my new kicks, tossed the old ones in the can, and joined my teammates on the court. I was back in the club as if my conversation with Mr. Cusimano had never happened. He even met me when I got off the court, apologized, and welcomed me back—*weird.*

Not knowing what the plan was with Vladimir, I waited outside after practice and assumed he would magically appear as he had in the park. I looked around for the Ferrari or G-Wagon, but he wasn't there.

As I stood in the parking lot, still perspiring from a tough practice, a souped-up black Cadillac with tinted windows crept up next to me. The glossy, aftermarket wheels glistened in the sunlight like black ice. The window came down and revealed the driver: Boris. There wasn't a more perfect car in the world for that beast of a man.

I opened the passenger door and slid inside. "Nice ride."

He had a stinky stogie between his teeth and was wearing a plaid pimp hat with a dotted feather tucked into the rim. As he rolled off the lot, I noticed his hair was pulled back in a ponytail, which revealed a tattoo of a black dagger inked on his neck. In his black suit, a fat gold chain around his neck, and an ominous expression that sneered, "Please give me a reason to kill you," I mentally cautioned myself not to do anything to piss off the big guy.

Russian polka music reverberated through the car, and I sat quietly in the passenger seat and processed the Big Fat Mess I'd walked into when I accepted Vladimir's offer. I was certain it was a gift, the problems I created for myself. Everyone had a talent; mine was doing the exact opposite of The Right Thing.

"What's all that?" Boris pointed to the wad of crap dangling from the lanyard around my neck.

I let out a little snort and held it up. "This is a rape whistle, and this is a mini thing of mace. I walk everywhere. I have to protect myself. And this is my house key, another key to my best friend's house, and a cherry-flavored ChapStick."

"Why don't you drive?"

Because Dad doesn't trust me. I lifted my shoulders. "I like to walk."

He let out a *humph,* which I suppose meant he was satisfied with my answer.

A wooden cross adorned with faux jewels and bound in a lacy pink ribbon dangled from the rearview mirror. It had Russian letters scribbled across it in a child's handwriting. Boris tapped his rings on the steering wheel when he noticed me admiring it. I wanted to ask him who made it, but I didn't think it wise to strike up a conversation with a snarling grizzly bear.

As we cruised down the hill past the church, I recognized the Chevy pickup driving past us on the other side of the road. The driver zeroed in on me as we passed.

"Shit." I slunk down in my seat to hide—two seconds too late.

Boris turned off the radio. "What?"

"I'm so sorry." I covered my face with my hands and sat up just enough to peek through my fingers and look behind. "Shit, shit, shit." The truck turned around.

Boris glanced in the rearview mirror. "Who is that?"

"It's too late. He saw me. Pull into the park up here on the right. I'm just going to let him shoot me and get it over with. I'm dead anyway." I curled my legs up to my chest and watched the truck closing in on us. I lifted my tennis bag up to my lap and unzipped the side pocket.

I may not win this round, but I won't go down without a fight.

Boris opened the glove box and pulled out a long black handgun.

"*Jeez.* What the hell?"

He glared at me like *I* was the crazy one. I pulled my fat orange-and-yellow Nerf gun out of my bag and waved it at him. "Chill, Putin, it's a game. Ever hear of dart tag?"

Boris eyed my toy and slid his gun back into the glove box. "You give up that easily?"

"The odds are against me. He and his buddies play video games like it's their religion. Plus, it's stupid and not worth my time. I surrender."

"Do what I say." Boris sped through the lot and parked by the picnic shelter. "Hide behind the wall." He pointed to the shelter. "*Davai.*" That meant, "Hurry the fuck up," in Russian, I supposed.

The truck pulled in and parked next to the Caddy. My friend Ryan and his gun-toting buddy got out of the truck and tried in vain to conceal humongous plastic machine guns behind their backs. When they approached the Caddy, Boris leaned against the car and puffed on his stogie. Ryan stooped down and peeked inside the car.

"Good afternoon, gentleman," Boris said. He exhaled a gray cloud of tobacco smoke.

The guys scrunched up their faces.

"Is there something I can help you with? You seem to have lost something."

"Just looking for our friend Carter, sir. Happen to know where she went?" Ryan asked, widening his stance commando style.

Boris crossed his arms. "You want me to be a rat?"

I covered my mouth to stifle my giggle.

"Who are you?" Ryan's buddy asked.

From my hiding spot behind the shelter, I snuck up behind my unsuspecting victims. First, I popped Ryan's friend in the back with my wimpy handgun and then took down one of my best friends with a kill shot to the head.

"Gotcha." I lifted the gun to my lips and blew away imaginary smoke from my two perfect shots. When they turned to meet their assailant, their shoulders slumped in defeat as the realization sank in that I had outplayed them.

"That's how you do it, boys." I smacked Ryan on the ass.

He reeled me in for a hug and spanked me back. "That was hot, babe." His muscles were strong and chiseled as if his body had been carved from petrified wood.

Ryan's friend headed back to the truck, not at all as good

a sport as his buddy. Boris watched their reactions with a glint of satisfaction in his menacing eyes.

Ryan wrinkled his forehead and sized up Boris. "You hired a bodyguard?"

I laughed. "Oh, right. Uh, this is Boris. He works for Dad's new boss. He's taking me to check out the office. Boris, this is my friend, Ryan."

Ryan shook his hand. "Nice to meet you, sir."

Boris didn't return the sentiment.

"Hey, what's our bet tonight, Cookie? San Francisco or Seattle?" Ryan asked.

I put my hand on my hip and twisted my lips as I thought it over. "Hmm, it's going to be close. Both have great offenses, but I think San Francisco's defense will dominate."

"Yeah, but don't forget, Seattle has the Twelfth Man factor at home."

"True. It'll be a tight game, so I'm going to have to go with my tried and true, no-fail approach—hottest QB wins. I'll take San Francisco."

"That guy has nothing on me." He flexed his bicep and kissed his bulging muscle. Ryan was a freshman running back on the UC football team and worked out more than I did.

"You wish." I shoved him in the chest. "What do I get if I win—I mean, *when* I win?"

"When *I* win," Ryan said, "you have to wear my jersey Friday night, and I'll treat you to dinner if you pull it off, deal?"

"Deal." We shook on it. "What time are you coming over tonight?" I asked.

"We have an end-of-season team thing, so I probably won't get to your house until the third or fourth quarter. Save me some pizza?"

"Yep."

His cowboy boots clicked on the blacktop as he walked back to the truck. Over on the basketball court, I caught a glimpse of this hot Spanish guy, Leonardo, shooting hoops with his friends. He worked out at the club and had been hanging around the smoothie bar for a couple of weeks. He spotted me and tossed me an up-nod.

I mouthed *¡hola!* and then sucked in my bottom lip and turned away, embarrassed that he had caught me checking him out. I leaned against the Cadillac next to Boris and held up a closed hand to initiate a fist bump. "That was badass, man."

Boris studied my gesture and knocked his thick, tattooed knuckle into my pale, bony fingers like an eighteen-wheeler crashing into a Smart car.

Ouch. I shook my fingers to relieve the pain. "I'm glad you're on my team."

6

HELL ONE, HEAVEN ZIP

When we arrived at the house, Boris ushered me to the kitchen and motioned for me to sit at the bar. He placed a teakettle over a gas flame.

"So, what's my first assignment? I can compose letters, do research, bookkeeping, slide presentations, spreadsheets—"

"You will use *vegetarian* skills and make dinner for the boss tonight." He handed me a pad of paper and a pen. "Make list."

Mentally, I prayed for guidance. "What happened to the chef?"

"He left us unexpectedly."

There was no way I could pull it off. My idea of a weekday dinner was a jar of peanut butter and a spoon. What the heck did Boris expect me to do?

For our first course, Mr. Ivanov, I have opened a can of condensed tomato soup, added some water from the faucet, dumped it all into a microwave-safe bowl, and nuked it on high for a minute and a half. For crunch, I have crumbled a handful of Goldfish crackers—

"*Davai.*" Boris tapped his finger on the counter next to the pad of paper. "Write down what you need. I will send runner to pick up groceries."

I cocked my head. "Can you give me a hint?"

He clicked his tongue like I was a moron. He held his hands out in front of the pad of paper. "Carrots, potatoes, beets, legumes, you know?"

I stuck a piece of gum in my mouth, chewed, and blinked at him like a dim-witted cow. He chuckled. Not like it was funny, more like he was stupefied by my ignorance. From behind the counter, he pulled out a stack of cookbooks. He set them down in front of me and motioned for me to get to work.

In the spirit of going along with it, I opened one up. "What's this, Russian?"

"*Da, Russkiy.*" He poured two cups of tea.

I could translate the Russian words into English on my phone—but still.

"What *kind* of vegetarian is Mr. Ivanov?" After a blank stare from Boris, I elaborated. "For example, I don't eat meat, fish, or eggs, but I do eat dairy. I'm a lacto-vegetarian."

"He's same vegetarian as you."

"Why doesn't he eat meat?"

"Why don't you eat meat?" He slid a teacup on a saucer over to me.

"Thank you." I spit my gum out into the trash can. "I find dead things unappetizing."

Boris sipped his tea and completely ignored my question. I gave up, rifled through the pages, and found a picture of a seemingly doable recipe for a vegetarian stew. As I scribbled down a list of ingredients, a guy pushed open the kitchen door and handed Boris a gym bag. With his slicked-back black hair and obnoxious swagger, the dude looked like a total player.

He conversed with Boris in their native tongue and pointed outside. I followed his gesture and snuck a peek out the window. There were two other shady-looking guys in tracksuits smoking and shooting hoops down at the end of the driveway next to the guesthouse.

The whole time he was talking, the guy stared at my body, salivating, like I was some tasty morsel wrapped in bacon. He made a smooching sound and motioned for me to come to him. I sucked in my lips and looked to the big guy for guidance.

Boris reprimanded him and snapped his fingers at the dude, who smelled like he had been swimming in a vat of Abercrombie cologne and cigarette butts. The playboy held up his hands in surrender and backed out of the room with a grin on his face.

"How do you say 'asshole' in Russian?" I asked Boris.

His red face softened, but I could tell he was still irate. "*Lapsha.*"

"*Lapsha* means asshole? I'll remember that." The devil on my shoulder poked me in the neck: *Get over yourself. It's a cultural thing.* Sophia said, *Get the hell out of there!*

If I had a car, I would've listened to Sophia—damn the consequences. I shouldn't have been in a house full of men who looked like they wanted to eat me alive. From outside, I heard the peacock alarm going off, and the orgasmic hum of the Ferrari engine. As I waited for the door to open, I wrestled with my conflicting emotions—excitement and fear.

The devil jumped over to the right side of my shoulder, grabbed Sophia by her wings, and shook her violently. Out of strength and resolve, Sophia flew away into the sky, leaving a stream of silvery white feathers in her wake. The devil kicked back and leaned against the crook of my neck —hell one, heaven zip.

"Boss likes a drink after work." Boris motioned for me to follow him to the bar. He lifted a bottle of vodka out of the fridge and turned over three shot glasses.

I heard the car door shut in the garage. The poodles cried, *Papa's home!* from the other side of the kitchen door. When Vladimir came in, I expected him to flash me a crooked smile, have a drink, relax—no such luck. He burst through the door, raging into his phone in Russian. He stormed through the kitchen and trailed off to his office on the other side of the house.

Boris listened and then excused himself to handle damage control. When Boris came back to the kitchen, he didn't specifically say what had lit Vladimir up, just that there was a minor issue back home in Russia he needed to handle. Apparently, he needed to handle it without me in the house. Boris took me home before I had a chance to screw up dinner.

7

WHACKED

Surprisingly, I'd slept soundly after The Situation on my first day at work. I shouldn't have been so relaxed. I had a crucial, must-win match that afternoon. Our team was tied for first place in our division, and our opponents were the co-leaders.

During warmups, Coach fed the basket and pounded balls at us to keep us aggressive. "Be ready for anything, ladies."

My statuesque partner, Rakhi, who had the wingspan of a condor, and I were up first.

"Play like it's for a trophy," Coach said. "Three balls, no mercy."

Coach nailed the ball down the middle on the first feed. I called Rakhi off it and sliced it crosscourt at Coach's gut. He pounded it back. I got my strings on it, but hit it into the net. He lobbed the next feed over my head.

"Switch!" I yelled.

Rakhi hustled back to chase it down, and I slid over to defend her spot. She popped back a floater right into Coach's sweet spot. In a match situation, I would've shuffled back to the baseline to return the overhead on the bounce, but I didn't want to look like a wimp in front of our opponents, who were warming up on the court next to us. I should've adhered to my personal mantra: "Live to fight another day," which meant don't set yourself up for an injury when it's not necessary, say match point or something. Stupidly, though, I held my position at the net, not willing to give up on offense.

Coach had his arm up, racket back as the ball came down. "It's coming to you, Carter. Shuffle back."

I bounced on my toes on the service line. No way would I back down.

Coach cranked the overhead shot. *Wham!* The ball nailed me on the right side of my cheek. The shock—more than the force of the blow—caused me to drop my racket. It didn't hurt *that* badly; it was a tennis ball, not a baseball. Coach apologized. He thought I could defend it. I told him it was no big deal, but I was embarrassed I'd lost the point in front of our competition.

After our match was over, I jogged out of the club and slid into the Caddy. I said a cheerful hello to Boris, pumped that we'd creamed our opponents.

"You won."

"Yep. We're officially in first place. We need three points next week to clinch playoffs."

"Congratulations." The car sat idle. He glared at me but didn't say anything. How unnerving. The only sound was the tapping of his gold rings on the steering wheel. "Everything okay?" Veins were bulging out on the side of his head.

"Yeah. Why?"

"Who did that?" He motioned to my cheek. He put off such a badass vibe. I was sure he'd seen or inflicted worse.

I put my hands up and laughed at his overreaction. "It's nothing. I'm fine."

"Answer me." He wrapped his big hand under my chin and turned my head to inspect the damage. I had iced it before and after the match, leaving my skin bright red from the cold pack.

I pushed his hand away. "I said I'm fine."

"Name."

What the hell was his problem? "Um, me. I did it. I hit myself with my racket defending a shot to the face. I feel like an ass."

"But you're right-handed. If you hit yourself, you strike left side of face." He picked up my right hand and demonstrated the swinging motion.

What the hell? Was he former KGB back in Mother Russia? "Okay. Jeez. Calm down. I got nailed with a ball during warm-ups. Can we go now?"

"A man did it." He rubbed his beard. "Women always lie when men hurt them."

I pulled a can of almonds out of my bag, noshed, and ignored his spot-on observation. Yes, a man did it, but he didn't mean to *hurt* me—he was just trying to scare me. As the saying goes in tennis, "High you die." My opponents would've never shown me mercy. "It was my fault. I should've backed up."

"Better get your story straight when boss asks."

8

SUCKA

A hefty Russian guy wearing a permanent frown on his face was carrying groceries into the house as we pulled up the driveway. He was the butler who had greeted us at the door on the night of the party. Boris took the bag from him and handed over the keys to the Cadillac.

Before the dude got in the car, he admired my bare legs and studied the red mark on my face. He shifted his gaze over to Boris, as if questioning the source of the damage. I sucked in my bottom lip and turned away.

"Did you bring change of clothes?" Boris asked, eying my tennis skirt.

"I can pull on some sweats. I'll bring something to change into next time."

Boris carried the groceries inside and then opened a leather notebook, put on a pair of reading glasses, turned on a sports program on the radio, and pretended he wasn't babysitting me. I kept a bag of ice next to me on the counter and pressed it against my face intermittently as I chopped up zucchini, onions, potatoes, beets, and carrots in the food processor for the stew.

While I worked, I returned a few texts. I tried to muffle my giggles, but my friends were cracking me up. Boris set out a plastic bucket on the kitchen floor and instructed me to toss the vegetable butts, skin, and extras in there for the birds. The peacock was out by the basketball court, strutting around with his feathers fanned out to impress the peahen.

"What's the peacock's name?" I asked.

"Igor."

"What's his girlfriend's name? Is she *Russkiy*, too?"

Boris glared at me over his glasses. "Natasha."

"Mr. Ivanov loves animals, huh? That's why he's a vegetarian?"

Not a peep from the big guy. *Jeez.* If I had ignored his question, he would have held me upside down by my ankles and shaken me until I came up with an answer. From where I was chopping, the feed bucket was about six feet away. Instead of scooting it closer, I tossed the leftovers out free-throw style. Yeah, I knew my game was annoying him.

"That's three in a row," he said, not looking up from his book.

"I'm on a winning streak."

He peeked over his reading glasses. "Care to make wager?"

"Seriously?" I would never back down from a challenge. "What's the bet?"

He tapped his pencil on the counter. "If you miss your next shot, you show me your phone. The way you and your friends waste time fascinates me."

"Fine. If I miss, which I won't, I'll let you see my phone for ten seconds."

He scoffed.

I put down the knife. "Okay, thirty seconds. What do I get if I make it?" I crossed my arms and leaned against the counter.

He scratched his bristly salt and pepper beard. "What do you want?"

Honestly, I didn't want anything from him, but since I was confident I would make the shot, I came up with a brilliant idea. "Truth or Dare." I put my hand on my hip and cocked my head, proud I'd outsmarted him.

He studied my pre-victory confidence. "I don't know what you mean."

"If I win, you have to pick truth or dare. So, if you say 'truth' then I get to ask you a question, and you have to answer it truthfully. You can't lie." I pointed a stern finger at him. "If you choose 'dare' you have to do whatever I say."

"What're you going to make me do?"

"Well, I can't tell you, but as an example, the last time one of my cocky friends chose dare, I made him chug an entire bottle of hot salsa. Once you're in, there's no backing out."

He tapped his fingers on the bar.

"Take it or leave it, tough guy." I held out my hand.

"I'll take it, of course." He shook—crushed—my hand and nodded for me to go for it.

I chopped off a piece of zucchini, lifted it over my head, and tossed it easily into the bucket. "Woo-hoo!" I did a victory dance. "Truth or dare, *sucka*?"

He removed his glasses and rubbed his temples. "Double or nothing?"

"No way, really?"

"What can I say? I don't know when to quit."

I felt kind of sorry for him. He was always listening to games on the radio and scribbling down notes or stats or something in a leather binder. Maybe he had a gambling problem. "Double or nothing it is." I agreed before he had a chance to come to his senses.

As I chopped off another piece, Boris got up and stood by the bucket to get a better view. I held the chunk up like before, aimed, and tossed a perfect shot. Just as it was about to float in, he batted it down to the floor.

"Hey, no fair."

Boris cocked his head. "Of course it's fair. Fan interference. You didn't make the shot. I win." He held out his hand. "Double or nothing means I get your phone for one minute."

"Whatever, cheater. If you want to snoop on my phone that badly I'll give it to you, even though we both know you played dirty." I turned my back, pulled my phone out of my sports bra, and slapped it in the palm of his hand. "Go." I counted out loud as Boris scanned my texts, taking in as much data as he could in the allotted time.

I peeked down to see what my friends were saying that had him so enthralled in our conversation, but he turned to block my view. "Fifty-nine, sixty." I snatched my phone back and scanned my texts in search of anything embarrassing. Nothing too bad, just some post-victory tennis texts, a few flirty texts from Ryan—he loved to tease me—and an urgent reminder from Kiki that I needed to secure a date for the ballet the following Friday. I slipped my phone back in my pocket and finished chopping up dinner. My mouth needed an off switch.

"Your boyfriend calls you *Cookie*?"

I ignored him and sautéed the veggies in a skillet to soften them up before I added the broth. After an eternity of awkwardness, he said, "Never make a bet you're not willing to lose."

Screw you, cheater. "I'll remember that." Preparing all the delicious food made my stomach growl. If I served dinner at eight, I wouldn't get home until, like, nine. I rifled through my tennis bag to scrounge up some emergency food rations. I found a cup of peanut butter and a bounty of Almond Joys, which my little sister had rejected from her Halloween candy stash.

I jogged downstairs to retrieve some vino from the wine cellar, which was the size of the entire second story of Dad's house. I found a bottle that likely cost more than my tuition and trotted back upstairs. I rounded up the poodles and put them in their crates in case Vladimir wasn't in a good mood.

I headed to the guest bedroom to shower. Once I was clean, I was about to help myself to the liquor cabinet to settle my nerves, when I heard the garage door open. I'd tried to conceal the red mark on my face with powder, but there was no way to cover it up. He would notice right away, and I didn't want to see him angry again. Over *what* I wasn't sure, but Boris had flipped out over it. Maybe Vladimir would react the same way.

Vladimir breezed through the door. "What's that delicious smell, Carter? Don't tell me you went to any trouble for me?" He hung up his coat, slipped on a pair of house shoes, and set down his briefcase in the mudroom next to the garage door.

"Oh, it's just a lentil stew."

He walked up to me, planted his hands on my shoulders, and kissed my cheeks. "I apologize for my late dinner—demands of my job. You must be starved."

I fluttered my eyes like a love-struck idiot; the kisses caught me off guard. Is that the usual greeting in Russia? Does *everyone* get the special treatment? "Oh, no. Don't worry about me," I stammered. "I'll eat later."

Vladimir lowered his hands and pushed open the swinging door to see the table set for one. His eyes sharpened. "You don't expect me to eat alone, do you?" He held the door open and ushered me to the formal dining room.

Boris appeared by the table, set down another place setting, and pulled a chair out for me. Before I sat, I whispered to Boris. "I can't stay too late. I have to be home by ten o'clock."

"You are grown woman and have curfew?"

"It's not a *curfew*, more like a respect thing. Dad worries about me."

"You'll be home by curfew."

Vladimir joined me at the table and set down the bread and dipping oil between us. "You got in a fight with your boyfriend?"

Oh, shit. Apparently, all Russian men think a bruise on a woman can only come from abuse. Suddenly, I worried this might twist back on Coach in some bad way. There were some serious cultural miscommunications going on. "No fight. No boyfriend, either, just a little competitive action on the court." I dipped my bread in the olive oil, like, a hundred times.

He gave me all of his attention. "You won your match today?"

My belly quivered. "Mm-hm."

He nodded his approval like *my* win was a positive reflection on him.

I bit my lip, unnerved that he wouldn't stop staring at me. "Oh, and thanks for the new tennis shoes. Pink is my favorite color."

"My pleasure. Tell me about your game."

"It was awesome. My partner and I took over the net and

won the first set, but in the second set, our opponents killed us with lobs and dominated two to six."

"How did you manage your comeback?"

"When you're losing, you have to change your strategy. Rakhi and I never do this, but we switched sides for the super tiebreaker. I played the deuce side, and she moved to ad. It messed with their minds. We won ten to two. Want to know the best part?"

"Isn't winning the best part?"

"No. The girls we played today creamed us in two straight sets earlier in the season." I leaned forward like I was about to reveal the secrets of the universe. "The *payback* is the best part." I slapped my hand on the table, which caused the wine to ripple in the decanter. "Sorry, I get carried away when it comes to competition."

"Don't apologize. I adore your passion." He locked his gaze on mine. "At what point in the match did your opponent hit you?" He brushed his finger across his cheek.

Boris appeared from around the corner and riffled through the china cabinet.

"It happened during warm-ups."

"Your teammate hit you then?"

Boris stalked behind Vladimir's back like the Big Bad Wolf peeking around a tree.

"Ummm, we had to win this match today to keep our playoff hopes alive, so Coach fed us some tough shots to keep us on our toes, and I was out of position. I should have backed up, so he treated it like a match situation and fired the ball at me—"

Vladimir inhaled sharply.

"Not to hurt me or anything. Just to teach me a lesson."

He blinked his cool blue eyes and tapped his fingers. He

looked angry enough to snap the table in half with his bare hands.

"No, no, bad choice of words. I'm sorry—"

Boris held up his hand to shut me up and spoke to the boss in Russian, presumably to calm him down. Whatever he said kicked his intensity level down a notch.

"Interesting technique Coach uses to train his girls." He lifted his glass to initiate a toast.

"Oh, I can't. I don't imbibe on school nights."

"Just a drink to be social. *Za tebya.*" Vladimir's glass hung in the air.

I didn't want to insult him, plus I seriously needed to relax. I lifted my glass and clinked. "*Za tebya.*"

9

MARBLE SLAB

On Friday, I had officially survived my first week as Vladimir's employee. My attempt to mimic the artistry of a chef was as laughable as me trying to return a serve from Serena Williams. After our first meal together, Vladimir told me to forget the recipe books and make what I liked to eat.

We had moved from eating botched fancy meals in the formal dining room to having a variety of appetizers and cocktails around the bar in the kitchen. With the new, less intimidating plan, I was busy with prep and assembly, and I could relax enough to hold a conversation without having an anxiety attack.

When Boris and I got back to the house after practice, I went to my room, the guest room, showered, and got ready Friday night style—jeans, bling, hair, and makeup. During the week, I donned my sporty-girl attire, but I made an effort to raise my stats at social events. I just had to get through dinner, a few cocktails, some chitchat, and in a few hours, I would be free from the Russians for an entire glorious weekend.

Once I was ready, Boris kept me company at the bar while he listened to a radio commentator jawing about college bowl games. UC was out of contention and finished for the season. He had his reading glasses on, a stack of papers fanned out around him, and was jotting down notes in a little black book.

"What are you, a bookie?" I joked.

He didn't respond.

Crap. Was he a bookie? I tied on an apron I'd found in a drawer and then opened a can of cannellini beans and dumped them into a glass bowl. I added salt, a dash of pepper, diced tomatoes, and a big bunch of finely chopped parsley. I folded the ingredients together, squeezed a lemon over top, and scooped spoonfuls of the mix onto bite-sized tortilla chips.

"You know, I'm capable of doing more than making dinner. I can do business things."

"You call that *dinner*?"

I placed a couple of them on an appetizer plate and set it next to Boris. "They're delicious." I stuffed one in my mouth.

He glared at me. "You're in good mood."

"It's officially the weekend. T.G.I.F.F.F."

His expression didn't change. "Is code for?" He tipped his hand.

"Thank God It's Finally Fucking Friday?" I grinned and popped another bean thing in my mouth.

"You have big plans tonight?"

I guess he'd observed the obvious uptick in my weekend style. "Oh, the usual."

"Which is?"

"Hanging out with my friends."

"Where?"

"Hockey game."

He stared at me.

"What?"

"I am waiting to hear the rest of your plans." He leaned forward. "You and your college friends don't go home to bed after the game, right?"

Yikes. I busied myself at the chopping block, dicing an eggplant for a dip. "Um, we just hang out and, you know, talk. What are your plans? Married? Got a girlfriend?"

"Who is driving you home?" Both his hands lay flat, palms down on the bar like an overweight panther ready to pounce.

Using the knife, I slid the eggplant into a clear bowl and microwaved it to soften before pureeing it. "I don't have to answer your questions, you know. I can do whatever I want in my free time."

"The big boy or the basketball player?"

I snorted at his shallow depiction of my friends. "Um, it's none of your business, but if it makes you feel better, a *girl* is driving me home."

"You're lying."

I tossed him a mischievous grin. "Why do you say that?"

"You always say 'um' before you tell a lie."

"Really? Thanks for the tip."

"And you suck in your bottom lip when men stare at your body, cross your arms when you're nervous, and pull your hair forward when you're paid a compliment."

"Jeez, stalker."

He kept staring at me like he was mentally downloading my quirks for his F.U.C.F.—Fucked-Up Carter File. The garage door opened. I went to the bar to prepare the drinks and to escape Boris's unnerving assessment. All I had to do was carry two small glasses and a bottle of vodka to the kitchen counter and set out some pickles, caviar, and black rye bread.

Instead of downing pure alcohol like a proper Russian, I paced myself and sipped on less potent mixed drinks throughout our evenings together. There was no way I could keep pace with these bad boys.

As I poured a shot of vodka into my glass, a knowing smile crept up on Boris's face. "Are you sure you should drink before you go out to meet boys?"

I topped my vodka off with a long stream of soda water, a lemon, and a lime wedge. "One drink isn't going to kill me. It helps me relax." I slurped down half my drink.

"One glass of *wine* helps you relax. One mixed drink makes you talkative, two drinks make you flirty, three drinks touchy-feely. I haven't studied your behavior after three, but I have a good idea what kind of mood you'll be in." He arched an eyebrow. "Watch yourself around the boys."

"You're an ass." I pushed past him and met the boss at the door. "Happy Friday, Mr. Ivanov."

"*Privet.*" He kissed my cheeks and checked out my upgraded style.

"How was work?" I placed my hand on my stomach to settle the butterflies that did a flyby every time he came home and greeted me *that way*. I finished my first drink while the boss hung up his coat and changed into house shoes.

After he turned around, he looked at me, then at Boris. "Is he bothering you, angel?"

I caught a glimpse of my evil-eyed babysitter and shook my head. "No problems here."

Boris spoke in Russian. Vladimir laughed at whatever he

said. *Do they know how rude that is?* Boris poured a couple of generous shots and said a toast. They clinked and downed.

The boss set his glass down and turned to me. "You have a date tonight?"

I must have seriously looked like a slacker during the week. "Just hanging out with friends." I popped some pita bread in the oven and set the appetizer tray in front of him. "Try these."

Playboy breezed into the kitchen from the back door unannounced. He had a heavy gym bag slung over his shoulder, a gash across his cheek, and a fresh, ruddy abrasion that looked like someone had clocked him. I subconsciously touched my own cheek, where the red mark had settled into a vague bruise that I covered up with foundation.

He held his hands up to the boss as if apologizing for the interruption. Vladimir waved him in. As Playboy seemed to be explaining what had happened to his face, he plopped the bag on the counter, unzipped it, and revealed the contents: stacks and stacks of fat cash.

Look away, look away, look away, Sophia said.

I wasn't supposed to see that. I turned a blind eye and busied myself in the kitchen. Vladimir patted him on the back and lifted his chin to get a look at his wound. My stomach turned. Playboy argued and raised his hands as if to say it was all good. The boss gestured for him to sit. Boris got some first aid supplies out of a drawer and set them out on the counter.

The boss saturated a kitchen towel with vodka, pressed it against Playboy's cheek to sterilize the wound, and stitched it up right next to the food I had prepared. Acid built up in my throat. After the boss applied a bandage,

Boris patted Playboy on the shoulder and poured three rounds of vodka.

Vladimir made the toast that time. They clinked glasses and threw back their shots. Playboy wiped his mouth, snatched a piece of bread off the counter like a ballsy seagull, and strutted back outside. I dropped my gaze to the floor and pretended I wasn't fazed, but my shaky hands ratted me out.

Vladimir stepped in to smooth it over. "As you can see, I run several different businesses. This one," he tipped his head toward the gym bag, "is a small cash-only side business."

I nodded and sipped my drink. Every single day that week, Playboy had delivered a stuffed gym bag to Boris. I'd seen plenty of gangster movies, and I knew whatever they had going on was no small side business; it was organized crime. It had to be. I mean, they didn't even want to take the guy to the hospital to get sewn up. What else could it be? I reminded myself to breathe, pulled the bread out of the oven, and set it on a marble slab to cool.

Boris rested his big hand on my shoulder. "Need some spending money for the weekend?" He offered up a bankroll of hundred-dollar bills, ready to shave off a few Benjamins.

"No thanks. I have some."

He slapped a stack of bills in my hand. "It's payday. I insist."

I tried to give it back to him, but he wouldn't let me. "It's too much," I said. "I hardly did anything. Besides, if I show up to the game with a hundred-dollar bill, my friends will think I'm a stripper or something." I laughed at my stupid, alcohol-induced sense of humor.

"Actually, dear, with a hundred-dollar bill, your friends will think you are *hooker*. Strippers carry twenties."

Keep your mouth shut, keep your mouth shut, keep your mouth shut...

Boris turned to Vladimir. “I have some business to attend to, boss.”

“Go. I will take care of Carter tonight. *Do svidaniya.*”

They threw back another round and ate some bread, then Boris put on his hat and coat, snagged the gym bag, and left the house. The boss and I were alone—*together.*

10

DUMPED

Vladimir loosened his tie and slid off his suit jacket. I jumped when I spotted a gun tucked into the left side of his pants. *Totally organized crime. Totally.*

"For protection." He placed it in the drawer where they kept the car keys. "Better?"

I nodded, trying my best not to look freaked out. Maybe I'd watched *too* many movies.

He unbuttoned the top button on his shirt, lazed against the counter, and studied the appetizers: beans from a can and store-bought tortilla chips. He was tolerant of my lackluster domestic skills. He picked one up, examined it, and then lifted it to *my* mouth. "Ladies first." His voice was soft, eyes playful.

I giggled. "Sorry, you surprised me. No one has ever—" God, my new boss was bad—*and hot.*

He lifted the tortilla chip again. "Good. I'm first." He winked.

My heart fluttered. "Wait." I picked one up, too. "At the same time."

"*Odin, dva, tri.*"

I opened my mouth, stepped out of my comfort zone, and let him feed me. Then I popped a chip into his mouth. His lips closed around my fingers, and he nibbled on my thumb. "You're delicious, Carter."

The fluttering sensation moved lower. *Much* lower.

He picked up my hand and admired my blue fingernails, each adorned with a tiny kitten motif. "How cute."

"Oh, you know, my little sister has a thing for cats. We match." I wiggled my fingernails and tried to blink away my embarrassment.

"She's lucky to have such a sweet sister." He patted my hand and then went to the bar.

I inhaled the scent of cologne left in his wake. *Heavenly.*

He poured himself a long straight shot of vodka. "Another drink, Carter?"

I loved the way my name sounded when each *R* rolled off his tongue. I already had two drinks, and according to Boris, three made me touchy-feely. Whatever. As long as I didn't get to four, I was fine. "Hmm. One more, but cut me off after that."

"Because you don't want to be tipsy for your date? Boris said you go out with a football player."

I pulled my hair forward and finger-combed my waves. "Boris thinks he knows everything. I told you, no date." *I wonder how tall Vladimir is?*

He poured what amounted to a double shot of Russian Standard into my glass. "Then why cut you off? It's the weekend." He topped off my drink with a splash of soda water, swirled the straw toward my mouth, and lifted it to my lips.

I sipped the fruity drink and stared into his sexy blue

eyes. Dad would fall into a tailspin if he found out his boss was serving me alcohol and treating me like a *woman*.

Holding on to the straw, he lowered the glass, rested his chin on his fist, and waited for me to answer.

"I'm trying to stay out of trouble."

"What did you do that you must *stay* out of trouble?"

Underage drinking, getting escorted home in a police cruiser, sneaking out of my bedroom window at night to meet my friends..."Um," I laughed.

He lifted his shoulders and waited for me to answer.

I exhaled. "Nothing. No big deal." I waved my hand.

He lifted the drink back up to my mouth. "Finish it, and I will make you something special—only for princesses."

I giggled. How could I resist? After I slurped it down, I followed him, propped my elbows on the bar, and watched him work. He unfastened his cuff links, rolled back his sleeves, and took off his Rolex. He had a tattoo watch under his real one and tats of Russian words and weird images all up and down his forearms.

I climbed onto a barstool and sat on my knees to get a better view of what he was doing. His gaze moved from the cocktail shaker to my chest. The way I leaned over, he had a perfect view down my shirt. I placed my hand over my heart, giggled, and buttoned my shirt up to my collarbone. "How tall are you?"

"One hundred and ninety centimeters."

My brain was temporarily out of order. "How tall is that in English?"

He poured several different kinds of liquor into a shaker. "Six feet and three inches. Why do you ask?"

"Just wondering."

Note to wasted self: never hand the keys to your sobriety over to a foxy Russian gangster.

"How tall are you, angel?" He poured my special drink into a tall hurricane glass and garnished it with an orange slice, a pineapple wedge, and lots of cherries.

Angel? "Five-seven." *Is that my pet name?* "When do you work out?"

He set the glass in front of me, but didn't answer. I slouched over and traced his ring tattoos with my finger. I peeked up at him. "Do you have tattoos all over?"

He tapped his fingers on the bar, then dumped my special princess drink down the drain. "Boris was right. You can't handle your liquor." He sneered, repulsed by my skanky behavior.

Lightning come...strike me down.

Vladimir scooped a big mound of white rice out of the cooker, dropped it into a bowl, and set it down in front of me. He shook his head in disgust like I was garbage writhing with maggots on his spotless kitchen floor.

I curled my legs up and shielded my eyes with my hands. "I'm so sorry. I don't know what I was thinking."

"You know Boris is my *sovietnik*—my trusted advisor. He was concerned for your safety around boys. I had to see with my own eyes, understand?"

Kill me.

"Do you have many partners?"

I choked. "Oh no, Mr. Ivanov. I'm not usually like this. No, no, no. I don't even have a boyfriend. I've *never* had a boyfriend. Seriously, let's forget this ever happened."

"You're a good girl?"

"Of course, I'm a good girl. Boris was right. I don't handle my liquor well. That's why I, um, never drink in public. If my dad found out I partied around guys, he'd lock me in my bedroom, dig a moat around the house, and stock it with meathead-eating crocodiles."

"Your papa is a good man. Maybe he should lock you away. *Yesh.*" He motioned to my plate.

I tossed the rice around with my fork. "I spend the night on campus with my best friend Kiki every Friday. We drink, but it's just us—no boys allowed. Are you still going to take me to the game? I promise I will not have one drop of liquor around the guys. I can see the error of my ways."

He dragged his fingers through his hair and contemplated his answer.

Boris had bullshit detectors built into his corneas. If I had tried that "error of my ways" crap on him, I would have been on lockdown until the day Russia outlawed the consumption of vodka. The boss, on the other hand, had a soft spot for me. I could wear him down.

"All my friends are going." I blinked innocently.

"Oh, Carter. How you bend my good judgment. Finish your rice and brush your teeth. I'll take you to your hockey game."

Victory!

11

LIES AND DISOBEDIENCE

On the way to the stadium, I played with the fringe on my tall brown boots.

Vladimir stole glances at me. "You're staying with Kiki in the dormitory after the game? Not going anywhere else?"

"Mm-hm."

The truth: Kiki and I were going to a house party with Ryan and his friends. If I'd told Vladimir the real plan, he never would've taken me to the game. It wasn't like I was *lying*, more like *protecting* him from worrying about me. He was better off not knowing about my wild side.

AFTER THE HOCKEY GAME, Ryan drove Kiki and me to Clifton. I played a country music playlist I put together for Ryan. He patted my leg and told me he liked my boots. I played air drums and sang the lyrics to his favorite song. From the backseat, Kiki reached up and pinched my arm to acknowledge the vibes between Ryan and me.

By the time we got to the house, the party was rocking. In a matter of seconds, Kiki and I had beers in hand while Ryan sipped a Coke. We headed out to the patio and danced with our friends. I was a sweaty mess in no time. Ryan christened me with his Bearcat jersey—my "punishment" for losing our bet—and shadowed me all night.

I sensed he wanted to be more than just good buddies. The shift felt awkward at first, but the alcohol loosened my nerves. Kiki caught me perched on his lap on a sagging couch, snapped a picture, and flashed a thumbs-up. I could get accustomed to having his strong arms wrapped around me like that.

When the party started getting crowded, and beer bottles were breaking, Ryan rounded up Kiki and loaded us into the truck just after one o'clock. He drove us back to Kiki's dorm and walked us to the door. He gave me a hug goodbye and told me to call him when I woke up so he could take us to breakfast. He was so nice. I felt comfortable around him. And damn, his body rocked. Still in his arms, I stood on my toes and planted a smooch on his lips.

Gently, he cupped my chin and backed away. "Not tonight, Cookie."

Ouch.

Once inside, Kiki set out her alcohol stash and helped me drown my sorrows with gin and juice. Her roommate stayed with her boyfriend on Friday nights, so I was free to crash. "Ryan is such an asshole," Kiki said, flipping her long black hair over her shoulder. "I mean, why was he all over you at the party and then why did he, like, body slam you WWE style when you kissed him goodnight?"

"I know, right? What the hell is this?" I tugged on Ryan's jersey.

"Bastard. You're ten times hotter than that fucking

Jessica whore he was with last month. She probably ruined him with her skank."

I laughed so hard I snorted. We cranked up the jams and danced until Kiki's RA shut down our party around four. We turned off the lights and got into bed. I closed my eyes but couldn't fall asleep.

What was wrong with me? First, I threw myself at Vladimir, and then I struck out with Ryan. Was I seriously that repulsive, not to mention desperate? At five-thirty, I gave up on sleep. Without waking Kiki, I headed out to get some coffee from the twenty-four-hour place on Calhoun.

Just as I began my journey down the sidewalk, a car rolled up next to me. Instinctively, I fumbled with the wad of crap around my neck to locate my rape whistle.

The car window hummed down. "Get in," Boris ordered.

I jumped at the sound of his voice. "What the hell, man?"

He glared at me. "Get in." His tone was louder and more threatening the second time.

I held my hands up in surrender, opened the door, and slid into the car.

"This is what you do in your free time, sneaky little weasel? Party with boys, drink yourself stupid, and hang around on dangerous street corners waiting to be attacked?"

"Easy, kick it down a notch." I winced. "You followed me all night?"

Boris took a deep breath, probably to stop himself from slamming my face into the glove box. "You lied to boss. What do you have to say for yourself?"

How insulting. "I don't have to answer to you. You can't tell me what to do in my free time." I put my hand on the door handle—

Boris grabbed my arm and glared at me like he wanted

to chomp me in half. "Lies and disobedience will not be tolerated. On the clock or off. Now you must answer to the *pakhan*."

I suspected the word *pakhan* translated to 'pissed off boss' in English.

This was not going to end well.

12

FILTHY

Back at the lair, Vladimir was not in the kitchen waiting for me as I'd anticipated. I seriously needed some caffeine before I faced the boss. "Want some tea?" I asked Boris. "You must be exhausted from prowling around all night."

"Is it possible for you to speak without slurring your speech?"

I cracked up—it wasn't funny. *Ugh.* I drank too much. "Tea? *Da? Nyet?*"

No response.

"Is Mr. Ivanov still asleep? I need a shower." I sniffed Ryan's jersey. "Gag. I reek."

"*Da.* I followed your scent. That's how I found you."

"Let's see, what scent attracts a man to follow around college girls?" I sniffed Ryan's party-seasoned jersey. "Mm. Cigarette smoke, stale beer, Calvin Klein." I inhaled again. "Tanqueray, wet dog—no wait." I sniffed again. "That's Ryan's sweat." I caught a glimpse of Boris's face and snorted.

"The boss is waiting in the study, *party girl.*" He held the swinging door open and scooted me out of the kitchen.

Shit. "Just wondering, on a scale of one to ten, how much trouble am I in?" Gustav and Anastasia danced at my feet, and I marched the walk of shame to the boss's office, escorted by a big, bad dude three times my size.

Boris glared at me before he answered. "Depends on how well you handle yourself. Could be two, could be ten."

"Great. No pressure then." Facing a ten-degrees-ticked-off Vladimir would be about as survivable as skipping up to a ravenous polar bear with an armload of barking seal pups. But what I did in my free time was none of his business, and I was going to tell him so.

The office door was closed when I approached the study. I could hear Vladimir clicking away on a keyboard, so I stood there, not sure if I should knock or wait until he opened it. Boris huffed, tapped on the door, and—with his big hand on the small of my back—ushered me inside.

Vladimir was seated in a leather chair with a steaming cup of tea in front of him on the desk. There was a map of Russia behind him, and a big, black box with wires and blinking lights connected to six computer monitors. I squinted to see if I could make sense of the information scrolling across the screen, but there were no *words*. Just a bunch of undecipherable programmer jargon and keyboard characters. His office was more high-tech than the cockpit of the International Space Station.

Even at an early hour, the boss had on a suit and looked fabulous, but he reeked of alcohol. He shook his head when he caught sight of my jersey-wearing ungodliness. "What's this?" He held up his hand, questioning my disheveled condition. Boris updated him in Russian and handed him his phone. Vladimir slid on a pair of glasses and thumbed through photos—of *me,* I presumed—on Boris's phone.

"You had a nice evening with the boys?" He leaned forward and folded his hands on his desk.

"Um—" I covered my mouth to keep from laughing.

The boss waited for me to respond, but I didn't know what to say.

Boris clamped his heavy hand down on my shoulder. "The *pakhan* is talking to you. The answer is yes or no."

"Yes?" I said, although I was sure it was the wrong answer.

Vladimir leaned back in his chair and folded his arms, looking sexy and smart in his dark-rimmed glasses. "When I agreed to let you go to the game, you made a promise, remember?"

I straightened my shoulders and swallowed. "I promised not to have one drop of liquor around the guys." My words came out slurred.

"So, you lied to me, in my house, in front of my face?"

My ability to twist a story was epic. With the Russians, however, I had to be careful. I didn't want to find out what would happen if I pissed either of them off too much. "Mr. Ivanov, I kept my promise. I waited to have cocktails until I got back to Kiki's. I just had a few beers at the party to be *social*."

Boris needled his fingers into my collarbone. "Don't you dare pull this shit—"

I squirmed to get him off me.

The boss raised his hand to silence him. "I made myself clear about drinking around boys. Want to learn your lesson with my *patsani* out back? Want to find out what happens when you lose your inhibitions around those animals?"

Was Vladimir threatening to sic his attack dogs on me? "They don't scare me."

"Did she do drugs?" Vladimir asked Boris.

"*Nyet.*"

"I'm sorry I've upset you, Mr. Ivanov. You taught me a valuable lesson last night. I don't know why you're so mad. What I do in my free time is not your concern, and it's not cool to have me tailed all night. I can take care of myself."

"Have you no sense?" Boris jumped in. "My boys out back would love to find a girl like you walking the streets at four in the morning, drunk on her own stupidity—"

"Give me a break." I shook my lanyard at him. "You're lucky I didn't unleash on *you*."

"Dear, *you* are lucky one. If a bad guy had found you stumbling down the street, you would have been bound, gagged, and locked in the trunk of a car before you could even scream rape whistle." He tugged on my lanyard until it was snug across my neck to prove his point. "You make it too easy."

I pushed his hand away. "What do you mean *if* a bad guy had found me?" I jammed my finger in his chest. "You're pissed because you waited all night for me to screw up and have nothing to show for it."

Boris caught my finger, turned my hand around, and poked *me* in the chest with my own finger, like, ten times. "Ouch! Stop it, you big bully." I grabbed him with my other hand and tried to pry him off me. Nice try. My effort to protect myself against him was as productive as a scrawny little monkey battling it out with a giant silverback gorilla.

"Blow your whistle, tough girl."

"Get off me."

"Enough," the boss said.

Boris let go of my finger and turned me around to face the *pakhan*. "When I hired you, Miss Cook, you became part of my brand. Your actions—on the clock and off—are a reflection on me. Perhaps I had a rare lapse in judgment when I hired you and your *papa*."

I understood the underlying threat in his words. I had pushed him too far. Fucking up and getting myself fired was one thing, but I couldn't risk sending Dad back to financial hell. "No, you didn't have a lapse in judgment. I'm sorry."

Vladimir stared me down. "For?"

"Lying to you about where I was going."

"And?"

"And for drinking around boys."

"And?"

I cocked my head as I thought. "And? No *and*. That's it." I peeked over my shoulder and looked up to Boris for guidance. "What else did I do?"

He tugged on Ryan's jersey.

I turned back around to face the boss. "Oh." I shook my head. "It's not what you think. We're just friends. Really good friends. Not friends with benefits, you know, just the *regular* kind of friends." I made a flat line motion with my hand to drive the point home.

Vladimir glanced up at Boris.

Boris responded in Russian and tugged on his belt. I imagined the boss needed clarification on the *friends with benefits* colloquialism, but Boris looked angry enough to kill someone.

Vladimir exhaled and pinched the bridge of his pointy nose. "This is exhausting." He ran his fingers through his tousled hair. "Remember the rules of our arrangement?"

"Good grades, keep up the sports, and stay out of trouble?"

He rested his elbows on the desk and tapped his fingers together.

"Two out of three?" I lifted my shoulders and grinned.

"She has proven to be untrustworthy. I want to see her schoolwork from now on," he said to Boris, then finished his orders in Russian. Then the *pakhan* set his sights on me. "I'm out of patience. I'll deal with you on Monday." He eyed me like I was yesterday's garbage and flicked his hand at me. "Get this filthy *shlyukha* out of my office."

13

DOWN

I used an app on my phone to translate the word *shlyukha*: whore.

I sequestered myself in my bedroom instead of going out with my friends Saturday night and stayed home all day Sunday. I wrapped myself in a blanket and camped out on the floor beside my bed. The wind howled, and a wintry mix of hail and freezing rain pelted the windows, providing a dismal soundtrack for my self-loathing mood.

Ryan kept calling. I didn't pick up.

I had a picture of us on my nightstand. I turned it down.

Dad sent Karen, the mediator, to check on me. I said I had a ton of homework.

My little sister Megan brought an armload of beanbag kittens into my room, but I was too emotionally wrecked to play with her.

As I lay on the floor, wrapped in my ratty old comforter, I chewed my fingernails down to the quick and tried to convince myself to talk to Dad about my arrangement with Vladimir. I knew it was crazy not to, but I was terrified Vladimir would fire Dad—or worse—if I told him the truth.

The thought of what the boss would do if Dad got up in his face made me sick. Dad and his New York temper were definitely better off not knowing what was going on. I hoped he wasn't unwittingly involved in anything illegal.

Since my Saturday morning Russian smackdown, I was so downtrodden I had completely lost my appetite. I couldn't stomach more than a handful of stale Raisin Bran all weekend.

By Monday, I still couldn't shake Vladimir's crass assessment of my character. Ryan probably thought I was a *shlyukha,* too. How could anyone think I was skanky? I was a virgin. So I drank and sat on Ryan's lap...Then I remembered...*Do you have tattoos all over?* Did I really say that to my boss?

I told Karen I had cramps and cut classes on Monday. I couldn't get tattoos out of my head. All the Russians had them. I spent the day searching the Internet for Russian organized crime. It took hours to filter through violent pornographic images, iconic religious motifs, and propaganda that revealed the Russians' secret criminal codes.

I had never given much thought to the ink Vladimir and Boris had engraved on their hands, but I did remember the watch tattoo the boss had on his wrist. Its meaning: time served in full. Vladimir had spent time in prison. Up until what I had witnessed on Friday, I never would've believed someone as sophisticated as Vladimir had a criminal past.

Star tats on the knees meant they would bow down to no one, stars on the shoulders meant they were high-ranking members of a prison gang, and a knife tat like the one Boris had on his neck meant he had killed someone in prison and was available for hire—a hitman.

I searched for Russian organized crime in Brooklyn, because Dad had said Vladimir had lived there at the same time we did. It turned out that an entire community of Russians immigrated to Brighton Beach near Coney Island. Multiple sites called it a hub for Russian organized crime.

The crimes associated with the *Bratva* ranged from drugs, prostitution, illegal gambling, and the usual offenses one would expect from the criminal underworld. Then, I stumbled onto something much bigger associated with the Russians—highly sophisticated cybercrimes and widespread scams led by the superintelligent ringleaders.

It didn't take a genius to figure out where Boris and Vladimir landed on the *Bratva* pie chart. Boris headed up the traditional way of doing business, and the boss led the intelligence side of the new technology-driven Russian mafia.

After I absorbed all the information I could stomach, I dragged myself out of bed and got ready to face the Russians. Boris would go King Kong on me if I failed to report to him after practice. Skipping work was not an option.

I should've forced down a protein bar or a shake before tennis practice, but I wasn't of sound mind. After an hour of drills, I went for a wide backhand shot, and my legs gave out. Down I went. Coach tossed me a sports drink and asked what was up. I tripped over my own feet, I explained.

"You're weak." He glanced down at my shaky hands. "The pressure of playing on court one getting to you? I can knock you down to three if you need a break." He was more concerned about *me*, not my tennis game, but "knock you down" still stung.

Court one was reserved for the top players. It was the most revered spot on the team, a competitive pressure cooker, and I would never let anybody knock me off my doubles pedestal.

I chugged the Gatorade and assured Coach everything was fine. I knew I looked like hell, so I said I needed to rest. He let me go, but I wasn't convinced he bought that excuse either.

Now—because of the Russians—I was blipping on Coach's fuck-up radar. There was no way I would let the boss and his locked-and-loaded sidekick screw up my court one status. As I marched to the car, I assessed my situation.

Vladimir wanted to spend time with *me*, but I didn't give a damn about *him*.

If I had my way, I would walk away from our arrangement and never look back.

The boss, however, couldn't handle losing his ex-girlfriend's little ghost.

Translation: I had the upper hand in our bullshit storm.

I was only a few minutes late for my rendezvous with disaster. I got into the car without speaking to my ill-tempered, grabby keeper. The Russians wanted to spy on me? Pelt me with insults? Threaten to teach me a lesson? Game on. They'd knocked me down for a round, but I was back in my ready position, ready to throw the next punch.

I *was* out of hand Friday night, but Vladimir had no right to berate me the way he did, and Boris crossed the line when he manhandled me like some asshole who owed him a C-note for a bad gambling debt. It was time to find out how the Russians would handle a taste of *my* poison.

Boris studied my pale face when I slid into the car. "Why did you ditch classes?"

I didn't answer.

He stared at me, waiting for me to change my attitude. "You're going to try this shit on the *pakhan*?"

No reply from me.

More death rays from him.

Once we got to the house, I skipped a shower. I would never be clean enough for the boss anyway. Instead, I pulled a stack of graded papers out of my backpack and, using a handful of kitten-themed magnets I'd brought from home, proudly plastered my overachiever test scores all over the fridge.

Then I got to work on an English lit essay.

Boris poured himself a shot of vodka. He didn't utter a word. He was probably devising an action plan to *make* me talk. I could just imagine his internal gangster dialogue: *She will beg to speak after I cut out her tongue.* "Want a drink? The boss wants you to learn how to handle your alcohol in a safe environment."

I resisted the urge to snort and kept working.

"Boss will be here soon. Better shape up."

I yawned.

Boris left the room, probably to stop himself from tossing me to the wolves on the basketball court. After I finished my homework, I started dinner. I kept myself busy doodling a picture of the lovebirds, Igor and Natasha, in my notebook. I worried about how Vladimir would react when I failed to greet him at the door and wag my tail like a golden retriever, but I refused to waver. I had to stick to my game plan. It wasn't like my situation could get any freaking worse.

The Big Chill was my weapon of choice with Dad. I wasn't naïve enough to believe it would work on Boris, but I was optimistic I could wear down the boss. I heard the garage door open. Vladimir was home early. He probably couldn't wait to see me so he could flay me some more. Was I prepared to go to war with the *pakhan*?

Stay strong. Show no fear.

I focused on the vegetarian chili I was stirring on the

stove. When the boss came in, he didn't say a word, but I felt him standing behind me.

He didn't speak.

I didn't move.

He wrapped his hand around my elbow and gently turned me around. He had a bouquet of two-toned red and pink roses in his hand. "Can you ever forgive me, Carter?"

No one had ever given me flowers before.

I dug my nails into the tips of my fingers. I couldn't look at him. He set the vase on the counter and gave me a hug. When I didn't hug him back, he picked up my limp arms and wrapped them around his body.

"I worry about you. You're so beautiful. Don't you see how the boys look at you? I couldn't think about anything since you left my house." He stroked my hair. "Then today, your papa said he was worried because you stayed in your room all weekend."

My breath caught in my throat. I squeezed my elbows against my ribs.

He lifted my chin. "He confided in me about your *problem*."

There. A kill shot to the head. Dad had told him what happened to Sophia. In sixth grade, I had gotten slapped with a detention for talking in class. I didn't want to get into trouble, so I begged Sophia to pick me up so Dad wouldn't find out.

Freezing rain fell from the November sky, and the temperature had dropped below freezing, but Sophia promised she would hurry so we would get back before Dad got home from work. Soaking wet, shivering, and chilled to the bone, I waited and waited and waited...

I covered my ears when a line of fire engines, police cars, and ambulances raced past the school and shielded my nose and mouth from the noxious odor of burnt rubber and scorched metal that hung in the air. It wasn't until later that I realized where the fire was coming from—and what had been burning.

On her way to pick me up, Sophia skidded off the road and slammed into a tree, which caused her car to burst into flames. She had survived the initial impact. It was the fire that killed her; she had been burned alive. The accident happened so close to the school that I could *smell* the wreckage.

My problem, according to my therapist, stemmed from the guilt over my sister's accident. My doctor calls the stupid things I do 'self-destructive,' and tells my dad I feel unloved, so he'll keep writing her checks. I *do* have self-esteem issues, and I *do* lose my appetite when I'm depressed. But I'm not punishing myself. That was a load of crap.

"I miss Sophia, too. Every single day. How can you possibly feel responsible for her death? It wasn't your fault, Carter. You're a perfect, beautiful soul." He rested my head on his shoulder. "Your papa said you were hospitalized after the accident. You didn't speak, didn't eat." My tears spilled free and dripped on his dark gray suit. He squeezed me tighter. "*Moy slomannyy angel*, what can I do to make this right?"

"Nothing. It's no big deal. Don't listen to Dad. He exaggerates everything. I need to finish dinner." I tried to pull away, but he wouldn't let me go.

"I want to take you out. Let's get you cleaned up. We'll go someplace nice."

"Dinner is ready." I picked up the wooden spoon and stirred the chili.

Vladimir put his hand on top of mine, scooped up a bite, and gave it a taste. He pursed his lips. "It's awful, angel."

I laughed, surprised by his candor. It did kind of smell like the inside of my tennis bag.

"There's your beautiful smile." He picked up my hands and lifted them to his heart. "For me, let me take you out to a nice dinner?"

Awesome. Call me a whore, point out you know my darkest secret, and then make everything better by buying me dinner.

"That's sweet of you to offer, but I didn't bring anything to change into today."

He held out my arms and examined my hideous green and yellow tracksuit. "Hmm, I might have something for you to wear." He steered me out of the kitchen and led me to the guest bedroom. "As I said, I couldn't think of anything but you all weekend. I told Boris to pick you up so I could see you, but as my *sovietnik,* he refused."

I wrinkled my forehead.

"I had to keep myself busy." He opened the door, ushered me to the closet, and revealed the surprise. There were boxes upon boxes of fancy shoes, purses, and gorgeous designer dresses.

All that stuff must have cost a duffel bag of cash. I had to think of the best way to respond. I needed to turn this around. I felt much safer around Nice Boss than I did around the devil-eyed *pakhan.*

"What do you think, angel? Can you find a dress to wear tonight?"

Game Plan Change Up: I hugged him. "You're too good to me."

"You deserve it all and more."

I pulled back. "It'll take me a while to get ready. I need to wash my hair."

"I'll wait a lifetime for you."

14

PURR

Out of all the glamorous dresses to choose from, I decided on a long, dark red velvet one with a slit up the side. I paired it with Prada heels with ankle straps and a Gucci crossbody purse.

I admired my reflection and wondered if Ryan would recognize me as girlfriend material if he saw me dressed as a sophisticated woman rather than a buddy-buddy gym rat in baggy sweats and a scraggly ponytail—my official weekday uniform. Then I wondered how Vladimir would see me. Was I just Sophia's spunky, fucked-up little sister who needed to be rescued...or in some messed-up way, her *replacement*?

I emerged from the bedroom with my hair falling over my shoulders. Boris eyed my outfit and gave me his *look*. I put my hand on my hip. "Boss picked it out."

"Ah, she speaks."

I flashed him a sarcastic grin.

"He's out back." Boris held up a shearling coat. I slipped my arms into the sleeves, and he issued a warning over my shoulder: "Behave yourself tonight."

"If you're referring to alcohol consumption, I won't be drinking. No one serves underage girls outside of this house."

"If you say so, dear."

Out on the patio, the heat lamps were ablaze, and the scent of burning firewood filled the air. Vladimir changed out of his work clothes and donned a slick black suit with a crisp white shirt unbuttoned a few notches. He *did* have tats on his chest along with a couple of gold chains around his neck. A blue-eyed, inked devil peeked at me from behind his shirt.

"You're stunning, Carter." His gaze moved slowly up and down my body. "Something is missing, though." Vladimir held up his hand, and dangling from his finger was a gold choker encrusted with champagne diamonds. "It accentuates your beautiful eyes." He motioned for me to turn around.

"I insist."

I gave in and lifted my hair so he could clasp it around my neck. Once it was secure, I let my hair down and brought my hands up to my neck to feel the necklace. "It's beautiful."

"Not as beautiful as you."

My heart pounded, and my stomach was all fluttery from a Molotov cocktail of emotions swirling in my gut. I'd been so lonely and depressed the last few days—because of Vladimir—and now I was filled with nervous excitement because he was treating me like his most prized possession.

He escorted me through the house, and when we reached the kitchen, he lifted the car keys from the drawer. "This is a Ferrari night. Want to drive?"

"I don't think so, Mr. Ivanov." I resisted all the way to the driver's side, but gave up, knowing I wouldn't win. "I don't have much experience."

"I'll teach you everything you need to know." He sat me down and adjusted the seat so I could reach the pedals. He slid in on the passenger side and positioned my hands on the wheel.

"Put your foot on the brake and push the button."

I did what he said. The engine purred.

"What do I do now?"

"Relax, angel. Listen to the sound of the engine. When it's ready to go, you'll feel it. The car has a mind of its own."

He was right. Moments later, the purr dropped lower. "Now?"

"You're a natural."

"Where's the stick?"

"No stick. To reverse, hold down the brake and tap the paddles." After a few more instructions, I rolled the Ferrari out of the garage, tapped it in drive, and pulled out onto the main road. Damn, it was intimidating. I felt like a jockey holding back a thoroughbred from breaking for the finish line, but after a few minutes, I got accustomed to the rhythm of a fine machine and got the beast under control.

When we rolled up to the valet, I spied the Cadillac parked up front. Boris must have left while we were on the patio. I had the impression the big guy was not just Vladimir's *sovietnik*. He was more like a bodyguard and was there to keep an eye on him—or *me*.

As we breezed through the dining area, all heads turned to us. Vladimir wrapped his arm around my shoulders, and we followed the manager past a couple of jumbo-sized bouncers and up a flight of stairs that led to a bar area.

Boris was there with a teacup in his hand and a bottle of vodka on the table in front of him. He was dealing cards to some old guys while another dozen seedy-looking Russians filled the room. There were girls there, too, wearing gobs of make-up, low-cut dresses, and ridiculously high heels. I jumped when I spotted Mr. Cusimano seated at the bar, locking lips with a busty brunette who was *not* Mrs. Cusimano.

Boris and his cohorts took notice as Vladimir and I passed through on our way up another flight of stairs to a fancy private dining room on the third floor. Artwork featuring Russian architecture lined the walls, shelves held an eclectic mix of shabby chic antiques and nesting dolls, and the room was illuminated by candelabras.

The boss had made it clear Friday night that he was not interested in me that way. Remembering his look of disgust flushed me with humiliation, but this setting seemed a bit romantic for an oligarch-protégé kind of dinner.

Was that why Boris had admonished me when he got a gander of my wardrobe choice? Was this a test?

The maître d' pulled out my chair and scooted me in. "How do you say thank you?" I asked Vladimir.

"*Spasibo.*"

"*Spasibo.*" I smiled at the sweet-faced old man.

Vladimir sat down across from me and set a napkin in his lap. "I hope you're hungry. The chef is preparing a traditional Russian feast—*lacto-vegetarian,* of course."

I knew what he was doing. He was trying to *fix* me.

A couple of bites of fancy food, and I'll be good as new, right? Well, it doesn't work that way. Food isn't the problem, nor is it the solution, and despite what my shrink says, I'm not engaging in self-destructive behavior...

A server set out a spread of pickles, skinny marinated mushrooms, sauerkraut, black bread with a crock of butter, and a small dish of salt. The waiter swooped in and set down a line of shots, each tinted a different color.

I wondered if the boss had gotten a head injury over the

weekend and suffered from acute memory loss. "Is this a joke?" I crossed my arms, ticked that he had the nerve to set me up like that again.

"Infused vodka. The house specialty. I want you to have the best of everything."

Okay, I felt like an ass. I could tell I'd insulted him. I gave in. "What are the flavors?"

"Pineapple, cucumber, and horseradish."

"Horseradish? For real?"

"Want to try?"

"I'm going to have to work my way up to that one. Let's start with pineapple." I pointed to the golden-tinted one.

"First," he said, "pick up a bread slice. Tonight, you will drink like a Russian."

He lifted the dark rye bread to his nose and sniffed. I followed his lead. Then, he buttered his bread and sprinkled it with salt. I did the same and set the bread down on the plate.

Vladimir raised his glass to mine and made a toast in Russian.

I held my drink back so he couldn't clink it. "Not until you tell me what it means."

"Something good." His glass hovered in the air.

I gave in. "To something good." We clinked glasses and downed our shots.

15

THE PAKHAN

Vladimir took a bite of bread. I tore mine into bite-sized pieces and glanced around the room, taking in the fabulous décor. "You pick the next one." I pointed to the shots.

He picked up the horseradish-infused vodka. "This one."

My throat still burned from the last shot. Since he had made the first toast, I held my glass up and initiated the next one. "*Za zdorovye*."

He clinked my glass, grinning at what I suspected was my horrid accent, and repeated the sentiment. We downed our shots. It tasted good, but my nose burned like when I put too much wasabi on my cucumber roll. "How do you say, 'the vodka is nice?'"

"*Vodka khoroshaya*."

"Say it again."

He obliged.

"*Vodka khoroshaya, Pakhan*. That's what Boris calls you. *Pakhan* means 'boss,' right?"

The truth: I'd looked it up. Specifically, it meant *godfather,* as in *crime boss*.

"You catch on quick, angel."

I picked from the appetizer tray and arranged little piles of marinated veggies on my plate. He wouldn't stop staring at me. I felt self-conscious and needed to loosen up so I could eat something. "Where did you meet my sister?"

"It was a long time ago."

I worried I might ruin the light mood, but I pushed anyway. "Dad packed away all of Sophia's pictures and never talks about her. I'm his only reminder she ever existed."

Vladimir brought a napkin to his face and patted his mouth. "That's why he's so protective of you. Your resemblance to Sophia is—"

"Haunting?"

"Remarkable."

"Do you see her when you look at me?"

His lips parted, and the answer was on the tip of his tongue. Then the waiter interrupted when he delivered trays of food: radish cakes, baked cheesy bread, eggplant caviar, and a beet and kidney bean salad. Vladimir welcomed the distraction and turned his focus on filling my plate with a sample of all the *zakuski* on the table. I still had internal bleeding from the verbal lashing he'd sliced me with early Saturday morning, but he was extending the olive branch, and I needed to take it.

Vladimir had apologized and was honestly trying to make it up to me. The gesture was sweet and genuine. I thanked him and plunged my fork into a saucy beet thing. I stabbed at it, trying to make it small enough to swallow without chewing. I set down my fork and picked up my water glass.

Unsure what my problem was, Vladimir lifted his shoulders and took a bite of the same dish I'd hacked to pieces. "It's good. No meat. No fish. No eggs."

I put down my glass when my hands began to tremble from being so nervous. "Stop trying to *fix* me." I tossed my napkin over my plate, bolted outside to the scenic patio that overlooked downtown, and welcomed the chilly breeze that cooled my clammy skin. As soon as I reached the railing, Vladimir wrapped his suit jacket around my shoulders as if he could extinguish my flame of insanity. I shook my head. "I'm so sorry—"

"It must be lonely to grow up without your big sister." He turned me around and tried to rest my head on his chest, but I stepped back.

"I felt lightheaded from the alcohol. I'm fine now." I took his hand and tried to drag him back inside. He didn't move.

"Coney Island."

I turned around.

"Sophia worked at a pizzeria near the boardwalk."

"She was a senior in high school when she worked there."

"And I was a seventeen-year-old Russian immigrant, living the American dream."

I mirrored his smile, encouraging him to continue.

"I'd never seen a more beautiful young woman in my life. Her golden eyes, her long, blonde hair waving in the wind." He looked up at the stars as he conjured up the memory. "When her shift ended, I approached her. The moment our eyes met, I knew we would be together forever."

"Sophia and I were very close, and she never mentioned you."

"She had planned to tell you everything, but our lives were interrupted when my work took me back to Russia. I had to stay longer than expected."

"Because you went to prison?" I lowered his hand and

pointed to the tattoo of a watch on his wrist, visible under his Rolex. "Time served. I noticed it when you took your watch off. I looked it up."

I worried he might be mad, but he seemed impressed. I picked up his other hand and continued. "This cross means you served one prison term. This ring tattoo of a crown means you're the *pakhan*. The Russian letters across your fingers spell out your nickname 'B-O-C-C' which translates to 'Boss.' The five dots represent four guard towers and you in the middle. I don't know what all the other stuff means, but Boris has way more ink than you do."

He squeezed my hands and lowered them to my side. "Don't dig too deep. It's not a pretty story. I wish you'd let me in on your secrets. So much pain behind your eyes."

"So, by the time you got out of prison, she was *gone*?" I asked, desperate to change the subject.

He smiled weakly, but I could tell he was holding back. "I think of her every day. Seeing you at my house the night we met, I couldn't help but wonder if—"

"If what?"

"Let's get you out of the cold." Vladimir put his arm around my shoulders, and I inhaled his cologne as he guided me back inside. Instead of sitting when we reached our table, he spoke to the manager in Russian. The guy nodded and led us back to the kitchen. At first, I didn't get it. I followed him curiously.

Our waiter cleared off a prep counter and brought in two barstools. Vladimir guided me to sit and scooted his chair next to me. The manager delivered a bottle of wine and set it on the table along with a corkscrew. Vladimir went to the bar and got a couple of glasses. He opened the wine, poured our drinks, and clinked my glass.

"Like home." He winked.

Finally, I understood. Our first dinner together in the formal dining room was noticeably painful for me. Sitting down at a fancy table and staring at each other didn't fly in my comfort zone. He'd picked up on my apprehension and moved our gathering spot to the kitchen. We ate *zakuski* at the bar, sipping drinks, and talking—like a Russian family.

"Thank you," I said, not specifying, but he knew anyway.

The chef gave us a quick cooking lesson. She even taught me how to grill kabobs, which I managed to do without gagging. Hearing the meat sizzle and watching the fat bubble up and melt down usually made my stomach turn. I guess Vladimir was the distraction I needed to maintain my sanity.

He even ate three skewers of meat and veggies and said it was the best thing he'd ever tasted. I'd had a sneaking suspicion he wasn't really a vegetarian. He'd dropped a few pounds since I'd become his personal chef. We took a break from cooking to sample the food and enjoy our wine as we did at home, and before the clock bonged *curfew*, the tension had lifted.

Vladimir and I were "over our bullshit," as Boris would say.

16

TICKED

The next day, it was drizzling outside, so I took a shortcut through the weight room to get to the back parking lot, where Boris picked me up. A shirtless Leonardo, the studly basketball player, nodded as I walked past. "*¿Cómo estás?*" He flexed his muscles.

"*Bien.*" Thanks to a good public education, I'm fluent *en español.*

"In a hurry?" He mopped a gym towel across his face.

Well, I would face the Wrath of Boris to hang out with you for a minute or two. "Not really." I set down my tennis bag and filled a cup of water from the cooler.

His dreamy green eyes lit up as his gaze moved up and down my sweaty body. "I haven't seen you. You don't work upstairs anymore?"

I shook my head.

"I just finished up. Want to grab a shake?"

My belly fluttered. "Oh, I wish I could, but my ride is here."

"Another time?"

"*Sí.*" I walked to the door but stopped and turned

around when a brilliant idea popped into my head. "I have an extra ticket to the ballet this Friday. I don't know if that's something you're into or not, but—"

"I'm into it if you are. *No puedo esperar.*"

I felt tingly all over. "*Yo tampoco.*"

We exchanged numbers.

When I met Boris, I was sure my aura was glowing. "*Privet.*" I plopped down in the front seat with more enthusiasm than usual.

He glared at me as if my good mood were a signal of imminent disaster. "*Privet.* Your day was good?"

"Yeah, practice was good. I got my calculus homework done in English lit. Good."

He didn't put the car in reverse, which made me nervous. I take after my dad. He rambles when he's nervous. I ramble when I'm nervous. "Yep. Good. Very good." I tapped my foot.

"What made your day *very* good? Something special must have happened."

Jeez. "Actually, yes. I have a favor to ask."

He nodded for me to continue.

"Well, Kiki's parents gave us an early Christmas present —tickets to the ballet."

"Ah, so thoughtful." His dark eyes were set on lie detector mode.

"Yes, they're fabulous. Anyway, the tickets are for this Friday." I waited to gauge his reaction, but his expression hadn't changed. "So, I was wondering if I could have the night off?"

He tapped his fingers on the dash as he processed the request. "To go to the ballet with Chinese friend?"

"Mm, hm."

"Of course, I will send a limo to take you in style. Two

lovely ladies shouldn't drive downtown alone. It is my gift to you and your friend."

"Oh, wow. That's so nice." Driver meant babysitter.

"My pleasure." He pulled back on the shifter to put the car in reverse.

"But—"

"*But*?" He slammed the car into park. The Cadillac engine revved.

I exhaled. "We're going with some friends."

Boris licked his lips. "Now the story changes?"

"No, no, no, the story didn't change." I tried to keep it light. "I gave you the abbreviated version instead of the long-winded one." I balled my fingers into a fist and put them in my lap.

He nodded at my hands. "This is how you mask your untruth?"

Everything was so serious with him. I laughed and patted him on the shoulder. "It's all good, Boris. It's just a night out with my friends. No alcohol, I promise." I put my hand on my heart. "I appreciate the offer for the car, but Kiki's date is driving."

"Your date is good guy?"

"Sure. Yeah. He's a nice guy."

"He goes to your college?"

Dammit. "No."

"Older boy?"

"We're about the same age." I turned on the music to try to change the subject. "What's that *Russkiy* song we listened to the other day? The one about the sky. I think I have the chorus memorized now."

He played the song. "*About* the same age? What does that mean?"

"Please don't interrogate me, Boris. No surprises—I promise."

He drove off the lot and tipped his head as he considered my request. "Friday night, I'll take you home early."

"*Spasibo.*" I clapped my hands.

He pointed his finger at me. "But you will serve the rest of your time on Sunday."

Ay caramba.

17

QUICK AND DIRTY

Since Vladimir and I had buried our little problem, he had come home early every night that week. We talked. We laughed. We celebrated my team's advance to the playoffs. We noshed on marinated veggies and bread and enjoyed our wine and vodka. Things were going so well, I looked forward to our time together. In fact, the Carter Love Fest bordered on obnoxious.

It was the last week before winter break, and Vladimir helped me study for exams. He wrote words of encouragement in Russian on my statistics practice tests—after he helped me correct my mistakes—and we engaged in mock business negotiations, Russian style, that involved generous shots of vodka chased down with dark bread slathered with rich butter. It was sweet of him to spend so much time with me, and I loved seeing him in boss mode.

For one of our negotiations, we pretended I was a produce supplier, and he owned a restaurant. I gave him an estimate for what I thought was a fair price for the order he placed, but he asked for a twenty percent discount. I countered with ten percent and, as a goodwill gesture, tossed in a couple extra heads of cabbage under the table.

"Twenty is my final offer," Vladimir said, pouring on his alpha male persona.

Determined not to squirm under pressure, I stared him down while I crafted a comeback. I kept my mental focus and extended my hand. "Thank you for your time, Mr. Ivanov. Regrettably, I am unable to accept your terms. Have a pleasant day." I tried to walk away, but he tightened his grip on my hand and wouldn't let me go.

"I'm sorry we couldn't have reached more favorable terms, Miss Cook. Now we'll do it my way."

"What? Are you—?"

"In one hour, *you* will personally deliver my order. I will receive a *fifty* percent discount off your lowest offer, and *all* cabbages will be delivered under the table. Pleasure doing business with you, Miss Cook."

I shook out of his grasp and made a T with my hands. "Timeout." I glanced over at Boris, who was seated across from us, writing in his black notebook. "Is he on my team or yours?"

Vladimir tipped his hand, offering me the big guy.

I straightened my shoulders and plastered my game face back on. "It certainly is a pleasure doing business with you, Mr. Ivanov." I checked my watch. "I have to run. Let's do this. I'll have my associate Boris go over the final details of your order. I look forward to a long, mutually beneficial business relationship with you, and I would hate for there to be any *bad blood* between us. Don't you agree?"

"Well played, angel. You're hired." He kissed my cheeks. "Welcome to the family."

I cracked up. Boris fired off some angry words in Russian, but Vladimir laughed it off. Boris hated to see the boss joking and fawning over me, but I thought it was sweet. I'm sure the boss had way more important things to do, but he liked spending time with me, too.

On Friday, the official kick-off to winter break and the night of the ballet, I heard the garage door open. I set out the drinks and *zakuski* and greeted the boss at the door as was our custom. "Happy Friday, Mr. Ivanov."

"*Privet.*" He admired my hair, styled in big, loose waves. "You look beautiful, Carter. Tonight, I will take you somewhere extra special to celebrate the end of your semester."

Holy shit. Boris hadn't told him about my date. I turned to my keeper for guidance. "Um—"

Boris spoke to the boss in Russian and poured a round of shots. Vladimir was silent, but his expression went from 'happy to be home' to 'lit stick of tattooed dynamite.' They downed their vodka.

"Boris tells me you are leaving early. You must have big plans?" He had fire in his eyes.

"Oh, not too big."

Boris poured another round and offered me a drink. I shook my head and lifted a water bottle out of the bar fridge. I was not going to have one drop of alcohol before I left the house.

"Tell me." Vladimir hadn't taken off his suit jacket or loosened his tie like usual.

Boris opened his betting book and pretended not to listen to our conversation.

"Kiki and I are going to the ballet with a couple of friends."

"Sounds nice. Girlfriends?"

I shook my head and launched a counterattack. "What about you? What are your plans?"

Boris looked up from his book, warning me to be careful. I smiled and waited for Vladimir to answer. He smiled back—not a cheery type of grin—more like a passive-aggressive response to my evasiveness.

"The boss asked you a question," Boris said.

"I heard him."

Boris glared at me.

"Sorry, I didn't mean for it to come out like that," I apologized to my keeper. "I'm not trying to be disrespectful, boss. Can we go to the other room and talk in private?"

Boris rattled off something in Russian.

I picked up Vladimir's hand and tried to pull him toward the swinging door. He didn't budge. I changed up my game plan and passed the ball to the boss. Why forge ahead into a losing battle? The *pakhan* didn't take orders. I let go of his hand and plopped down on a barstool in defeat.

Vladimir savored his victory. "You want to speak in private?" He tugged on my elbow. "Come. We'll sit by the fire."

Safe in the company of the boss, I flashed a grin to Boris. Vladimir led me out of the kitchen to the couch in the living room.

"I know you worry about me," I said. "After last weekend, I get it. Epic fail on my part, but really, I'm not like that." I squeezed his hand. "I need you to trust me."

"I do, Carter."

"I mean all the way. Tell Boris not to follow me tonight."

The boss let go of my hand and walked to the fireplace. He stacked up a couple of logs in the hearth, arranged some kindling, and struck a match to light the fire. "The thought of you running around the city at all hours—"

"See? That's my point. You worry too much. We're going to the ballet and maybe out for coffee after that. Then Kiki and I are spending the night at her parents' house—alone. The dorms are closed until break is over. There's nothing to worry about, Mr. Ivanov. I won't relax if I know I have a tail."

"You can't think of any other reason why I might be concerned?"

I shrugged.

"My dearest Carter, you are so naïve."

I stood up and met him by the fireplace. "I am capable of going to the ballet without a babysitter."

The boss put his hands on my shoulders. "There's something you said last Friday. I feel like you weren't being honest with me."

"About what?" My heart pounded.

He swept my hair over to one side and smoothed my waves. "You said you've never had a boyfriend. A girl as beautiful as you—it's not possible. Want to change your story?"

I held my hands up dismissively. "Boss, I hate to break it to you, but you have some distorted view of my status with the boys. I promise you, I have never in my entire life had a boyfriend."

His eyes were saturated with disappointment. He didn't believe me.

"Okay, I am going to let you in on a secret, but if I tell you, you have to promise to drop it. It's not something I want to talk about." I guided him to the couch. "The picture of Ryan and me last weekend didn't tell the real story. He didn't kiss me. *I* kissed him."

His jaw tensed.

"And when I did, he declined my offer." I covered my mouth to hide my quivering lips.

He rested my head on his chest. "Is he homosexual?"

"No, he likes girls, just not *me*." The humiliation of that night felt fresh.

He rubbed circles on my back with his warm hand, encouraging me to give him more. "He can pretty much go out with any girl he wants to. It's no big deal. I'm over it." Tears dripped down my cheeks.

Vladimir dabbed away my tears with his silk pocket square. "The boy is crazy. If a beautiful girl like you gave me so much as a glance, I would give her the world. Designer clothes, fine jewelry, fancy cars—"

"You already do that for me." I smiled through my tears. "Seriously, is the matter settled now?"

"Of course." He walked me back to the kitchen.

Boris didn't look up from his book as we breezed past him at the bar.

"Tonight wouldn't happen to be your *first* date, would it, angel?" Vladimir asked.

His question caught me by surprise. "Well, you know I go out all the time with my friends—guys and girls—but I guess officially tonight would technically be my first *real* date."

He bit his bottom lip, then snapped at Boris in Russian. And kept snapping. *Damn.*

The boss is obviously ticked about something, but is he mad at Boris or me?

"Is something wrong?" I had wrestled with the idea of inviting Vladimir to the ballet, but I couldn't handle him rejecting me again. If he said yes, Kiki would wonder why I was hanging out with Dad's boss. My employment situation was a secret, Dad would kill me...

Boris replied, "*Nyet,*" and shot me the evil eye.

Vladimir shook off the crazy, slid on my coat, and kissed

my cheeks. He lifted my hands and checked out my upgraded fingernails. I'd gotten a manicure at the club, courtesy of him, after I'd chewed my nails off. They were painted pale pink with light purple French tips and a hint of glitter.

"So, what about my special request?"

"I will leave it up to my *sovietnik*. Whatever the two of you work out is fine by me. *Do svidaniya*."

My keeper cracked a smile and spun the Cadillac key ring around his finger.

Double damn.

I had fourteen minutes to make my case. I gave Boris the quick and dirty version of the plea I'd made to Vladimir. I'm in college, perfectly capable of going to the ballet without a babysitter, I appreciate Vladimir's concern...

"Your papa approves of this young man? Knows the family?"

"That's not how things work here."

He gave me a sideways glance. "Your papa knows you have date tonight, right?"

I fumbled with the zipper on my coat. "He knows I'm going to the ballet with Kiki."

"I don't recall you mentioning this nice boy's name." I could tell by Boris's tight lips and white knuckles that the big studly picture was coming into focus.

"Uh, the basketball player. Leonardo—"

He ranted in Russian, swerved onto a side street, and slammed the car into park. "This will not happen under my watch." He rubbed his beard. "You have two choices. One: You will go back to the house and explain to the boss why a nice young lady is interested in dating a twenty-four-year-old man *with a criminal record*."

"I didn't know, I swear." It's not like I asked for his birth certificate and resume. I had no idea how Boris knew so much about Leonardo, but I believed him. The big guy had his faults, but lying wasn't one of them.

"Option two: Call the Spaniard right now and tell him you will not be going out with him tonight or *ever*." His deep, angry voice had enough torque to uproot a tree.

My survival instincts took over. I tapped Leonardo's number. I spoke to him in Spanish and made up a bullshit excuse for canceling. I ended the call. Boris seemed even more pissed than before. "What did I do now? I called it off."

By his expression, I should have already known what I did wrong.

"Oh, come on," I said. "We always converse *en español*."

He pointed his thick finger in my face. "Dear, one day you are going to push me too far."

I looked away.

He cupped my chin and turned my head until I met his eyes. "Trust me. You don't want to see what happens when I lose my temper."

18

CRASHED AND BURNED

After my awesome date with an empty chair, I couldn't wait for a Saturday night do-over. My friends wanted to do something *memorable* over winter break, so we planned a sleep-in-your-car, all-nighter camping trip. I had told my dad that, as per usual, I was spending the night with Kiki, and Kiki told her parents she was staying at my place.

We'd made the lake plans weeks ago, before I'd even met the Russians. After my failure last weekend, I didn't want to subject myself to another lecture, but if I didn't drink and/or throw myself at anyone, I could flash the stupid girl card on the trespassing crime. I mean, damn, I could go camping with my friends without Vladimir and Boris's approval.

With our alibis in place, I told Kiki to text me when she got to the house, and I would meet her outside. I didn't want to give Dad an opportunity to ask questions. A knock came from the front door. *Jeez, Kiki.*

I yelled goodbye to the family, hoofed it downstairs, and opened the door. Ryan was standing on my porch. His shoulders were slumped, making him look like a dejected

Teddy bear. *Awkward.* I'd been avoiding him since The Kiss. He had called and sent me a billion texts, but I didn't have the guts to own up to my drunk behavior.

"Please talk to me." He reached out and tugged on my coat sleeve.

His sweet brown eyes wore me down. "Okay, but not here." I hopped inside Ryan's truck and texted Kiki I would catch up with her later.

We made small talk as he drove us to our favorite pizza place. Turned out he was spending winter break with his dad, who lived across the street from me. Once we got a booth and ordered a large white pizza with artichokes and black olives, with a side of meatballs, Ryan put his hand on top of mine. "I didn't turn you down that night."

I looked away, ashamed. "Ryan, I'm totally embarrassed about the whole thing. Can we please drop it?"

He shook my arm to loosen my constant anxiety. I couldn't look at him. I took a sip of my Sierra Mist.

"You're not hearing me, Carter. I've been crushing on you since high school."

"Ryan, stop it."

"Seriously. I only said no because I have too much respect for you to take advantage of a situation like that. But, if you were my *girlfriend* and wanted to attack me, I'd be all right with that." He tapped my foot under the table and squeezed my hand.

I peeked up at him. He had the cutest dimples. "*Your* girlfriend?"

At that exact moment, a guy bumped into Ryan's chair. When the dude turned around and held up his hand to apologize, I recognized him—Playboy. He tossed me a wicked grin and camped out at the table behind Ryan.

After Playboy took a seat, two of his cohorts joined him

—the big, grimacing fellow that lurked around Vladimir's house, and a wiry guy with a shaved head and a trail of black tats running down his neck. Playboy waved behind Ryan's back and snapped a pic of us. A not-so-subtle reminder for me to be on my best behavior.

That trio of Russian outcasts must be the *patsani* Vladimir had warned me about last weekend. My God, would he really use them to teach me a lesson?

As we walked back to his truck after dinner, Ryan said, "Can I talk you into a movie instead of going to the lake?"

Hanging around with Ryan would be a solid way to stay out of trouble. I hated the thought, but the Russians were right about drinking around boys, and there was potential for the trip to end badly—and I sure as hell didn't want Playboy and his posse to get involved.

"Come on. I'll buy the Milk Duds."

"You're tempting me with the promise of a sugar buzz and a mouthful of cavities? Smooth. I'm a sucker for bad boys. Your bribe is accepted."

As Ryan drove to the theater, Dad's ringtone erupted in my purse. "What's up? I'm with Ryan." I paused, listening. "Cowan Lake? On my way."

"What's wrong?" Ryan asked.

"The cops busted Kiki and a bunch of the others for being at the lake after hours. Some jerk brought beer, so everyone had to call their parents to pick them up. Kiki's dad was worried because I was M.I.A. and called Dad."

"How angry is he?"

"Oh, you know Dad. Somewhere between an overprotective rhino and a ticked-off Coach Harbaugh." The drama was getting exhausting.

"But you weren't even at the lake."

"Stop applying common sense. We're talking about my dad, here."

When Ryan got me back to the house, Dad was waiting on the front porch in his pajama pants, house slippers, and a winter coat. He couldn't even wait for me to get inside the house to interrogate me. Ryan offered to walk me to the door and be my witness, but I convinced him to go home. I liked the idea of knowing he was across the street.

"You lied right to my face, Carter?" Dad asked before I even made it up the steps. "How dumb do you think I am? You do this sort of thing every weekend with your wild college friends?" He held the door open, I stepped inside, and he locked it behind me. "Does Ryan lie to his dad so he can sneak around all night? So, the two of you are an item now?" Even though he was shouting, he sounded excited about the prospect of me dating the Perfect One.

I didn't answer any of his questions. The one night I didn't do anything wrong, I got busted for lying to my dad for no good reason. Karen peered at me from the kitchen table.

"You don't want to talk?" he went on. "Fine. You're grounded. Give me your phone. If you don't have anything to say to me, then you don't need to talk to anyone else."

I handed my phone to him without pleading my case. Grounded. Like a kid. Total bullshit, but I didn't have it in me to fight back. In fact, I could think of nothing better to do than sit in my room and rot all weekend.

He glanced down at my screenshot and let out an exasperated sigh when he saw a selfie of Kiki and me making fish faces. "The two of you," he mumbled under his beer breath. "It'll be such a relief when you're finally out of this house, so I won't have to put up with your goddamn shit anymore."

My hands flew to my mouth.

"Oh, Rick," Karen said. "Apologize."

"I didn't mean it. Sorry," Dad said to Karen. He was more motivated to appease his wife than he was to take back what he said to me. *Because it was the truth.* He reached out and laid his hands on my shoulders.

"You're not sorry." I shoved him. "You hate me. You've always hated me. It's my fault Sophia's dead, and you'll never forgive—"

"Oh no you don't, Carter." Dad held out his hands. "Don't you dare try to deflect—"

"Admit it. You wish *I* had crashed and burned instead of your *good* daughter."

"Carter, how could you—"

"I'm sorry I made your life suck." I retreated to the safety of my room, dropped to the floor, and did push-ups in rapid succession to ignite the burn in my muscles.

The devil clung to my shoulder and hissed in my ear.

You're a fucking loser...Sophia was a better person...you should have been the one who died...it's your fault...it's your fault...it's your fault...

Sophia's voice was silent. She blamed me, too. "I'm so sorry, Sophia," I whispered. "I would trade places with you if I could." My muscles were on fire, but I deserved the pain. I kept going until my body quit working, and I collapsed on the floor.

I could not do one thing right to save my fucked-up life.

19

AFTERMATH

Before my disastrous Saturday night, I'd agreed to Boris picking me up at our usual spot on his way home from church Sunday morning to make up for the time I'd missed on Friday. Since I was *grounded*, for God's sake, and without a phone, I had to think of a way out of the house to let him know I wasn't going with him.

Instead of making it complicated, I bundled up and told Karen I was going out for a run. The December deep freeze hadn't set in, so jogging outside was still plausible. She didn't try to stop me. Dad wasn't around anyway. He was probably across the street in search of The Truth. He was best buds with Ryan's dad.

When I got inside the Cadillac, Boris gave me the once-over. I wore gloves to cover up my shaky hands and sunglasses to mask the fact that I had bawled well into the morning hours. Even though Playboy and his wolf pack had surely followed me, there was no way Boris could have known what had gone down after I got inside the house.

He waited for me to speak first.

"You don't have to say it." I held my hands up in surrender. "I can't do anything right. I hear it all the time." My eyes welled up again.

Boris put his hand on my shoulder, and I caught a whiff of incense on him from church. "The boss is proud of you for making a good choice to stay out of trouble." He patted me on the back in an attempt to calm me down or, possibly, be *supportive.*

I wiped my nose on the sleeve of my gray jacket. "Kiki's dad called my dad and busted my story. He said he can't wait for me to move out so he doesn't have to put up with me anymore."

Boris tapped his rings on the steering wheel and stared at the handmade cross dangling from his rearview mirror. "You shouldn't have lied to your papa."

"If I told the truth, he would never let me leave the house. He still thinks I'm a little kid. I can't wait until I move out. Besides, if I had caved and told him about the party, I would have ratted out fifty of my friends. You *know* I'm not a rat." I appealed to his sense of loyalty.

"Your papa taught you a lesson?" He strangled the steering wheel.

"What?"

He pointed to my sunglasses. "He hit you?"

"Of course not." I lowered my shades to show him my red, puffy eyes. "I'm grounded, but he didn't say for how long. He took my phone, too. Will you tell Mr. Ivanov I'm sorry?"

His veins were popping out. I couldn't tell if he was mad at my dad, me, or the situation in general. "Get home before you get into any more trouble."

When I got back, Dad met me in the foyer. I tried to slide past him and escape to my room, but he blocked me.

"Hold on, Carter." His eyes were rimmed in red like

mine. "First, I'm sorry for what I said last night. I didn't mean it. I was just mad, okay?" Dad's apology was as sincere as a warning label on a pack of cigarettes.

I had always felt like a burden on my dad, especially after he married Karen and Megan was born. They were a family, and then there was me—the aftermath. "No problem. Sorry I lied." I tried to escape, but he wouldn't move his arm.

"Secondly, when we have an argument, it's not fair to use your sister as a weapon against me. You've been to enough counselors to know better than that by now."

Ouch. "My bad." I went with what I was *supposed* to say rather than what I felt. *I learned that in therapy, too. Check the right boxes, and you don't have to spend your Saturday mornings trapped in a shrink's office.*

Dad reeled me in for a hug. I didn't hug him back. "Boris called a few minutes ago. Vladimir wants us to come over and watch the Bengals game today. Feel like going?"

Leave it to Boris to untangle my mess. "I thought I was grounded." I stepped back.

"Karen and I talked about it this morning. We decided not to punish you. Technically, you stayed out of trouble."

Technically, I'm not twelve years old. I clamped my lips, though. I was getting out. I suppressed a smile as I passed him to go upstairs.

"One more thing," he called out. "Boris said to bring your tennis racket and a bathing suit."

I ran to my room, careful to keep the pep in my step down a few notches. Being at Vladimir's house, soaking outside in the hot tub, and watching a Bengals game sounded like utopia compared to hiding out in my room all day at Dad's—and I had Boris to thank for it. A reward for staying out of trouble? Maybe. I'd take it.

20

SOLITARY CONFINEMENT

Boris and the poodles were waiting to greet us at the front door. Megan was at a birthday party, so she wasn't with us. Dad and Karen walked ahead while I trailed behind, carrying a grocery bag full of snacks and fruit. When I passed Boris, he maintained his usual contemptuous expression but initiated a celebratory fist bump behind my dad's back.

Ouch.

The poodles cried, "*Mama! Mama!*" and danced in circles, overjoyed to have me home.

"The dogs remember you, Carter," Karen said.

"I have a way with animals." I turned to Boris. "Do you mind if I use the kitchen?" I nodded to the bag. "I need to cut up the fruit."

"Of course, Miss Cook. I'll show you the way. Rick, Karen, the game is on outside. It's sufficiently warm with heat lamps and fire. Vladimir will join you momentarily." Boris picked up the bag from my arms and led the way to the kitchen.

Considering my track record, I worried I might be in

trouble for something, but Vladimir put me at ease right away. He smooshed my face against his crisp blue shirt and wrapped his arms around me. He stepped back, cupped my head in his hands, and swept his thumbs under my puffy eyes. "No more sad Sundays for my good girl."

"Thanks, Mr. Ivanov." I suppose hanging out with Ryan wasn't a crime, or Boris chose not to tell him. I had a feeling the boss wouldn't share my joy about the fact that we had officially started dating, so I decided to keep my mouth shut.

As Boris unpacked the grocery bag, I pointed to the refrigerator to bring attention to my schoolwork still on display. He dismissed my concern with a tip of his head. I got out a cutting board, a sharp knife, and a platter for the fruit.

Vladimir rubbed his hands together and moved to the bar. "Let's make Mama and Papa a drink." He turned over two champagne flutes.

"Wait. If you want to have some fun, serve Karen a margarita. Trust me, Dad will be completely preoccupied."

He took my advice and mixed a strong batch into a pitcher, and Boris carried it outside. When we were alone, the boss set down the knife I was using and pressed a new phone into my palm. "If you ever need anything, you call. My personal number, as well as Boris's, is programmed into the phone. Day or night, for any reason, promise?"

I slid it into my pocket. "Thanks, Mr. Ivanov."

He mirrored my tortured expression. "Oh, my angel. How could your papa ever want to be rid of someone as wonderful as you?"

I should never have told Boris what Dad had said. "Mr. Ivanov, he didn't mean it. He was just mad. It was totally my fault, anyway. We're over it."

"You deserve to be cherished and adored, not like some

pest unworthy of your papa's love." He stroked a long strand of hair that had fallen from my messy bun. "I want you to live here with me."

Say what? "Everything is fine. People fight. It's no big deal." I forced a smile. "And I appreciate the offer. It's tempting, but I can't move out of Dad's house and live here with you."

"Of course you can." He squeezed my shoulders. "Let me take care of you."

"Mr. Ivanov—"

"I'll buy you a car—"

"I can't just—"

"I'll pay for your college education—"

"That's very generous, but—"

"I can give you everything your heart desires. Say yes."

I'd known him for two weeks, and he wanted to move me into his house and make all my dreams come true. "I can't, Mr. Ivanov." I gave him a broken smile. "It means a lot that you care, though." I fought another round of tears. "You're the best boss ever."

His eyes clouded over with disappointment. "Oh, Carter, is that what I am, your boss?"

I placed my hand on my belly to settle the butterflies. "Let's go watch the game." I tried to move on from our awkward conversation. "I made a bet with Boris that the Dolphins QB will get sacked in the first quarter. I want to see his face when I win."

Vladimir picked up my hand and guided me to the bar, visibly deflated by my rejection. "What can I make you, angel?"

I tapped my fingers as I thought it over. "I think I'll wait. I need to eat something first."

He checked his watch. "It's after one o'clock, and you

haven't eaten today? Is your punishment starvation as well?" His mood had flipped in an instant.

At times, he was like two completely different people: Vladimir and the *pakhan*. Vladimir was the sweet, caring man who loved to make me happy, but then there was the ruthless, take-no-prisoners crime boss—a dangerous man, never to cross.

"Oh, no. I got up late. It's not Dad's fault. He would never do that." I had to remember who I was dealing with. I could never let my guard down. I never wanted to find out what would happen if he thought someone had hurt me.

"I'll make a tray of cheese and olives to go with the fruit. We'll eat together on the patio," I said. "See you out there in a minute?" I pleaded.

"Sounds good." He turned over a shot glass and poured a long swig of vodka. "Don't be too long."

I hacked up the fruit, cubed some cheese, and dumped a jar of olives on the platter. Boris was outside, so I knew he would keep the peace between my dad and the boss. Nonetheless, I didn't want to linger.

I set down the tray on the coffee table between Dad and Karen and the Russians. I filled a plate and offered it to Vladimir, but he motioned for me to go ahead. He downed another shot. Boris flashed me a look to remind me not to act so familiar with the boss, then he downed a shot of vodka, too.

Vladimir narrowed his eyes at Dad. Boris shouldn't have told him about our fight. "You know, Ricky, we have a deer overpopulation problem on the grounds. Maybe you and I should take out a couple of them."

"No way!" I jumped to my feet. "I mean, *no fair*. Dad gets to see you every day. I was hoping we could hit some balls." I directed my gaze to the tennis court.

Boris downed another shot and then said something to Vladimir in Russian.

"I'm sure Vladimir wants to relax on his day off, sweetie," Dad said.

The boss still had the crazy in his eyes. He needed convincing. "Please? Can you teach me how to nail that wicked backhand slice of yours?"

Dad wrinkled his forehead. "When have you seen him play?"

"I spend half my life at the tennis club, Dad. He hits with Mr. Cusimano."

"You could skin a cat with your backhand slice," Dad said.

"Please, Mr. Ivanov? We have our playoff next Thursday."

"You didn't tell me you made playoffs," Dad said.

"Surprise." It came out snarkier than I had intended.

Dad gave me a weak smile. "Congratulations." I could tell I'd hurt his feelings.

"Will you, Mr. Ivanov? I need all the pointers I can get." I batted my sad, watery eyes.

"I would love to teach you something."

Boris invited Dad and Karen to enjoy the hot tub. He refreshed their drinks and showed them where to change. I smiled to thank him for helping to diffuse the situation.

Out on the court, I set up the ball machine to fire shots at us—the boss and I had to be on the same team. I could never allow us to be across the net from one another. He wouldn't take losing well, and I had no off switch when it came to competition. We had to stay united.

We warmed up our arms, and then I let him 'teach' me how to nail a crosscourt slice. I flubbed it a few times, which prompted him to wrap his arms around me and position my racket to help me get a feel for the right touch. I peeked up at the patio and saw Karen sexy-dancing in her swimsuit with a drink in hand—mission accomplished. Dad was preoccupied.

Vladimir loved to wrap me up in his strong arms and sneak kisses on my cheeks. It was a cultural thing. Still, Dad didn't need to see it.

The boss followed my gaze. "Your papa has a way with the ladies."

"He's a total stud." I laughed. "Thanks for making this happen today." We switched to a doubles position and fired back shots at the orange markers I'd set up on the other side.

"Anything for you, angel."

Once we worked up a sweat, we headed back up to the patio. Karen and Dad stepped out of the hot tub, and she was all over him. Boris brought out a platter of Russian appetizers. He must have ordered a tray from the restaurant we dined at the other day.

Dad loaded up a plate with buckwheat, marinated mushrooms, and a big dollop of sour cream. "Here, Carter, you need to eat something."

I was about to unleash on him for insinuating I *needed* to do anything, but the *pakhan* didn't need another reason to be ticked off at Dad.

"You'll love it. It's from Vladimir's restaurant."

I took the plate from Dad. "*Your* restaurant?"

"I like to diversify my business interests." He winked.

I dug into my new favorite food. Vladimir mirrored every bite I took. He loved to see me smile. Boris prevailed at the art of distracting Dad and Karen, but it must have been exhausting since the boss didn't quit.

Dad looked antsy as the fourth quarter wound down. I

wanted to stay. There was no way to pull that off, but I tried to prolong the visit. I went inside and changed into my pink polka-dotted bikini. I had on a cover-up, but Dad's eyes widened as if I had strutted across the patio in a Playboy Bunny costume. I stepped out of my matching wrap and sank down in the steamy water.

"Don't get too comfortable, Carter. The game is almost over," Dad said.

Vladimir twisted his lips as he watched me relaxing in the tub. I could tell he was working out a scheme in his head. I decided to help him out. Why not? I had solitary confinement to look forward to back at the house.

"Okay, Dad." Then, I turned to Vladimir. "You're not going to go back on our deal, are you, Mr. Ivanov?"

Everyone turned to him.

His eyes were positively glowing. "A Russian never goes back on a deal."

"What was the bet?" Dad's gaze went back and forth between us like he was watching a tennis match.

"I bet Mr. Ivanov I could get ten consecutive shots down the alley."

"And?" Dad asked.

"And I did. Now he has to drive me home in the Ferrari."

Boris shook his head. I didn't need him to reprimand me. I knew I was pushing it.

Dad probably wanted to yank me out of the hot tub by my messy bun and drag me to the car. "Vladimir was teasing, sweetie. The game just ended. We need to pick up Megan."

I stood up in a cloud of steam.

Water dripped down my body.

Dad whizzed a towel at me.

I stepped out of the hot tub, covered up, and waited for Vladimir's reply.

"I will take you home in the Ferrari, Miss Cook, but I have one condition."

I bit my lip, eager for his reply.

"*You* must drive."

21

BERSERK

Once on the road, Vladimir cranked up some Russian jams and laughed when I made up my own lyrics in time to the music. I knew early on that he was involved in illegal activity, but the man I'd gotten to know was caring and someone I enjoyed spending time with. My dad, however, wished I would evaporate.

Vladimir and I cooked together, dined out, and spent time just being together. At home, we didn't do family dinners—at least not ones that included *me*. I loved my dad, but I couldn't wait to get out from under his roof.

Instead of following the Camry, I took the long way around. Since it would take time to pick up Megan, I decided to surprise the boss. For once, I had control over him. I felt so wild and free and *bad*.

"Where are you taking me, angel?"

I peeked over at him. "It's a surprise." I turned into an ice cream shop and parked the Ferrari sideways in the back of the lot. When we got out, a little boy with light-up racecar shoes and blue ice cream caked on his cheeks bounced over to us. "I wike your Fewawi."

“Thank you, cutie,” I said. “Actually, the car belongs to him.”

“What’s mine is yours, Miss Cook.”

The boy looked up to Vladimir with his mouth open as if I had introduced him to Batman. The boss’s complexion glowed as he admired his star-struck admirer. “Cool shoes, young man.”

The boy stomped back to his mom’s minivan. “The Fewawi guy wikes my shoes.”

Vladimir put his arm around me, and we walked to the door. I led him to a table by the window and ordered a triple-scoop raspberry sorbet sundae topped with pineapple sauce, yogurt chips, and extra cherries. Two spoons. When the server brought it out, she set the huge bowl down between us. I clinked his spoon and toasted “to your health” in Russian.

Vladimir fished out a cherry, held it up, and dangled it in front of my mouth. I followed his lead and picked one up for him. “At the same time,” I said.

“To sweet surprises,” he said.

“To sweet surprises.” We clinked our cherries and fed them to each other. Just as I wrapped my lips around it and the tips of his elegant fingers pressed against my mouth, a voice boomed behind me.

“Are you really going to eat that *garbage* before playoffs, Cook?”

I almost choked. “Hey, Coach.” I spit the cherry out into my napkin. “Don’t worry, I’ll burn it off.” I sat up straight in my seat.

He flashed me *the* look.

“I’m sure Miss Cook knows what she’s doing, friend.” Vladimir leaned forward, tapped his fingers together, and stared down Coach.

Coach put his hands on his hips. "I'm not sure she does, comrade."

Oh, shit. "Coach, it's cool." I stood up and backed him toward the freezer section. "Mr. Ivanov is my dad's boss. Please, don't embarrass me."

He glared over my shoulder. "I know who he is." He turned his focus back to me. "And he paid off your debt at the club out of the goodness of his heart?"

I studied Coach's accusing eyes. *What is he insinuating?* "He's the most generous person I've ever—"

"You have a lovely family, Coach Williams. Jerome Williams," the *pakhan* said.

Coach's wife waved. She and the kids were building their sundaes at the topping station.

"Your family lives across the street on Deer Cross Lane, right?"

How did he know that?

Coach's expression soured, then he softened his stance and walked back to his family. "See you at practice tomorrow, Cook."

When we got back to my house, Dad and Karen hadn't arrived yet. Vladimir got out of the passenger side, walked around the car, and opened the door for me.

"Thanks again for an awesome day." I gave him a quick hug. "See you tomorrow."

I turned to go inside, but he pulled me back to him. "Take me to your bedroom."

"What?"

"I want to see where you spend your time when you're away from me."

"It's nothing. Dad will be here any second. What if he comes home and finds—" Before I could make my case, the boss headed up the sidewalk to the front porch. I hurried, got out my keys, and twisted the lock. Once inside, I bolted upstairs. He followed.

When he entered my room, he marveled at my décor as if he wanted to remember every detail: My purple bedspread, a stack of fashion magazines, dusty stuffed animals, a Barbie Doll shrine, a corkboard with pictures of my friends and me, a bookcase loaded with trophies, and a life-size poster of Rafael Nadal next to my bed.

A picture of Sophia and me on my desk caught his eye. I was five, sitting on my thirteen-year-old sister's lap. Sophia was smiling with her arms around me, and I was snuggling my poodle twins in my arms. The picture had belonged to Sophia. When she died, I took it from her room, hid it in my bed, and slept with it under my pillow for months.

"That was Sophia's favorite picture."

"Mine, too."

Vladimir's gaze moved to a collage of my life growing up with Kiki. The big picture in the center of the frame was of us at a hibachi table holding up crossed chopsticks.

"Look at you, Carter. Such a tiny angel." He ran his fingers over the glass.

"That was my twelfth birthday party. Dad traveled a lot, so Kiki's mom and dad, Doc and Mary, took us out. They practically raised me after Sophia died. They call me their 'other' adopted daughter."

He read the caption under our photo. Chopstick Twins.

"It was our nickname back in grade school." I held up two fingers. "Stick thin and always together."

"So cruel."

"Now you understand why I've never had a boyfriend? I

looked like a stick-side-down mop until I started working with a trainer."

"Is that why you look so sad?"

"Is this the face of an unhappy girl?" I pointed to some of the other pictures. "Kiki and I did gymnastics, soccer, ballet, and vacationed together. We're like family."

"Why do you fight with your papa?"

I felt like I was at confession. A fresh round of tears welled up in my eyes. Vladimir put his arm around me, led me to the edge of my bed, and sat us down. "Tell me."

"Kiki and I have been best friends since we moved here. Up until the accident, Sophia had taken care of me while Dad worked long hours. Since we didn't have family close by, Mary offered to help. During the week, I lived with Kiki's family—where I was happy—then Dad dragged me back here on the weekends. I hated him for it."

"He's your papa."

"It got worse when he married Karen. He made me stay here with her full-time instead of going back with Kiki's family. I felt like I didn't belong in my family anymore, so I hid up here."

"I'm sorry you had to go through that."

"It was a long time ago. I'm totally over it. Dad, however, is not. He drives me nuts. I can't wait until—" I stopped midsentence when Vladimir's breathing had gotten heavier.

"I can't stand the thought of you being mistreated."

"Whoa, whoa, mistreated? I'm not mistreated. All kids fight with their parents. It's our job to make their lives suck so they won't miss us when we move out." I joked to lighten the tension.

"You're different. A fragile angel like you—"

"I'm not fragile, and don't you think he's *right* to be hard on me sometimes? Let's be real. Dad thinks I'm at the tennis club, whipping up smoothies so I can buy a car. If he knew about our arrangement and how I've been lying to him, he'd go berserk." Worried I had insulted him, I shut my mouth and waited for him to respond.

"I will tell him when he comes home. I won't let you face his wrath because of me." Vladimir headed for the door.

"No way. Promise you won't say anything." I jumped in front of him and blocked my bedroom door. "He'll be so ticked. Probably madder at you than me, and trust me, you don't want to see him angry."

Vladimir crossed his arms and studied my freaked-out, arms stretched across the doorframe stance. "You think *I* am afraid of your papa?"

"Of course not, but why do you want to provoke him? Everything's fine. If he finds out, he'll never let me see you again. Please, I *need* you."

Vladimir peeled my fingers off the doorframe, held my wrists, and brought my arms down. He kissed my cheeks, but not in the usual way. His warm lips lingered on my skin while he massaged the nape of my neck. The closeness of our bodies and the heat emanating from his skin caused a groan to escape from my lips. Vladimir rubbed warm circles on my back and whispered Russian words in my ear to soothe me.

"What does it mean?" I whispered.

"Something good."

Blood rushed *down there*. I wanted to tackle him on my bed and run my fingers through his sexy hair and touch his chest and feel the warmth of his lean, muscular body. Lately, I'd felt The Urge. Right or wrong, Vladimir lit my sexual fire. It wasn't his body or his incredible blue eyes, it was how he made me feel—like the important person in his universe.

"What kind of good?" I laid my hand on his chest and

snuck my finger inside his shirt to touch his skin. I traced the outline of the devil with my fingernail. Vladimir inhaled sharply, excited by my touch. I unbuttoned the top button of his shirt—

He lowered my hand. "Your papa will be home soon." He left the house a minute before Dad turned into the driveway. I replayed the day's events from his smoldering eyes, to his strong embrace, to the taunting words, "Oh, Carter, is that what I am, your boss?"

What did he want to be? My friend? Boyfriend? Lover?

I spent the rest of the evening melting under the covers, dreaming about how awesome it would feel to have Vladimir there with me. He was guarded on my turf, but if we'd been at his place, there would have been nothing to hold us back. I was dying to feel the weight of his body on top of me and the warmth of his skin and his hands rubbing me all over...

I tucked my special phone under my pillow in case he called to say goodnight.

He didn't.

22

WEDGED

On Monday morning, Kiki and I went to breakfast and vented about the bullshit from Saturday night. She'd been lectured by her parents about the lake thing, too, even though she didn't even drink.

"Here's the deal, Carter." Kiki dumped a heaping spoonful of sugar into her coffee. "We need to fast-forward our apartment situation. The food on campus is heinous, my closet is the size of a rat hole, and my roommate and her boyfriend think our dorm is a porno studio that's open 24/7."

"Sounds like you're jealous," I laughed and scooped a bite of oatmeal and bananas into my mouth.

"Absolutely. I need a boyfriend—or a fuck buddy."

I cracked up. "What's happening with Toby?"

"God, he's big and beautiful. I want to strip down, curl up on his chest, and settle in for a catnap right there in chem lab."

I laughed so hard I snorted.

"For real, his belly sticks out perfectly like a warm lump of bread dough rising in a bowl, waiting for me to knead it into shape." Kiki wiped imaginary drool from her chin.

"He's obviously intimidated by your hotness. Help a brother out and *casually* mention you're craving Thai food and lure him to that cozy place across the street."

"Oh, that's good. I will, but let's get back on track. I made an appointment for us to take a tour of an apartment complex off Calhoun Street. They have a unit coming available mid-January. That gives us about a month. We need to put down a deposit and first month's rent today to hold it. You in?"

Mentally, I tallied my financial situation. I had enough in my savings, thanks to my generous boss and the money I'd saved working at the club. "In."

"Really?" Kiki asked.

"Way in."

We squealed. Finally, I had secured my ticket to freedom. I could do whatever I wanted, come home when I felt like it, and start living my adult life.

We signed the rental agreement, put down our deposit, and went shopping to get some decorating ideas. Then we went to lunch and made a list of all the stuff we needed to get started. I hated to end our strategic planning session, but I had to go to tennis. I went through the motions at practice, but I was so nervous—the excited kind of nervous—I couldn't think about anything except Vladimir and my newfound freedom.

When I slid into the Caddy, I avoided Boris's omniscient eyes and rambled on about our tennis tournament, which was taking place on Thursday. His advice: Teach your opponents a lesson early in the match. He brushed the side of his cheek where Coach had whacked me.

I was hoping Vladimir would be home waiting to greet me, so I could share my news—which I hoped would turn into a romantic, celebratory dinner somewhere fabulous.

Instead, I found a bouquet of red and pink two-tone roses along with a card on the bar. I tore open the envelope and pulled out an elegantly scrolled note:

My dearest Carter,
In preparation for your match, Boris will go over your game stats so you may understand your high and low percentage shots. Listen to him. He is a good coach.
Regards, Vladimir

THAT NIGHT, Vladimir worked late. Boris sent out for pizza from my favorite restaurant, and together we came up with a game plan for my match. I'd kept a couple of slices warm for Vladimir in the toaster oven, but he never came home, never called, never texted. Not exactly the romantic evening I'd hoped for.

On Tuesday, another bouquet of roses and another note.

My dearest Carter,
Find your way to the bedroom. I have arranged for a masseuse to help relax your muscles. I regret that I will be working late again this evening.
Regards, Vladimir

ON WEDNESDAY, the eve of the tournament:

My dearest Carter,
Overthinking your game is the kiss of death. Get ready for a relaxing evening at home. Meet me in the living room. I am waiting for you.
Regards, Vladimir

I TOSSED the note in the trash. Since our *moment* on Sunday, the boss had strategically kept his distance and set up diversions so he didn't have to face me.

Hint: my passion was unrequited.

"Can you please take me home?" I asked Boris.

"*Nyet.*" He flung open the swinging door and nudged me out of the kitchen. Vladimir was seated on the sofa, sipping a golden drink on the rocks.

"Join me, Carter."

I plopped down on the couch, keeping a cushion of distance between us.

"Feeling shy?" He swirled his drink. Ice cubes clinked against the glass.

I averted my gaze to a trio of candles glowing on the coffee table.

"About the other day—"

"I don't want to talk about it." I ripped a page out of his playbook and kept my emotional distance, too.

"Carter, if things were different—"

"Please stop. You don't have to explain. I don't need this right now—the tournament." I picked up the remote. "Let's watch a movie." As I browsed the comedy list, I wrapped up in a throw blanket and wedged a pillow in the open spot between us.

I am such an idiot. Why didn't I take the hint the first time he rejected me? How fucking humiliating...

He touched my shoulder and whispered my name. I pretended not to notice.

23

GAME OVER

The next day, my teammates and I huddled around Coach for our pre-game pep talk. "Come out strong. Make them play your game. Be aggressive. Even if you make a mistake, they'll be afraid of what you'll do next. Go for high percentage shots, and keep the ball in play until you can put away a clean winner. And most important of all: Don't back off if you're losing. Make your opponent beat you. If you're going down, go down swinging."

Coach held out his hand in the center of the huddle.

We piled our hands on top of his.

"Bring it on three. One, two, three—"

"Bring it!"

We brought that energy onto the court. Our team finished strong in the first round and moved on to the finals. It boiled down to this: Court three won, and court two lost. On court one, Rakhi and I had won the first set and lost the second. The Super Tiebreaker—first to ten, win by two—would determine the winner.

We dominated and got the score to nine to six. If we won

the next point, we would win not only the match but also the trophy. It was our opponent's serve. We came out strong and rallied cross-court, but I blew it when I dove for a poach and tipped the ball out, nine to seven. Then on their next serve, Rakhi blasted an easy put-away out, nine to eight. Our turn. We would win if Rakhi held serve on the next point.

I took a deep cleansing breath and looked up to the viewing gallery. Vladimir was standing next to Mr. Cusimano. He flashed me an open hand, which meant one of two things: One, he was waving hello. Or two, he was signaling for me to poach.

It didn't matter. This was my game, not his. As Rakhi bounced the ball on the baseline, preparing to serve, Boris's stats revealed that when we played Australian—when I lined up in the service box on the same side as Rakhi—we had won the majority of points when she served from the deuce side. I jogged to the baseline. "Let's do Australian."

She continued to bounce the ball and nodded. When we lined up, I flashed her an open hand behind my back, signaling I was going to poach. When she served, and the ball slammed down on the line, I shuffled left to field the return. When the ball came through the middle, I pounded back a punishing volley and nailed the net player in the gut.

Winners.

I knew we would take the trophy and, since it was a special occasion, I came prepared with a bottle of French champagne I'd taken from Vladimir's wine cellar: *What's mine is yours.* After our handshakes and post-victory powwow with Coach, I rounded up the team and led them out back to Rakhi's minivan.

Once everyone piled in, I popped the bubbly. I poured the champagne into the mouth of our trophy cup, and the girls squealed. We laughed and passed the chalice, reveling in our triumph. The cup made it all the way around back to me. As I sipped, I saw Rakhi's caramel skin blanch. Somebody banged on the car window behind me. Coach opened the door. Every single one of us was underage. We were stone-cold busted.

Oh, shit. I dumped it out and said I was the only one who had a sip. I didn't want anyone else to get in trouble for my stupid idea. He dismissed my teammates with the threat that they were not absolved of guilt yet.

"Give me the bottle." Coach's face burned with condemnation. "Looks expensive. Where'd you get it?"

I was sure he already had a pretty good idea of where I got it. "I take full responsibility. The girls didn't know I brought it until we got out to the car."

"I'm giving you a chance to come clean. Name your source, or you're off the team."

I crossed my arms and stared at him with pursed lips. I was no squealer.

Coach waited a moment and gave me a chance to change my mind. When I didn't waver, he pulled the trigger. "Turn in your uniform tomorrow."

"What? Coach, please—"

"End of discussion. Is your father here or at work?"

My *father*? Another man treating me like a kid. *Ridiculous.* When I didn't answer, Coach scanned his phone. I reached out and tried to lower his hand. "No."

He held it out of my reach. "Underage drinking is a crime. I have to report this. Would you rather I call your father or the police?"

Hold your tongue, Carter, Sophia said. *There's still a way out of this.* "Dad—but don't tell him at work. Can you call him later tonight at home?"

After a searing stare down, he agreed to call him later. At

least that would give me time to figure things out. "Thanks, Coach. I'm so sorry about this."

"I'm not done with you, Carter. I'm not stupid, and I'm not blind. One way or another, you're giving up your source. All I can do is kick you off the team. The police, however, can press charges." He shook his head. "What you—what *he* is doing is not right."

My loyalty took over. Vladimir had given me a job. He'd let me drive his Ferrari—his *Ferrari*. He even invited me to live in his mansion. Vladimir was the most *right* thing in my life. "I'll *never* tell."

"I'm sure your father will convince you otherwise."

I pushed past him and ran off toward the park. There was no way I could face Vladimir after I took his alcohol without permission. He'll be crazy mad that the police could be involved. I wanted to evaporate.

When I reached the park, I heard a vehicle pull up behind me. Vladimir honked and rolled down the window. "Well done, angel." When he caught a glimpse of my tortured face, he parked, jumped out of the G-Wagon, and rushed over to me. "What's wrong?" He squeezed my shoulders.

I looked down, ashamed to utter the words. Tears dripped on my uniform. He led me toward a park bench, wrapped his coat around my shoulders, and sat me down. By the way I was acting, he must have thought someone had died. "You won."

Bawling, I squeaked, "I'm so sorry."

"For what?"

No matter what he thought of me, I had to warn him. Once Coach called my dad, game over. I would never be allowed to leave the house again. "Coach caught my teammates and me *celebrating* with champagne after our match."

"That's it? You had a drink? What's the problem?" He blotted away my tears.

I took a deep breath. "The problem is I'm nineteen. It's illegal for me to have it. Coach said if I didn't rat out my source, he'd kick me off the team. I told him I wasn't a narc, so I'm out. He's going to call Dad tonight and tell him." I covered my face to mask my shame.

He lowered his hand from my shoulder. Over the last few weeks, I'd spent more time at his house than at my own. I'd gotten comfortable. He treated me like a princess. Nice way to repay the man—steal a bottle of his fancy champagne.

"Why didn't you tell him where you got the alcohol?"

"Because I got it from you. I wanted to toast my teammates. Not to get drunk or anything, just to celebrate." The weight of my shame could have squashed a rhino.

"You got kicked off your team to protect *me*?"

"You could get in trouble. I understand if you never want to see me again."

He put his hands on my shoulders. "Your loyalty amazes me."

"No. Don't you dare be nice to me." I pushed his hands away. "I did a horrible thing. You trusted me, and I let you down."

He brought a finger to my lips. "Your coach would have let you stay on the team if you had named me?"

With his finger on my lips like a loaded gun, I nodded. He hugged me as if I'd taken a bullet for him. Then, he pushed me back and towered over me. "I'll speak to your coach. He won't call your papa. Go to practice as usual tomorrow. I'll take care of your problem."

I sucked in a mouthful of air. "Oh, no. I made a mistake. I'll suffer the consequences."

My rambling didn't deter him. The *pakhan* pulled out his phone. I felt sick as I listened to him bark out orders in Russian. He sounded as angry as he had on my first day of work.

"Who are you talking to? What are you going to do?" *What have I done?*

He ended the call. "Go home and rest. Celebrate your victory. I give you the day off."

"Please—"

"Coach is a reasonable guy, right?"

I nodded like a wind-up monkey.

"You look pale. What has your coach done to you?" He brushed my cheek in the exact spot where Coach had whacked me with a tennis ball a few weeks ago.

"Really, I'm fine. I'm going to go now, you know, in case Coach calls."

An expression as sharp as the tip of a knife sliced across Vladimir's face. With those cold blue eyes boring through my soul, my pulse quickened.

"I told you, Coach will not call." The *pakhan* gave my shoulders a tight squeeze. It seemed kind of hard for a "don't worry" gesture. Then I brushed off the thought. He was strong and really agitated. He would never *intentionally* hurt me. Slowly, he relinquished his grip and forced a smile. "Everything will be fine. Trust me."

24

HOOKS

The next day was Friday, and I showed up to practice just as Vladimir had instructed. When I walked on the court, the girls were huddled around Coach. He stood on the baseline with a splint taped across his nose.

"Calm down, ladies. I'm fine. Just tripped on a ball."

"How many times?" Rakhi asked. "Looks like someone cracked a racket across your face."

Coach glanced at me. "No. Just an accident."

I had never seen fear in his eyes before, but when he looked at me, that was fear.

"Start warming up." He held his ribs as he made his way off to the sideline.

"I can't believe you didn't get into trouble," Rakhi said.

I pretended I didn't hear her. My hands were shaking so badly that I could barely hold my racket. *Did Coach and Vladimir get into a fight? Or did Boris rough him up for threatening the boss?* I was ticked at Coach for treating me like a kid, but I never wanted any harm to come to him—and he certainly didn't deserve broken bones.

Rakhi fed the ball to me in the service box. I couldn't move. The ball bounced and hit me in the gut. Coach was lucky to be alive.

My stomach churned. Enough. People were getting seriously hurt because of my twisted game with Vladimir. This thing, our arrangement, my weird dance with the boss had to end.

Confession time: I was an idiot for not trusting my dad from the start.

High on fear and adrenaline, I bolted from the club and headed home. I had over an hour before I was due to meet Boris, and in that time, I had to steal Dad away from the boss before Boris figured out I'd bailed.

When the house came into view, I gasped. The Cadillac was parked in the driveway behind Dad's Camry.

Plan B: I burst through the front door. "Dad!" I ran into the kitchen.

"You're home early, pumpkin. Look who's here."

My gaze drifted to Boris.

"*Privet*, Miss Cook." He popped the cap off a bottle of beer.

Karen sat next to him. "Hi Carter, how was—"

"What's he doing here?" I panted, winded from my run.

Dad wrinkled his happy face. "Vladimir and I knocked off early today. I invited the guys over for dinner tonight to celebrate your big win."

"Where's Mr. Ivanov?"

"He'll be here after he wraps up a conference call. Something wrong?"

Boris zeroed in on me and drummed his prison-tatted fingers on the table. With the other hand, he patted his side where Vladimir kept his gun tucked. I understood his silent threat. If I ratted him out, I would pay with the blood of my family members.

"Sorry, that didn't come out right. I was surprised to see you home so early, Daddy." I crossed into the kitchen and gave him a hug.

Boris nodded, congratulating me for sparing him the task of murdering my family.

At that point, the Russians had officially sunk their hooks under my skin. I was in, and there was no way out. The lives of my family rested in my hands. Until I could figure a way out of the mess I created, I had to play their game.

It was like a tennis match; it wasn't the hardest hitter or the best server who came out on top, it was the player who recognized her opponent's weakness and used it to her advantage. With Boris, there was no way I could beat him, but the boss? His weakness was me.

Game on, Vladimir.

25

NEON SIGN

"Can you pick up a few things from the store, Carter? Something vegetarian for you and Vladimir?" Dad wiggled his fingers in the air like vegetarianism was some mystic concept that required a black cauldron, eye of newt, and a bat eyelash to conjure up. He held out the car keys, but Boris stepped up and insisted on driving me.

Once we were in the Caddy, my rambling began. "I'm sorry. I didn't mean to screw up. I know what happened to Coach is all my fault. What's going to happen now?"

He pulled into the parking lot and turned off the car. "You know what my job is, dear?"

Your dagger tattoo says you're a hitman. "It's none of my business."

He came around to my side and opened the passenger door. I stood, but he blocked me before I could take a step. "My job is to protect the boss."

I looked down at my feet.

He lifted my chin. "And to clean up his mess when things get out of hand—including *dirt* his pet princess drags him through. By all means necessary. Want to find out what happens if you cry to papa?"

I shook my head.

"Good girl." He patted me on the back and steered me toward the store entrance. "Remind me to pick up champagne." He softened his ominous tone. "We haven't celebrated your team's victory. Unless, of course, you have any more of the boss's fancy bottles stashed?"

I sucked in a deep breath. "No. I'm clean."

WHEN WE GOT BACK from the store, Dad and Vladimir were in the kitchen, talking, laughing, and drinking. The boss appeared to be in a good mood, despite all the bullshit I'd dumped on him in the last twenty-four hours.

"Hi, Mr. Ivanov. Great to see you again." I met him in the kitchen. "What are the odds you and Boris are here, and I'm free on a Friday night?" *Sorry, Ryan. No bowling and burritos for me tonight.* I set down a grocery bag and moved in for a hug. Partly to let him know everything was cool and partly to feel the gun tucked at his side: affirmative.

"A beautiful girl with no date? The boys must be crazy."

I slunk away before Dad took notice of the neon sign flashing, "I'm having an inappropriate relationship with your daughter" above Vladimir's head.

I survived dinner that night with Boris and Vladimir—and so did the rest of my family. The boss fawned on me the way he always did, but he also doted on Megan and Karen. Although I knew what the *pakhan* was capable of, *Vladimir* was a joy to be around. I wished there was a way to extract the dark side while keeping the goodness intact. My family adored him—and Boris.

The next day, Vladimir treated the family to dinner at a fancy restaurant downtown, and on Sunday, he took us on a private cruise up and down the Ohio River. By the end of the weekend, the Russians had fully immersed themselves in our lives. Megan even started calling Boris *Ded*, which he taught her was Russian for *Grandpa*, and she dubbed Vladimir *Dyadya,* which meant *Uncle.* Based on appearances, we were One Big Happy Family.

Nyet.

26

COCKY

On Monday, I had one goal: get through the rest of the week without getting into any trouble. Dad was taking the family on the road to Karen's parents' house on Friday. It was an annual pilgrimage I dreaded, but at least it would put separation between the Russians and me for four glorious days.

When we got to the house, I dove into a steamy romance novel my teammates and I were reading for book club. I usually worked on homework, but the semester was over.

"Congratulations." Boris dumped a pile of household bills and a checkbook on the bar in front of me. "You've been promoted to Household Bullshit Manager."

"Gee, thanks." I thumbed through the bills—cable, electric, trash. "Got it."

I made out the checks and slid them across the bar for Boris to sign. As I finished up my task, the boys out back started hollering. I turned and looked out the window. "Anything else I can do?"

"Truth," Boris said.

"What?" I swiveled my barstool around.

He tipped his head. "Truth or dare. You wanted to play the other day. Truth. What do you want to know?"

"Seriously?" There had to be a catch. More likely, I reasoned, he wanted to find out something from *me* and not the other way around.

The wolves started barking out back again. I glanced out the window. Right as I looked down at the basketball court, Playboy heaved a rock at Igor. Luckily, he missed by an inch. "Hey!" I tapped on the window.

Playboy looked up at me, waved me off, and laughed.

Boris lifted his eyebrows. "What is it you want to know, dear?"

I twisted my lips as I thought about how to phrase my question. I was worried about Dad. He worked with Vladimir every day. If *I* knew about Vladimir's side business, wouldn't Dad know, too? "I'm not sure I should ask. If you don't want to answer—"

"If I don't want to answer, I won't." Boris tipped his hand, encouraging me to continue.

"Is my dad involved in anything at work that could get him into trouble?"

Boris glared at me. I knew I shouldn't have asked. "I mean, it's none of my business what you and Mr. Ivanov do, but Dad—"

"No," Boris said. "What your papa works on with the boss is legit."

"Good. Thanks." I exhaled, relieved Dad wasn't an accomplice in Vladimir's *other* business.

"I'm curious," Boris said. "What if I'd told you he *was* involved in something else?"

I kept my attention on the basketball court. "I would have asked Mr. Ivanov to fire him."

Playboy threw another rock at Igor.

"Hey!" I pounded on the window. "Boris, tell him to leave the peacock alone. He's emasculating him in front of Natasha."

He turned on the radio, unaffected by my bird drama.

Playboy tried to kick Igor, but the bird dodged him.

"I'm not kidding, Boris. Tell him to stop, or I'm going out there."

He lowered his reading glasses. "Not your problem."

I went to the mudroom and lifted my tennis racket and a can of balls out of my bag.

On my way outside, Boris caught my arm. "Stay out of it."

His threatening tone meant business, but I'd pledged to hold my own with these Russians. I could at least do that with a bird on the basketball court, for god's sake. "The boss will be super ticked when he finds out *he* was bothering his bird, and *you* didn't stop him." I tried to shake off his hand, but he wouldn't let go.

"Or maybe boss will be ticked because *I* told you to stay out of it, but *you* defied me."

I tried to pull away again, but instead of letting up, he squeezed tighter.

"Let me go."

He looked down at my tennis racket. "If you act against that bad boy, I won't stop him when he comes after you, understand? Time you learned your place."

My mouth gaped. "My *place*?"

The peacock shrieked. "*Help! Help! Help!*"

He let go of my arm and gave me one last warning. "You'll be sorry."

I stuck to my convictions and marched out on the balcony. With my racket hidden behind my back, I yelled at Playboy and pointed to the peacock.

He flipped me off.

The peacock charged him.

When Playboy turned to find another rock, I got out a ball, bounced it, and took aim like I was ready to serve up an ace. I tossed the ball up and slammed it down on the basketball court.

Wham. I hit Playboy point-blank on the side of the head. *Shit.* I'd aimed at his feet. The other two goons laughed, but Playboy stared me down like he wanted to kill me. I squinted at him, went back inside, and locked the door behind me, with a tremor in my legs. Playboy can sure look menacing when he wants to.

Boris had gotten out his betting book and was scribbling down notes when I shuffled back to the kitchen. I fumbled with my book and pretended I wasn't terrified. Just when I thought it was safe, that Playboy wasn't stupid enough to come after me, the swinging door flew open, and he stood in the doorway with a sinister grin.

I was ninety-nine percent sure Boris was bluffing when he'd said he wouldn't protect me. There was no way the boss would be okay with one of his *patsani* coming into his house and hurting me. And if Boris stood there and watched, he would be in trouble too.

Playboy stepped toward me with his hand behind his back.

Wait. Wasn't the boss the one who said I needed to *learn a lesson* with his boys out back? *Shit, shit, shit.*

I stood strong, though. I was tough. Whatever happened, I could take it. Boris continued to work, unaffected by Playboy's threatening posture. What did that jerk have behind his back?

A baseball bat?

A knife?

A gun?

Playboy moved toward me and said something creepy in Russian. Then, from behind his back, he showed me his closed fist—and then he opened his hand to reveal his prize.

Brown and white feathers fluttered from his grip and floated to the floor. Fear and disgust twisted in my gut as I realized where the feathers had come from.

Natasha.

Playboy pointed in my face and barked at me.

"Boris, tell him to get out of here." I backed up as Playboy cornered me against the stove. He grabbed my hand, dragged me back to the pile of feathers, and waited for me to do something about it.

"Boris, please."

"I warned you."

"What does he want?"

"He wants you to clean up the mess you made."

"The mess *I* made? Are you serious?" I stepped around the bar and fired back at Playboy. "Screw you, *lapsha*. The *pakhan* is going to be ticked when I tell him what you did."

Boris spoke to him in their native tongue. Playboy's face burned red when he got the translation that I'd threatened to rat him out. He picked up a cookbook from under the counter and whizzed it at me. I covered my face and ducked, narrowly dodging a blow to the head.

I jumped up to escape, but before I could get away, Playboy clutched my ponytail and yanked me to my feet. He put his other hand on my back and steered me toward the mess on the floor.

He picked up my hand. I fought him—with all the strength I had—but it was no contest. He pressed my hand down into the feathers. "Your mess," he said. "*Do svidaniya, ptichka.*"

I turned my head and squeezed my eyes shut. In defense, I bent my knees and pushed my back against him, but instead of letting up, he jammed me against the counter and locked me in place with his thick arms. The stench of cigarettes, cologne, and greasy hair forced acid up my throat.

"Ready to apologize and clean up your mess?" Boris asked.

Would the boss blame me, too? "I'm sorry."

"Say it in Russian. *Izvinite.*"

"*Izvinite.*"

Playboy yanked me upright, pointed to the pile of feathers, and flung open the trash drawer. With shaky hands, I collected the feathers and followed his orders.

"Why did he do this? She's innocent." My voice trembled.

"To teach the peacock a lesson," Boris said. "That cocky bird will think twice before picking a fight with him again, don't you think, dear?"

Playboy snapped his fingers and waited for me to finish the job.

I buried my nose in my jacket and zipped it up all the way. Trying not to gag, I tied the bag shut and took it out to the garbage receptacle in the garage.

When I came back to the kitchen, Playboy was gone. "Where did he go?"

"It's over. You're even," Boris said. "Not a word of this to the boss."

27

POPPED

In the morning, snow fell as Dad loaded up the car for the trip. A winter storm was on the way, so he left work early to beat the traffic. Last minute miracle: Ryan scored tickets to the Bengals game on Christmas Eve and invited me to go. I flashed the I'm-an-adult card so I could stay home from the family road trip.

Reluctantly and with a stern warning, Dad agreed. Kiki was in Florida with her family, so I guess not having my partner in crime eased his mind. I decided to wait until after the trip to break the news to him about the apartment.

Before the family rolled away, we said our goodbyes. Megan squeezed her little arms around my waist. She looked adorable in a frilly green dress with reindeer prancing around the hemline. "If you see Santa, tell him I'm at Grandma and Grandpa's house."

"I will, kitty." I kissed her on top of the head, and she bounced to the car.

"We'll miss you." Karen gave me a hug and slid me some spending money. "I wish you would come. My parents have been asking about you."

"Next time," I said.

Then it was Dad's turn. "No alcohol. No boys. No parties." Dad perched his hands on my shoulders. "Don't mess this up, Carter."

Potential fuck-up: Had Dad mentioned the change of plans to the boss? I was betting no. I'd waited until the last minute—when would he have had a chance, or even the inclination, to call Vladimir to report this? I should be fine, and God, did I need that freedom for one stinking weekend.

In case I had a tail, I asked Dad to drop me off at the club on their way out of town, so if someone were spying on me, it would appear I'd left with the family as planned.

The club was a ghost town. I hoped to hit some balls, but none of my friends were there. I peeked down at the basketball court—empty. The elliptical put me to sleep, so I decided to shoot some hoops instead. A few minutes into my workout, Leonardo crashed the court.

"*¿Cómo estás?*" He swaggered up to me and rebounded my rim shot.

Shit. "Hey, what's up?" I tried to keep it light.

He bounced the ball at the free-throw line and swished in a basket. He retrieved it and passed it to me. "Let's see you make two in a row."

"Oh, I was just leaving." I passed it back to him and headed for the exit.

"*Cluck, cluck, cluck.*" Leonardo made a chicken sound.

Seriously? My competitive drive kicked over to autopilot. I turned around and put my hand on my hip. He passed me the ball. I took a shot from the free-throw line but missed. I cursed and chased after the ball.

"*Fácil, LeBron.* Let's play a game. *Uno a uno.*"

Of course, I should have said no and left the club. Boris

had made it clear I was not to see him again—but the big guy thought I was on my way to Akron.

Game on.

I faked left and went up for a layup. Leonardo raised his hand and jumped to block the ball. When he came down, he landed on my ankle and twisted it sideways. I crumbled to the floor, groaning in pain. I didn't hear a *pop*, so it probably wasn't broken, but it was throbbing like crazy. No way could I walk home in a blizzard with a busted-up ankle. So, I accepted a ride from Leonardo.

I buried my face in my jacket as he carried me out so word wouldn't get back to my college team coach, Erin. She would be pissed if she found out I was screwing around with the meatheads from the gym. Team practices were set to start up again in January, and she had sent out a team email warning us to behave over winter break:

"Don't screw around ice skating, snow skiing, bungee jumping, cage fighting, or engaging in other unnecessary activities that could jeopardize your health. You're athletes, not wild chimpanzees. Have a great break. Go Bearcats!"

The heavy snowfall was accumulating, and the roads were slick on the ride home. The forecast predicted eight to twelve inches. Leonardo parked in my driveway, and I tried to put some weight on my ankle and walk in on my own, but it was too sore. I resorted to hopping.

Leonardo laughed. "I've got you, *loca*." He folded me up in his arms before I could protest. Ryan had a perfect view of my house from his living room and would not be pleased to see The Spanish Stud carrying me into the house. Since Ryan and I had kind of started dating, we had barely seen each other. I wanted to go back to just being friends for multiple reasons, but I hadn't had a chance to talk to him about it.

Once inside, Leonardo set me on the couch and went to the freezer for an ice pack. "Are we alone?" he asked, tossing his gym bag on the floor.

I ignored him and untied my laces to assess the damage. Sliding off my shoe made me cringe. My ankle was swollen so badly that it appeared I had a softball stuffed under my skin. I feared it was more than a sprain.

Leonardo winced. "Oh, baby, that's not good." He twisted the top off one of my dad's longnecks and took a swig. "You'll need to get an X-ray tomorrow." He popped the top off another beer and offered it to me.

Boys and beer: Dad's first two rules broken in record time.

28

MIXED COMPANY

"My dad will kill me if he finds out I drank his beer."

Leonardo set the bottle on the table and dropped onto the couch next to me. "Relax." He wrapped an ice pack around my ankle, his fingers lingering on my leg.

I should have called Ryan to pick me up.

"Thanks for the ride, but I'm exhausted. I need to rest."

His undaunted expression told me he didn't take the hint.

"And I have a boyfriend."

Leonardo chugged his beer, leaned over, and pressed his weight onto me. "You don't act like a girl who has a boyfriend."

"What the fuck? Get off me, pig!"

"I'll make you feel better." He pushed my hair back and licked my ear.

"Back off, asshole. You're hurting me."

At that moment, all the lights went off in the house. The digital display on my dad's desk went black. The storm had knocked out the power.

"Nice timing." He cupped my breasts.

I tried to slap him in the face, but he caught my hand.

My phone rang.

I tried to shove him off.

"*No seas mala.*" He held my wrists down and sucked on my neck.

A loud knock came from the front door.

Leonardo covered my mouth.

The knock came again.

I bit down on his hand until he let go. "Come in!"

The door opened. "Carter? It's me. Are you all right?" A flashlight cut through the darkness.

"In here, Ryan."

When Leonardo heard Ryan's deep voice, he rolled off me and sat up like nothing was wrong. "Keep your mouth shut," he whispered. I didn't need to see his face to know it was a threat.

"I tried to call," Ryan said. "The power is out on the whole block. Whose car is in the driveway?" He stepped into the room and shined a flashlight on the couch.

Ryan shined the flashlight across my swollen ankle, up my heaving chest, and to my panic-ridden face. Then he turned it on Leonardo. "What the fuck did you do to my girlfriend?" Then the flashlight dropped, and the primal sound of fists on flesh echoed through the room.

Oh, shit. I crawled across the floor and pulled myself up using the edge of the table. The coffee table slammed into the wall in the living room. I hopped over to the door and pressed the police button on the alarm box.

"Ryan, are you okay?"

He didn't answer.

"The cops are on their way. Ryan?"

Panic surged when I realized the alarm button might not

work without power. I crawled to get my phone out of my purse. The guys were still wrestling and swearing at each other. I needed someone to get between them.

"The police are coming. Get out of here, Leonardo." I found my phone and started to dial 911, but thought better of it. Leonardo deserved an ass-kicking, but I didn't want Ryan to get into trouble. Another crash. I had to call Boris.

He picked up on the first ring. "I need your help." I heard the tinny sound of glass ornaments shattering when the Christmas tree went down. "I'm at Dad's. Please hurry."

I hopped into the living room. "Ryan?" I used the light from my phone as a flashlight.

"Stay back, Carter," Ryan said. I could see in the faint light from the window that he had Leonardo in a headlock.

Sirens were nearing the house; I had activated the alarm after all.

I tugged on Ryan's arm to loosen his grip. "Don't hurt him. Everything's okay."

Leonardo struggled to get free, but Ryan had him good. "Give me my bag, and I'll go."

"Fuck you, loser," Ryan said.

"Give me my fucking bag!" Leonardo shouted.

"Okay, okay." I found his gym bag on the floor and started to toss it his way, then stopped. Why was he so worried about what I assumed were his sweaty gym clothes? I unzipped the bag and stared at the contents: a bounty of baggies of weed and coke, at least twenty rubber-banded bankrolls, and a small black gun.

Oh, shit. "Let him go, Ryan. Now. Do it before the cops get here."

"Are you crazy, Carter?"

"Trust me." The harshness of my tone startled even me. The image of Playboy's vicious order to clean up my mess came to mind. I pushed the nightmare away, hopped to the front door, and opened it.

Ryan dragged Leonardo to the front door and tossed him into the snow. I whizzed his car keys at him, but kept the gym bag. No way would I toss him a lethal weapon to use on us. I locked the door and then squeezed my arms around my hero. *What would have happened if he hadn't shown up?*

The sirens were getting closer. I shined the light on Ryan's face. Blood oozed from a cut above his eye. *My fault.* I begged him to go home. "Hurry, Ryan, they're almost here." Reluctantly, he agreed. He could get kicked off the football team for fighting. I promised to call as soon as I could to explain everything.

When the patrol car rolled up, I met the officer on the front porch with the hood of my jacket over my head and Leonardo's felonious gym bag slung over my shoulder. No way could I leave illegal drugs, a small fortune, and a fucking gun in Dad's house.

Shit. I recognized the cop's chubby, freckled face and bushy black hair—Officer Montgomery. She had busted me drinking last summer and drove me home in her cruiser. "Sorry to bother you, ma'am. I was home alone, and the power went out. I kind of freaked out."

"What made you freak out?"

I pointed to my swollen ankle. "I was running to the kitchen to get a candle and kicked the coffee table."

The officer ran her flashlight down my leg. "Looks like it might be broken." She raised the light to my face.

"I know. My grandpa is on his way over to take me to get an X-ray. There he is now." I pointed to the Cadillac. *He must have been close by.*

"Have we met, miss?"

Oh, shit. "Um, not to my knowledge, officer."

"You live here with your parents?"

"Yes. They're visiting relatives in Akron."

Boris made his way up the sidewalk. The police officer eyed his big body up and down.

"Thanks for getting here so quickly, Gramps. Can you take me to the hospital to get an X-ray?" I pointed to my foot and nodded.

His gaze drifted to the driveway and to the tire tracks in the snow from Leonardo's car. "Good evening, officer. Thank you for checking on my precious granddaughter." His coat collar was popped to conceal his knife tattoo, leather gloves covering his prison ink. "Let's go, dear."

My dad's ringtone had been erupting from my phone nonstop for several minutes. He must've gotten a call from the alarm company.

The officer held up her hand. "Just a minute. Can I see your ID, young lady?"

I fished my license out of my purse and handed it to the cop. As she examined my info, a knowing smile crept up on her face. "Carter Cook. I didn't recognize you with your hair covered." She tapped my license in her hand. "I've busted you before. You and your feisty little friend, right?"

Shit. "My mistake, Officer Montgomery."

"Have you been drinking tonight?"

I felt Boris's villainous glare bearing down on me.

"No, ma'am. Not a drop. I learned my lesson. Can we go now?"

"A pretty girl like you can get into a lot of trouble drinking in mixed company. You're lucky we busted up your after-hours pool party last summer." She glanced at Boris, then at me again. "Glad you straightened out. Hope your ankle is okay."

"Thanks." I reached up and put my arm around Boris's

shoulder so I could hop to the car, but he was out of patience. As I clutched the gym bag, Boris scooped me up, carried me to the Cadillac like an infant, and dumped me in the passenger seat.

I tucked the gym bag at my feet, and Boris drove away like everything was cool. I forced a smile and waved to the officer, still parked in front of the house, filling out her report. She squinted at Boris's license plate as he rolled away.

"I don't need an X-ray." I pulled out my phone. "I have to call Dad."

Boris drummed his fingers on the steering wheel.

"Hi, Dad. I'm fine. The power went out. I accidentally hit the alarm button when I tried to turn on the light...I'm sorry. I didn't realize I did it until the police showed up...Yes, they just left. Everything's fine."

Dad had already turned the car around and was on his way home. I convinced him to get back on the road. Dad was sharp, though. "If the electricity is out, you'll freeze to death. You'll have to stay somewhere tonight."

"Okay, I'll call around—"

"I've already got you covered. When I couldn't reach you, I called Vladimir. He has a generator. Boris is on his way. You can stay with them until the power comes back on."

I hung up the phone. Boris looked like he was ready to kill someone. That someone would be *me*.

29

HOMICIDAL RAGE

"Your lies won't work on me." Boris removed his gloves and tossed them on the floor.

"I'm not planning on lying to you, please—"

"*Nyet.*" He held up a finger to my face. "Who was at the house?"

"Um—"

"No *um*. Just name."

My fear spilled over into tears. "You don't have to interrogate me."

"Sneaky little weasel." His fist pounded the dashboard. "I take my eye off you for one hour, look what happens."

The Caddy swerved on the icy road. "Everything is okay. I'm okay. I promise." My ankle was throbbing. Ryan was home with a bloodied face. I had a bag full of drugs and a gun—yeah, everything was cool. *How did I get myself into this mess?* "Please, pull over. I'll tell you everything."

I had to buy some time. If I told him what had prompted the fight, he would hunt down Leonardo and kill him with his bare hands. The guy was an asshole, a sexual predator, and a drug dealer, but I couldn't be responsible for his murder. I had to think of a convincing lie. When Boris pulled into the park, he turned the car off and put the keys on the dash—an intimidation technique.

"Hurt anywhere besides your ankle?" His prison-tatted hands strangled the steering wheel.

I shook my head.

"You called me for help. You made up a story to police officer. You lied to Papa. You will not pull this shit on me." He grabbed my coat and growled in my face. "Truth. Now."

I tried to pull away.

"Last chance."

"If I tell you what happened, I'm afraid of what you'll do."

"Who was at your house?"

"Nobody."

He let go of me and took a deep breath. He was trying to control his temper. It wasn't working. Veins were popping like champagne bottles.

"I'm begging you, Boris. Leave it alone. Everything is under control." I rubbed my wrists where Leonardo had pinned me down.

Boris studied my body language, then lifted his hand like he was about to deliver a backhand to the side of my face. "You disobeyed me?"

"Not on purpose, I swear. I didn't plan it."

He lifted his phone out of his coat, tapped the screen, and yelled in Russian. That's what Vladimir did when I had trouble with Coach. I couldn't let this happen again. In desperation, I snatched the gym bag, opened my door, and hopped toward the tree line like an injured animal. I needed to find somewhere to dump the evidence.

"Did he touch you?" He removed his gun from the glove box and tucked it in his pants.

"No. Ryan kicked his ass." I didn't want to tell him. "I got hurt playing basketball and needed a ride home, okay? That's why he was at my house, I swear. Ryan came to check on me after the power went out, and they got into a fight. There's blood and glass all over the house. I lied to the cop to protect Ryan, not Leonardo." Unable to keep my footing, I toppled into the powdery snow. Pain shot up from my jacked-up ankle to every nerve in my body.

Boris snatched Leonardo's bag out of my arms and unzipped it. Homicidal rage burned in his eyes as he scrutinized the contraband. "Starting a little side business of your own?"

"No, no, no—"

The heat emanating from his eyes could've melted plutonium. "On a scale of one to ten, *Lapsha*, how well do you think the *pakhan* is going to take this?" He yanked me to my feet and dragged me back to the Cadillac.

30

UNPLEASANT BUSINESS

The whipping wind blew the snow sideways, covering the double yellow lines on the road. It looked like we would get the full foot of snow the weatherman had predicted. As we sat in silence, I focused on the windshield wipers swiping the snowflakes away, erasing any trace they'd been there.

I was terrified of what would happen to Leonardo. I glanced over at Boris. His knuckles were white, body stiff, jaw clenched.

He tapped his fingers on the steering wheel. "How's your ankle?"

"Fine. Totally fine."

He made that menacing, dismissive *humph* noise.

I knew he wanted to hunt Leonardo down and run over him a hundred times. I tried to think of something to lighten the mood, but anything out of my mouth would have irked him.

"Working out a lie to tell the boss?"

"I twisted my ankle on the court. *Tennis* is a competitive sport."

"I see." His tone was uncharacteristically placid.

Is he calming down?

When we got to the house, Boris opened the garage door and parked in the vacant spot normally reserved for the G-Wagon. I convinced myself I could walk no matter how bad it hurt, but before I took one step, Boris picked me up, tossed me over his shoulder, and carried me into the kitchen like a sack of beets.

He set me down on a stool, headed straight for the bar, and pulled Old Faithful out of the fridge. He poured a long shot and drank it down. He refreshed his glass and filled one for me. He threw back another, with his other hand resting on the bottle. My clothes and hair were wet from my trek through the snow, and I felt dirty from having Leonardo's hands all over me. I took off my soggy shoe and sock from my good foot. I needed to take a hot shower to chase away the chills, but I didn't want to ask.

Boris ordered me to drink up. I did. Then he poured me another one.

There was a knock on the kitchen door. I jumped. Boris opened it and let in a hunched-over gray-haired man holding a black bag. They seemed to be having a serious talk. They must be business associates. I sat there nursing my drink, oblivious to their conversation.

"This man is a doctor, Carter. He's going to examine you."

"Oh." I didn't expect that.

The door opened again, and the wolves from out back slunk in through the kitchen door. Playboy and the other two rounding out the pack, shook the snow off their coats and stomped their boots on the floor. How un-Russian of them to drag that mess into the house. Vladimir wouldn't have approved. *Animals.*

Boris picked me up and carried me past the living room into the guest bedroom, where he laid me down on the bed. He had his wet boots on, too. The doctor sat next to me. The goons slid into the bedroom and locked the door behind them.

Five bad dudes surrounded me as I lay defenseless on the bed.

"What's going on?" Did this have something to do with the lesson the *pakhan* thought I needed to learn after the Friday night fiasco? Where was he, anyway?

The doctor felt my ankle and then moved it up and down.

"Ouch!" I sucked in a mouthful of air.

"Not broken. You will wear air cast for week or two," he said in a thick accent.

As the doctor wrapped a bandage around my ankle, the goons were looking away—not at me—like they were trying to act casual. Something was very, very wrong.

When the doctor finished, I turned to Boris. "Is Mr. Ivanov home yet?" My words caught in my throat. I felt so tiny and fragile in the midst of the *Bratva*. There was only one reason I could think of why all those dangerous men had closed themselves in the bedroom with me.

I sat up to get away, but the doctor held up his hand. "Need to check one more thing."

Boris snapped his fingers at the goons. Playboy jumped on top of me and pinned down my wrists. I tried to scream, but the weight of his body pushed the air out of my lungs. In between gasps, I pleaded for help, but Boris just stood there with his arms crossed, watching his *patsani* terrorize me.

When I felt the other two trying to rip off my sweats, I wrapped my good ankle around the injured one to keep my legs together. "Get off me." My pants slid down my hips to my thighs. I gave up on defense, switched over to offense, and tried to kick them. The big, grimacing dude, along with the wiry skinhead with tats trailing down his neck, tugged off my pants with ease; they probably had a lot of experience violating girls in their line of work.

I can't let them take off my underwear. I held my knees together and screamed, "No! *Nyet, nyet, nyet.*" Playboy lifted his hips and scooted forward. Grimace slid his hands across my bikini line and yanked off my panties.

When my clothes were on the floor, the goons each took a leg and spread me apart. I thrashed and kicked to defend myself, but I wasn't strong enough to fight them off.

"I'm sorry, Boris. Tell them to stop," I screamed. "*Izvinite*! *Izvinite*!"

The doctor closed in beside me and ran his fingers along my V. I clenched my body tight to keep him out, but he brought in his other hand and spread me apart. Then, he thrust his filthy fingers inside me and felt around. I cried out to Boris once more, but Playboy grasped both of my wrists in one hand and covered my mouth with his free hand to silence my screams. While the doctor violated me, he taunted me in Russian.

Why did I think it was perfectly fine to play around with gangsters? I was naïve, just like the boss said I was. My reward for being an idiot? I was about to be gang raped. Did the *pakhan* order them to do it, or was this all Boris's sick idea?

I don't know if it was the shock, fear, or lack of oxygen, but my body stiffened up as if rigor mortis had already set in. There was no way I would be going home after these monsters were done with me. I squeezed my eyes shut and prayed for a miracle.

"She's clean—and pure," the doctor announced. He

withdrew his nasty fingers, wiped his hands on the sheet, and left the room.

Boris dismissed the goons, leaving just the two of us alone in the room. *No, no, no.* I needed to make a run for it, but my muscles were shredded, and I could barely breathe, let alone move. Boris sat beside me and tapped my cheek. “Next time, tell the truth, so we can avoid this unpleasant business.”

Gently, he sat me up, slid my arms into a plush pink robe, and tied it around my waist to cover my naked body. “I had to be certain. Everything out of your mouth is a lie.”

I struggled to fill my lungs with air.

“Take a deep breath.” Boris patted me on the back. “Calm down. Breathe.”

I flinched away from him, then managed a few short breaths. My heart was thumping so violently, it felt like I was about to burst.

“You need to bathe before dinner. Need help?”

I shook my head.

“I sent a runner out for your cast. It will make getting around easier.”

Where is Vladimir? He wouldn’t have let this happen. He protects me. He always protects me.

“That vile drug dealer is lucky the big boy showed up. If I found out he’d touched you—”

I wrapped my arms around my legs to stop from shaking.

He softened his demeanor. “I will send my men to clean up mess at your house.” He moved to the bathroom and turned on the water to draw a bath. He came back, scooped me up off the bed, and set me down on the edge of the tub. I couldn’t look at him. “I will set some clean clothes out for you. Want me to stay?”

I shook my head.

"Not a word about this to boss."

31

HOUSEGUEST

I sank into the tub and corralled the bubbles to shield my nakedness. How could I face Boris? He warned me not to rat him out to Vladimir, but there was no way I could shake off the assault and act like everything was okay. Everything was *not* okay.

After I cleaned up, I hopped to the bedroom, dressed in fresh clothes, and strapped on the air cast left out for me on the bed. Still in shock, I sat on the floor, crossed my legs, and practiced a Ujjayi breathing technique I'd learned in yoga to calm my nerves. I had to stop shaking; I was stuck there. I had no choice.

Dad wouldn't be home with the family for three more days. In that time, I had to play it cool, and hopefully, things would go back to the way they were before.

I willed myself to open the bedroom door and make my way to the kitchen, but I didn't have enough energy to pick myself up off the ground. I felt like every muscle in my body had been removed, leaving a fleshy pile of *shlyukha* matter. I curled myself up into a ball on the floor, breathing as deeply as I could manage between gasps to fuel my body with oxygen. Someone knocked on the door.

"How is my poor, injured girl?" Vladimir knelt beside me and rubbed my back.

"I'm fine. Just trying to get my blood flowing." My voice cracked.

He sat next to me on the floor, cradled me in his arms, and rocked me gently to calm me down. If Vladimir had been home when we got back, he would've protected me. Absolutely.

"What can I do, angel?" He kissed my cheek and stroked my hair. He hadn't been affectionate with me since our special moment in my bedroom. I melted on his chest and welcomed his soothing embrace. In his arms, no one could hurt me—not even Boris.

"You're light as a feather. Let's get you some nourishment." Vladimir helped me to my feet and guided me into the kitchen. Instead of eating at the bar, we sat at the breakfast nook by the balcony to watch the snow fall. I picked at the butter-laden potatoes, zucchini in cream sauce, and pickled beets loaded on my plate while Boris lurked around the kitchen, probably to make sure I wasn't going to nark on him. Since the boss wasn't crazy eyed, I doubted he knew about the Leonardo stuff or what Boris had ordered that dirty old man to do to me.

If my instincts were correct, Boris had given Vladimir a revised version of The Incident to protect himself. When he came to my house, he'd said, "I take my eye off you for one hour." Meaning, the big guy screwed up.

Vladimir eyed my plate. I choked down a few bites to stay off the emotional wreck radar, but I was traumatized and freaked out about sleeping at the house. Boris had the entire lower level all to himself. He could threaten me, spread my legs apart, but if he tried anything in front of the boss, the *pakhan* would kill him.

Did I want him dead?

I shook off the thought. I was turning as crazy as these Russians. Murder wasn't a problem-solver.

"Change of plans this weekend? Last we spoke, you were going to visit relatives."

Shit. "Yes, totally a last-minute thing. My friend scored tickets to the Bengals game and invited me to go. It's on Christmas Eve."

"Kiki?"

I shook my head. "My other friend, Ryan." I snuck a peek up at the boss as I smashed my potatoes down with the back of my fork. He still seemed in good spirits. I thought he would be pissed at me for trying to pull a fast one on him, but the fact that I would be his houseguest for the next three days probably made up for my bullshit.

Vladimir set down his fork and patted his mouth with a napkin. "You're exhausted. Let's get you settled in the living room."

"Perfect." I picked up our plates, but Vladimir took them out of my hands and insisted I rest. He rolled up his sleeves, loaded the dishwasher, wiped off the countertops, and took out the trash. The way he was there for me...I wished I could tell him the truth about what had happened, but if he knew what Leonardo tried to do or about my *examination*, he would have a Chernobyl-sized meltdown.

"You left this in my car." Boris handed me my phone. "Your papa is trying to reach you."

I checked my missed calls. It wasn't Dad. Ryan had called eight times and sent about twenty texts. "I'd better call him back. I'll be quick. Can you get a fire started?" I asked Vladimir.

"Anything for you, angel."

Once the boss left the kitchen, I got up from my chair, turned my back to Boris, and tapped out a text.

"What are you doing?" he asked.

"If I don't get back to Ryan, he'll call my dad," I snapped. I felt empowered knowing Vladimir was home to protect me.

Angry at my disrespectful tone, he whirled me around, clamped onto my shoulders, and jammed his thumbs into my collarbone. My ankle exploded in pain. "Be careful. It takes seven pounds of pressure to break the clavicle bone. I'm at five and a half."

I squirmed to slip out of his lethal grip. He didn't let up. I dropped the phone and tried to pry him off me, but me trying to defend myself against Boris was as productive as trying to yank a brick out of a house with my bare hands. "You're hurting me. Let me go, or I'll scream. The boss will be pissed when he finds out what you did to me."

He loosened his grip. I made a run for the swinging door to dive into the safe arms of the boss, but before I took a step, Boris grabbed my ponytail and slammed me back against the pantry door. He towered over me and covered my mouth with his hand.

"If you ever threaten me again or breathe one word to anyone about your examination, I will hurt you in ways that will haunt you the rest of your life. Don't forget who you're dealing with, little girl. I am not a man to cross." He pointed to my phone and snapped his fingers.

Panting, I picked it up off the floor and handed it to him.

He motioned to the door. "Don't keep boss waiting."

I skittered back to the living room, picked up the remote, and browsed the movie channels. I stopped when I found my favorite movie of all time: *Moonstruck*.

I snuggled up with a throw blanket on my side of the couch. The poodles joined the party and curled up on the rug. Vladimir caressed Anastasia with his foot.

"Will there be anything else tonight, Vladimir?" Boris towered over us, holding two glasses of red wine.

My body started to shake. I lifted the blanket up to my neck.

"No, we'll be fine." Vladimir took the vino from Boris and handed a glass to me.

"Have a wonderful evening with boss, Carter."

Something in Boris's suggestive tone freaked me out. In the last twenty-four hours, I had sprained my ankle and almost been date-raped. Ryan and Leonardo beat the shit out of each other in my house, where drug-dealing Leonardo was never supposed to be, and Boris and his thugs had done the unthinkable. I would love to have a wonderful fucking evening, Boris.

A half hour into the movie, I gave up. "I don't think I can make it to the end, boss." I let out a big yawn.

"You're a tough girl. You can make it." He lifted his glass. "*Za tebya.*"

"*Za tebya.*" We clinked and sipped.

At the point in the movie when Ronny enters the story, I blinked to stay awake. My body felt so heavy. Vladimir pulled me over to his side of the couch and nestled my head on his chest. He tipped the glass to my mouth, encouraging me to take another sip. As Loretta and Ronny argued onscreen, he stroked my hair and sipped his wine.

I yawned again. He removed the glass from my hand and set it on the coffee table. He lowered my head to rest on a pillow and brushed my hair off my face. I fought to keep my eyes open, but before Johnny Cammareri came back from Sicily, I blacked out.

32

FILTHY ANIMALS

It was almost noon the next day when I regained consciousness. I had no memory of how I got tucked into bed in the guestroom—or how I ended up in clean pajamas. I felt like a steamroller had mowed over me. I groaned as I sat up. When I leaned over to snag my cast, vertigo set in. I tipped off the bed and crash-landed on the floor with a thud.

I don't remember drinking that much.

My body needed more sleep, but my brain urged me to get moving. I slid on my cast and made my way to the bathroom. I undressed and checked my body for damage. I had deep purple and red marks on my collarbone, a bounty of finger bruises dotted my arms and legs thanks to Playboy and his crew, and I was sore *down there* from my examination.

I replayed what had happened over and over in my mind. I understood—in *Bratva* terms—why Boris wanted to know if Leonardo had forced himself on me, but why did he want to know if I was *pure*?

As I considered the thought, I got down on my knees

and hovered over the toilet in the morning-after ready position. The last thing I remembered was dozing off on the couch. Then the realization hit me—

They drugged me.

I shuddered to think what they'd done to me while I was unconscious. Once again, only one reason came to mind. I dry-heaved into the toilet. I had to keep it together. I was trapped there. If I didn't emerge soon, they'd come get me. I had two and a half more days there, and it wasn't in my best interest to conjure up the *pakhan.*

Live to fight another day.

I got dressed in one of my home-away-from-home outfits, plastered on my game face, and limped to the kitchen. Vladimir was seated at the bar, sipping a cup of tea next to a box of pastries and a fresh fruit and cheese display. "Good morning, angel."

I couldn't look him in the eye. "Sorry I got up so late. I don't usually sleep in." I motioned to the food. "You didn't have to do that. It's my job." My voice sounded hoarse.

"Nonsense. You are my guest. Sit. Eat."

Boris wore a hat and coat and clutched Leonardo's gym bag in his hand. He stood by the door, spinning the Cadillac key ring around his index finger. "Well rested?"

Careful not to let on that I knew they'd drugged me, I played dumb. "Best night's sleep I've had in ages." I smiled. "Oh, have either of you seen my phone? I must've misplaced it."

Boris held it up. "It's been going off all morning."

I slid over to him, snatched my phone from his hand, and shuffled back to get some distance between us. I had five missed calls—all from Dad and Ryan—and about a hundred texts. Kiki, Rakhi, Coach Erin...*Leonardo.*

Coming over at noon to pick up the bag. NO COPS.

My stomach turned. I wiped my sweaty palms on my pants.

"Boss, I have an appointment to get to at precisely *noon*. Do you need anything before I attend to business?" Boris asked.

"No, of course not. We'll be fine. *Do svidaniya*."

"*Do svidaniya*." Boris tipped the rim of his hat.

"Wait," I blurted. "Can you take me to the club? Coach Erin asked if I could stop by today so the trainer can check my ankle. She's leaving early for the holiday weekend."

"It's up to boss."

I have to get out of this house. "We can go downtown when I get back. There's a Christmas display at Fountain Square and ice skating, a nativity scene with real reindeer, and a band—"

"We will do all of that and more." He laughed. "Don't be gone too long."

I got a water bottle out of the bar fridge and grabbed a pastry. "*Do svidaniya*. That's how you say goodbye, right?"

"Perfect. You see, Boris? She's one of us."

Boris shook his head as if the idea of *me* being like *them* was enough to make his brain bleed.

I slid on my shoe and followed Boris out the door. When we got into the car, he turned on the music. I turned it off. "What's the plan? You're just going to give him his bag, right?"

Boris drummed his fingers on the steering wheel. "Not possible."

The *patsani* who had held me down the night before were waiting for us in a white van with blacked-out windows, the kind murderers drive in movies and true-crime shows.

"Are they going to follow us?"

"*Shush*. No questions."

Boris turned the music back on. I whizzed the pastry out the window.

I got the evil eye. "Why can't you eat like normal person?"

"I don't feel good." I squeezed my arms around my legs.

Boris studied my body language. "You drank too much."

"What did you do to me after you drugged me?" I buried my face in my hands, frightened by my own words.

He grabbed my forearm. "Don't come up with crazy ideas. Not what you think."

I shrugged him off and turned my back on him.

"Look at me."

Fearful of backlash, I peeked over my shoulder and met his unsympathetic eyes.

"Filthy animals do things to girls against their will, not boss."

I wiped off my tears and snot on my coat. "There's no other reason. Once that dirty old man told you I was a virgin, the two of you decided to help yourselves—"

"No one touched you."

"You mean *again*?"

By the death glare on Boris's face, I was skidding dangerously close to the Point of No Return.

"I needed to make certain you stayed put in your room."

I gasped. "Why?"

"I don't like giving you freedom to roam the house while

we're sleeping." He glanced sideways at me. "I'm not a trusting person, you know?"

"It was *your* idea to drug me?"

"No, dear. *My* idea was to handcuff your wrists to the bed frame."

I covered my mouth with my hands.

"Lucky for you, boss didn't like that idea either. He's too soft on you."

The idea of the two of them discussing the best way to immobilize me made me ill, but I believed the motivation behind it. Considering their illegal activity, I was a liability. "Which one of you took my clothes off?"

"No more questions."

My thoughts turned back to where we were headed. Leonardo was in grave danger. He deserved what Ryan had dished out to him last night, and in my eyes, we were even. As casually as I could, I slid my right hand into my pocket and pulled my phone out just far enough to manage a text to warn him not to go to my house.

Boris busted me, twisted my wrist, and squeezed my hand until I let go of my phone. The Cadillac veered down a secluded road and parked in front of an old, dilapidated barn. The murderer van slid in behind us. I unlocked my seat belt and hopped out of the car. I had only made it a few feet before Playboy had me in a chokehold.

Don't go to the house I will

"I will what, Carter? Give him another opportunity to disrespect you? Want to go have some fun with these bad boys?" He nodded to the barn.

The goons circled around me.

"Please stop. You're scaring me to death."

"That dirty Spaniard will be sorry for what he did."

"I'm sure he's sorry already. His face was bloody the last time I saw him."

Boris licked his lips. "He contacted you because he wants something, but failed to apologize for hurting you and for the damage he caused to your house."

"Let's make a deal," I said. "If he apologizes, you call off the wolves. If he tries anything, you have my blessing, okay?" I held out my hand for a binding agreement.

Boris scoffed. Playboy steered me back to the Caddy. Before I could get there, I dropped to my knees and vomited in the snow. Mentally exhausted by my bullshit, Boris handed Playboy Leonardo's bag and gave the *patsani* their orders. The white van rolled away and kept its course toward my place. Leonardo was going to learn a lesson about the consequences of fucking with the *pakhan's* most prized possession—*me.*

33

UNDER HIS SPELL

When Boris and I got back to the house, Vladimir greeted me at the door. "Ready to celebrate?" His eyes were lit up and dazzling. I believed Boris when he said he didn't drug me for the reason I'd assumed. Vladimir would never hurt me—*that way*.

"I'll wait while you change into something clean."

Such tact. In the car, I noticed I had vomit splashes on my clothes and reeked like a frat boy on a Sunday afternoon. "Yes. I'll hurry."

Once I showered and dressed in fresh designer clothes, Vladimir took me to lunch at a trendy high-rise restaurant that overlooked the holiday festivities on Fountain Square. We had a cozy U-shaped booth tucked in the corner. The best seat in the restaurant.

I choked down a couple of bites of bread and a few spoonfuls of vegetable barley soup, but I was so anxious from all that had gone down in the last twenty-four hours, I doubted I could keep anything in my stomach. Not to mention, I had the Big Papi of all hangovers caused by whatever Boris had slipped into my drink last night.

A text from Boris came in on my special phone. It was a photo of Leonardo lying on the ground with a busted-up and bloody face, holding his ankle in agony; it was clearly broken. Acid built up in my throat, and chills rocked my body.

Any more messes need cleaning up?

No.

Not a word, understand?

Yes.

Good girl. Delete this now.

I trashed the picture and tucked the phone back in my purse.

Vladimir pushed his soup bowl aside and folded his hands on the table. "Talk to me, Carter. I need to know what you're thinking."

I must have looked as crappy as I felt. I tucked my hands into my shirt sleeves and stared out the window. I held back tears, trying to come up with something to say that wouldn't get me into trouble. Ever since Leonardo had given me a lift home, one fucked-up thing after another had been set into motion. I didn't know how to make it all stop.

Coach, Natasha, Leonardo—no more mistakes.

Our twenty-something-year-old waitress with bouncy pigtails and artsy tats came back to the table. "Are you finished with your first course?"

Vladimir motioned for her to take his bowl. "Please."

"Cool tats." The waitress flashed a flirty smile. "Goes great with the accent."

"*Spasibo*," he replied.

She tilted her head and giggled.

"I'm finished, too," I said.

After the waitress skittered away, I asked, "Jeez. Do all girls throw themselves at you like that?"

"Jealous?" He winked.

I crossed my arms over my chest. "No."

"Ready to talk?"

"There is something I want to ask, but I'm afraid—"

"Don't be." He scooted closer to me in the booth.

I wrung my hands in my lap and tried to think of how best to phrase my question.

"Tell me." He put his hand on my back.

His touch startled me. I lowered my gaze, slumped my shoulders.

He wrapped his arm around me. "Please don't fear me. I would never hurt you."

"Did you come to Cincinnati because of me?"

He squeezed my shoulder. "You have quite an ego, Miss Cook."

Why had I bothered? He wasn't going to tell me the truth anyway. "Yeah, whatever. Can we go now?" I stood up to leave, but he held on to my arm.

"Wait." He pulled out his wallet, flipped it open, and cupped something in his hand.

I sat back down, and he revealed a striking picture of Sophia with the New York skyline behind her.

"I spent five years of my life in a Siberian prison camp. The idea that this vibrant young woman was waiting for me to return kept me alive."

"You thought she was waiting for you?"

He tipped his head.

"When did you find out she died? Before or after you got out?"

"After. Boris thought it best not to tell me. He knew she meant the world to me."

"You must've been devastated."

"With the love of my life gone, I had no will to live until —" He flipped over a second photo of me, holding a tennis trophy. I was in high school, and I'd just won my first tournament.

"Whoa, whoa. You've been stalking me all these years?"

The restaurant went silent. All eyes were on us.

"Not *stalking*, looking after you."

I blinked as if I'd been conked over the head with a blunt object.

"Sophia loved you so much, Carter. With her gone, I felt it was my duty to watch over you. Knowing a part of her lives on through you has helped me get past the grief." He picked up my hands. "My family convinced me to stay away from you, for your own good. My line of work can be *unpredictable*."

"Why'd you change your mind?"

"I've kept tabs on you over the years. When I found out your papa had been out of work for so long and your family was struggling, I couldn't sit back and do nothing, could I?"

"You came all the way from Russia to help my family?"

"You know me well enough to know there are no limits. There is nothing I wouldn't do for you." He folded my hands into his, lifted them to his lips, and kissed the inside of my wrist. "You are my world."

The idea that this man—this powerful man—cared so deeply for me that he left his country, disrupted his world, and came to Ohio to rescue my family and me left me speechless. "Then why do you keep pushing me away?"

"*Moy slomannyy angel,*" he whispered. "I'm not pushing you away. I'm trying to resist you, Carter. You're better off without me in your life, but you've captured my heart. I can't breathe when we're apart."

We stared into each other's eyes.

"A young woman as beautiful as you can choose any man she desires. Stop wasting your time on losers who don't deserve you. Choose me." He leaned down to kiss me.

Under his spell, I closed my eyes, parted my lips—

The waitress bounced back to the table with our entrees. "Oh, sorry. I didn't mean to interrupt."

I opened my eyes.

"No apology necessary," Vladimir said. "I have a lifetime to show my angel how much she means to me." He kissed my cheek and whispered something sexy in Russian.

The waitress's cheeks flushed. "You are the luckiest girl in the universe. I wish *my* boyfriend treated me like that."

Boyfriend? Oh, God. What have I gotten myself into now?

34

NATURAL DISASTER

When we rolled up the driveway, Igor cocked his head and blinked at me from his perch in the tree. Like me, the peacock thought it best to keep his mouth shut and quit strutting around like he owned the place.

While we were away, the house had been transformed into a winter wonderland. The aroma of warm spiced cider filled the air, *zakuski* lined the bar, and Christmas decorations dangled from the row of mini chandeliers in the kitchen. In the dining room, the table had been set, and a feast stayed warm in chafing dishes. A real Christmas tree stood by the fireplace, decorated with sparkling glass ornaments and illuminated with soft white lights.

The poodles whimpered to be let out of their crates.

"No crying, babies." I released them and took them outside. When I came back and locked them in their crates so their paws could dry, Vladimir patted the vacant spot next to him on the couch, drawing me to him. I kicked off my air cast, plopped down on the couch, and wrapped myself up in a blanket.

"I never want there to be any secrets between us." Vladimir scooted my body down until he had my back spooned against his chest, and my head rested in the curve of his neck. He curled and tucked me into the contours of his body like I was the weak turtle meat and he was the hard, protective shell.

He brushed his hand across my cheek. "I'm looking forward to spending a lovely evening with you." He leaned us back into a more relaxing spoon position and kissed my cheek. "Want to do something special tonight?"

He got a call and checked the screen. "It's your papa."

I sat up and retreated to the other side of the couch.

"Ricky, my friend. How are you? How's the family? ... She is here. Right here. Let me have you speak to her." Vladimir handed me his phone.

"Hi, Dad. I'm sorry. I can't find my phone. We're having a wonderful time...Everything is great...No, no problems... Give everyone my love." I hung up and handed the phone back to Vladimir. He had a serious look on his face.

"He didn't ask about how your ankle is feeling?"

I exhaled. "Well, I didn't mention it."

"Where is your phone?"

"Uh, Boris has it."

"Why?"

"You know him. He's paranoid."

"*Hmm*," he said.

"What's *hmm*?" I asked.

He got up from the couch and walked into the kitchen. I followed, hopping on my good leg. He poured himself a shot of vodka and downed it. Mentally, I prepared to protect myself against one of his alarming mood swings.

"Why don't you tell your papa about your injury? Have you something to hide?"

"I'm not hiding anything. If I told him I was hurt, he would cancel the trip and come home. I don't want him to worry."

Vladimir downed his vodka and set the glass on the counter. He moved toward me with penetrating eyes like a cobra. "Do you keep things from *me* so I don't worry?"

Shit. I knew he would figure out something was wrong. If I could make some noise, maybe Boris would come up from downstairs to check things out. "No, of course not."

I knocked over the almost empty vodka bottle. It bounced a half-dozen times before rolling to a stop. "I'm so clumsy." I slipped out of his grasp and followed the bottle over to its resting place by the stove. I picked it up and set it back on the counter. "I would never betray your trust. You know me better than that, right?"

"Of course, my dear. I'm sorry to question your loyalty." He pulled my body into his and squeezed his arms around my back. "Tell me *exactly* how you hurt your ankle."

Shock, panic, and fear rippled through my body. "How did I hurt myself? Didn't Boris tell you?" Shit. Did Boris tell him the truth, or was he going along with my tennis story?

"I want to hear it from you."

"I twisted it on the court."

He waited for the little weasel in me to elaborate. I opened my mouth to speak, but before the words came out, Boris swung open the kitchen door. "I heard noise."

"Sorry to bother you, Boris. I knocked over a—"

Vladimir raised a hand to silence me. A sixth sense alerted me to take cover, like when a natural disaster is about to strike, and animals escape to higher ground. I, too, needed an exit strategy before the testosterone tsunami hit and swept me away.

"Come in, friend. We were just talking about you. Sit. Have a drink."

Boris had the same feeling I had. I could see it in his eyes. "What are we talking about, boss?" He turned over a couple of glasses on the bar and filled each with ice-cold vodka. He slid one to Vladimir and swirled one in his hand.

He answered in Russian.

Boris nodded. They clinked glasses and downed their shots.

I put some weight on my ankle to test it out. It was tender without the cast. Boris wasn't the most trustworthy person in the world, but I hoped the idea of mopping my blood off the kitchen floor would deter him from steering the boss south.

Their conversation continued, and the mercury was rising. Vladimir held out his arm for me to come to him. Obediently, I hopped to his side. He wrapped his arm around my waist and aligned my body against his.

"You're right, boss. Carter is a special young lady." Boris switched back to English. "I would never allow any harm to come to her."

The boss responded in Russian.

Boris narrowed his eyes.

Vladimir unwound me. "Set the table for dinner, angel." He kissed me on top of the head and shoved me toward the dining room.

It was going to come down to some massive Optimus Prime versus Megatron showdown. There was no way those two control freaks could coexist peacefully on one planet. I hopped past the dining room into the living room, sat on the couch, and strapped on my walking cast. Then I searched around for a weapon to protect myself: the poodles. I released them from their crates. I went to the dining room and found a carving knife in the china cabinet.

The argument had escalated, but I didn't hear any physical fighting. I tapped open the door with my good leg to see what was happening. The door swung open, and for a moment, I saw the look of surprise on two old friends' faces. What must I have looked like to them?

The door swung back open, and Vladimir and Boris stared at me as I stood there with a twelve-inch knife in my hand, a gimp leg, and two pampered pooches whimpering and wagging their tails.

"What's this?" Vladimir asked, unable to keep a straight face.

"I thought you might...need some help."

"You thought we were going to *kill* each other? Over an argument?"

"What are we, animals?" Boris asked.

"Oh. I..." I lowered the knife. The dogs continued their yipping and wagging.

The two men slapped each other on the back, unable to keep it together. The boss came at me with his hands up, careful not to freak me out. He took the knife from my hand and set it on the counter. The poodles bounced around, excited to see their papa.

"So what was the plan, Carter? Were you going to slice my *sovietnik* to death or order the attack dogs to rip out his jugular vein?"

I took a couple of deep breaths to relax my pounding chest.

"How do you feel about that, Boris? Will you be able to sleep tonight knowing we have a vicious *devushka* living under the same roof?"

"I'm sorry I—"

Boris draped his arm around my shoulder. "It's okay, dear. You're good girl. I am grateful you spared my life."

"*Lapsha*." I shook off his arm.

"Noodle?" Vladimir translated.

I shot Boris the evil eye. "You told me it meant *asshole*."

Boris held up his hands in surrender. "Why trust me? I'm bad guy."

Vladimir laughed. "You need a drink, angel. Wine or vodka?"

"Vodka." I mimicked his accent. It was going to be a long night.

35

SOPHIA

An empty vodka bottle sat on the floor, and Boris cracked open a second. I had turned over my glass after the inaugural shot to keep my mind clear, but the two of them were not holding back. I was seated at a barstool, and Vladimir stood behind me with his arm draped across my shoulder while he and Boris reminisced about the good old days. I could tell when the story turned dark because they switched to Russian. I wondered how long Vladimir had been *bad*.

After about the fifth toast, Vladimir's hand slid from my shoulders down to the back pocket of my jeans. Everything had been happening in rapid-fire succession, and I hadn't had a chance to talk to him about...*that*. And I knew better than to bring up anything that might piss him off while he was drinking.

After they polished off the second bottle, Boris flipped over his glass. He gave me a stern look and then spoke to the boss in Russian. I had a feeling they were discussing security measures.

I pleaded my case to Boris. "Please, don't drug me again.

My head has been throbbing all day." I turned to Vladimir. "I promise I'm not going to do anything stupid."

Vladimir's eyes were at half-mast. "Of course, angel."

"*Nyet*," Boris said. If you don't want drugs, then we'll do it my way. Your choice, dear."

"No, no handcuffs."

"Enough. I will not leave you unattended—"

"I'll sleep in his room." I clung to the boss. The second the words dribbled out of my mouth, I knew I'd fucked up.

Boris shot me the look.

Vladimir wrapped his arm around me. "It's settled then."

Boris gave up the battle and swerved down to his lair in the basement.

The boss and I were alone. He ran his fingers through my hair and tried to kiss me, but I turned my cheek.

"Something wrong?" I sensed the *pakhan* had taken over. Careful not to piss him off, I patted him on the back and sidestepped out of his reach. "Everything's fine. I'm going to get ready for bed now." I made a run for my room, but he caught me.

"Don't you dare leave me." He tightened his grip around my upper arms and squeezed like a python coiling around its prey.

I wanted to scream. He was so strong. My bones felt like they were going to snap. "I won't." I panted as his hot breath beat down on top of my head. After a moment, he released his grip when *he* was ready to let me go.

"Don't keep me waiting, Sophia."

Oh, God. "I won't, *Vladimir*." I scurried away, rubbing my aching arms and contemplating my next move. I had two options: One, I could lock myself in my bedroom and hope he would pass out before he could bust down the door. Two: Boris.

There was no way I could protect myself against the *pakhan*. I decided on the latter. I tiptoed downstairs into the pitch-black nothingness of the basement and felt my way around to avoid bumping into the pool table. "Boris?" I whispered. I found a door and opened it. "Boris?"

I heard the ruffling of sheets and then a *click-click.*

"Jeez! Don't shoot. It's me."

"That's it. I'm getting the handcuffs."

"No, I need your help. Please, it's serious. Get up."

He huffed, stumbled to the door, and turned the light on. "What did you do now, stupid girl?" He tied a belt around a black silk robe.

I took a deep breath. "I'm scared. He called me Sophia."

He chuckled. "What did I tell you about your teasing? Do what he says. Being with a man will help you relax. Get out of here, *lapsha*."

I tugged on his arm. "He's out of his mind drunk. He almost snapped my bones in half. I know he doesn't want to hurt me. If you don't help me—"

He clicked his tongue. "What do you think happens when you entice men? It's time to pay up, Carter. Have a nice evening."

He put his hand on the doorknob and tried to shut me out. In desperation, I lunged forward and clutched two fistfuls of chest hair. He retaliated by grabbing my ponytail and dropping me to the floor.

"Ouch!" I stood and clung to his arm. "Listen, I need a mulligan on this. I'm not on the pill. What if I get pregnant? Dad will find out."

Boris pointed his finger in my face. "Get back upstairs. Now."

"No. No way. If you don't help me, I'm taking my chances scaling the Berlin Wall out there. Please, he's not himself. If this happens, it will be against my will. You said only filthy animals do that sort of thing. Is that what the boss is—an *animal*?"

"Oh, Carter, why are you so much trouble? The other girls are easy."

Other girls?

The truth of my words registered in his eyes. "Get a bottle of wine from the cellar, open it, and come back."

I did as Boris said. When I returned, he tapped a couple of pills out of a small plastic bottle and dropped them into the wine. "One glass will knock out an elephant. Serve half a glass, and you both will drink, understand? I don't give a shit about your headache."

"Thank you, thank you, thank you." I scurried upstairs.

"Carter."

I turned around on the landing.

"You owe me."

36

PINCHED

I awoke late Christmas Eve morning, sprawled out on the couch in the living room—on top of Vladimir. My face was nestled in his chest, and my fingers were buried in his soft, wavy hair. I lifted my head. His shirt was soaking wet with my drool. *Dad would be so proud.*

I had no memory of what had happened after we drank the wine, but we both still had our clothes on from the night before. Carefully, I slid off him, mopped the slobber off my face on the sleeve of my sweat jacket, and made my way into the kitchen.

I brewed a pot of tea, lit a pine-scented candle, and slid a tray of croissants into the oven. Boris was up shortly after I had started rustling around in the kitchen. "*Privet*. Merry Christmas Eve." I greeted him with a cheery smile.

He glared at me. "*Dobroye utro, lapsha*. Sleep good? You and boss looked cozy when I checked on you last night." He glanced at his watch. "He's usually up with the sun. How much did he drink?"

I averted my gaze to the oven. The pastries were burning around the edges. I thought it would be nice to cut the dough into the shape of Christmas trees, but the flaky layers were too thin on the outside to cook evenly. I pulled them out of the oven and set them on the counter.

"Carter?"

"I have no clue. I made a toast, drank two sips, and everything after that is a blur."

"You're playing with fire, stupid girl. He's going to know you did something."

I peeled my fractured forest off the metal baking sheet and piled the half-baked dough on top of a sheet of wax paper to cool. "Well, technically, *you* did it." Worried he might dive across the bar and stuff my head into the oven, I kept my eyes on him, poured him a cup of tea, and pushed it across the bar.

"This is all going to catch up with you. I look forward to the day." He lifted his teacup and sipped the steamy English Breakfast brew. "Wake him in an hour if he's not up."

"Wait. Are you leaving?" I asked more desperately than I'd intended.

"I'm going to church."

"Any chance I could get my phone back?"

"Not today." He walked to the mudroom to retrieve his hat and coat. "Just a bunch of bullshit texts." He bundled up and issued a warning. "The boys out back are keeping an eye on things for me. Don't try anything stupid. There's already blood in the water."

I glanced out the window to see if they were out. Playboy was leaning against the murder van, bouncing a tennis ball. Skinhead took a drag off his cigarette and waved hello. I curled my legs up on the barstool and tried to make myself invisible. "How am I going to get to the Bengals game?"

"Boss will take you."

"What if he's mad at me?" I wrapped my arms around

my body, rested my chin on my knees, and chewed on my fingernails. What would happen when Vladimir woke up and found out what I'd done? Would he put his hands around my neck the next time I ticked him off?

Boris hung up his hat and coat and moved toward me. He put his hand on my jacket and tried to unzip it. I flinched, grabbed his hand, and pleaded with him not to do it.

"*Shush*," he whispered. "Just want a look."

Out of fear of retaliation, I stopped fighting and let him remove my jacket. My limbs were blanketed with bruises in various stages of healing from being manhandled over the last few days. They were so colorful they could have passed for tattoos. The bruises on my collarbone from Boris's correction the night before last were a disturbing deep purple. The most recent finger marks from Vladimir's death grip were blood red.

"Boss did this to you last night?"

My gaze dropped to the floor. I kept quiet, unsure of how to answer.

He put his hand on his face and rubbed his beard. "You look like a corpse. I can't return you to your papa in this condition." He moved his hands to my waist and felt my ribs.

I squirmed and shoved his hands off me. "You haven't eaten a thing since you've been our guest, have you? This will not do. Skin and bones, skin and bones." He went to the refrigerator and took out a carton of eggs, a stick of butter, heavy cream, and a block of cheese. From the cabinet, he pulled out a clear mixing bowl and a whisk. He turned on the gas burner and placed an iron skillet over the flame.

"I thought you were leaving."

He cracked an egg into the bowl. "You need protein."

Then he cracked another one. "A stray dog has more meat on its bones. Your papa will think we've mistreated you." He whipped the chicks into a dizzying pulp, beating them until they blurred together into one communal bowl of *ick*.

"I won't eat that. Eggs make me gag."

Boris tipped his head. "Most days you don't eat eggs. Today you do."

"Stop it. I have some nuts in the cabinet. I'll eat the whole can."

"You will eat eggs."

"No, I won't. You can't make me." I stood up and side-stepped toward the door. "I'm going to get ready now. I'll eat when I get to the stadium."

He aimed the spatula between my eyes. "Why do you fight me? I have given you freedom to speak your mind, but now you're pissing me off, little girl. Take a seat and shut your mouth."

I kept moving.

"Last chance." He unfastened the buttons on his long-sleeved shirt and rolled them up to his elbows. He had an inky blue chain link tattoo that wrapped around his wrist like a serpent. He prowled toward me with the unsympathetic eyes of a killer.

I slunk closer to the door.

Sit down. Let him win this one, Sophia said.

"You're going to be sorry," he warned, closing the gap.

The intercom buzzer beeped. We looked at each other, sharing our mutual *who the hell could be* look.

The poodles whimpered.

"Did you make any calls?"

I shook my head.

He glanced at the security monitor, mumbled something in Russian, and tossed me my jacket. "Cover your arms and keep your mouth shut." He typed in a security code to open the gate and left to meet their guest. I slid to the swinging door to try to hear the conversation in the other room. "Hello, friend. Good to see you. Come in, come in," Boris said.

"Thanks, sorry to bother you."

I threw open the kitchen door and ran into the living room. "Ryan." I crashed my face into his Bengals jersey and wrapped my arms around him. "How did you know where to find me?"

"I was worried when you didn't get back to me about where you were staying. I texted your dad, and he told me you lost your phone. He gave me this address. Why are you shaking?" He unwound my arms and held me back so he could see my face. "You look like hell, babe. Are you okay?"

Boris was trying to act casual, but I knew he wanted to hogtie me and stuff me in the trunk of the Cadillac. I had to be careful. "I know, right? I caught whatever is going around. I haven't been able to keep anything down. Boris has been trying to get me to eat something, but I don't have an appetite." I coughed and rubbed my nose for effect.

Ryan's gaze drifted down to the air cast on my foot, probably considering if Leonardo had something to do with my sudden illness. "Is it broken?" His expression was both angry and hurt. I never had a chance to explain why I had been hanging out with Leonardo in the first place.

"No, it's no big deal." I waved my hand dismissively.

Boris scoffed at the lies that so comfortably rolled off my tongue.

"We need to talk about what happened, okay?" He tried to kiss me, but I covered his mouth with my hand to block him. "I'm contagious. Trust me, you don't want what I got."

"Why didn't you call me? If that bastard touched you—"

I felt the heat of Boris's rage resonating around me. I had to keep Ryan out of this. "We'll talk later. Everything's fine. Let's have breakfast. I think I can eat something now that you're here." I looped my arm around his elbow and guided him toward the kitchen.

Vladimir sat up on the couch, glared at Ryan, and spoke to Boris in Russian.

I jumped. "Sorry we woke you, Mr. Ivanov. My friend is here to take me to the game."

Vladimir got up, smoothed his hair back, and staggered toward us. His skin was pale, eyes bloodshot. "This must be the football player Carter is always crying about. Ryan, right?"

Ryan tossed me a quizzical look. "Nice to meet you, sir."

The boss studied the cut above his eye from the Leonardo incident. "You had a fight?"

"Carter didn't tell you what happened?"

I pinched Ryan in the side. Boris eyed my hand and spoke in Russian to Vladimir.

While the two of them were preoccupied, I stood on my toes and whispered to Ryan. "Don't bring up anything I wouldn't want Dad to—"

The weasel detector went off.

The Russians stopped talking.

My gaze darted nervously between them.

"You are a good friend to our dear Carter." The boss was careful to keep his crazy in check. I had no idea what Boris had told him, but I was certain it wasn't the truth.

"You got that right, sir." Ryan reeled me in and smooched my cheek.

Judging by Vladimir's seething expression, my game clock had officially wound down to zero. Boris had already physically hurt me, and as of last night, so had Vladimir. My messed-up situation wasn't a game anymore. I feared for my life and the lives of my loved ones. I needed a distraction before Ryan caught on. "Let's go to the kitchen. Boris made breakfast. We don't want his good efforts to go to waste."

I knew I would pay for it later for the egg thing, but I filled my plate with fruit, nuts, and cheese to appease Boris. He circled the kitchen, watching me eat like a goddamn vulture. Vladimir shot daggers at me as he sipped a cup of strong black tea.

As we stood around the bar, I wanted to curl up in Ryan's arms so he could protect me if Boris tried to hurt me. If it came down to it, I think Ryan *could* take him. He was younger and all muscle, but Boris was bigger and meaner—and he had a gun. Plus, he probably kicked ass daily—and he had no soul. Maybe I was overly optimistic about the odds.

While I would be safer with Ryan, I wouldn't allow my poor choices to drag him down. The boss was no doubt ticked that my *friend* was in his house in the first place. Boris couldn't have missed the death rays Vladimir was firing at Ryan, so he diffused the situation by striking up a conversation with him about his take on the statistical probability of the Bengals scoring a playoff berth. I seized the moment and excused myself to get ready for the game.

I dusted on some powder, shadow, blush, a swipe of mascara, and a spot of pink lipstick to try not to look so sickly. I put on the smallest jeans I had to compensate for my weight loss and picked a stylish plaid sweater to go over it. I couldn't ditch the cast, but I put on three pairs of socks to keep my toes warm on my bad foot and slipped a toasty Ugg boot on the other. When I got back to the kitchen, the conversation died. My sixth sense that something fucked up was about to happen kicked in. "Ready to go, Ryan?"

"There's been a change of plans." Vladimir walked to the mudroom and came back holding a full-length fur coat whose original owner was some sort of spotted cat. I let him slip it on me.

Ryan's brown eyes twinkled when I lifted my hair out of the coat and let it fall over my shoulders. "This is going to be the best Christmas Eve ever."

Or our last Christmas Eve ever.

37

WAGER

If Ryan hadn't come to the house when he did, I might not have been breathing by kickoff. Instead, the boss called up a connection and reserved a private box at the stadium for the four of us. To top it off, Boris arranged a limo to take us there in style. En route to the game, Boris popped a bottle of champagne. What we were celebrating, I did not know, but I was certain it had something to do with Ryan.

The boss must have had one hell of a hangover as I did, but he hid it well. He dressed in a dark blue pinstriped suit with a long, luxurious sable fur coat over it. He was acting cool, but the crazy was shooting out of his eyes like a laser light show. Boris had on his usual all-black ensemble with a fat gold chain around his neck and a black leather fur-trimmed winter coat. The deep freeze had officially set in.

Boris always looked like he wanted to kill someone—usually me—but the boss was way beyond his usual frustration level. And when the game was over and we said our goodbyes, I would be back at the mansion with the big bad gun-toting Russians, out in the middle of the woods, surrounded by barbed wire and a pack of wolves. I didn't stand a chance.

"That's a nice coat," Ryan said. He knew I'd never choose to wear real fur.

"It's a loaner," I said.

"Does that belong to your girlfriend, sir?" Ryan asked the boss.

A devilish grin crept up on his face. "Yes, my beautiful girlfriend."

"I'm sure she looks just as hot in it as *my* girlfriend does," Ryan said.

Oh, God.

"*Your* girlfriend?" The boss was officially on the verge of losing his mind.

Ryan slid his foot across the aisle and tapped my boot. "She made me chase her, but I finally wore her down. Isn't that right, Cookie?"

Vladimir glared at me like an executioner hovering over his victim, axe raised, ready to make the fatal swing. Boris said something in Russian to try to calm him down.

My Game Plan: keep it light, and maybe they would let me off easy for good behavior. I laughed. "You're such a joker, Ryan."

When we got to our private box at the stadium, I couldn't decide where to sit. All three of them wanted a piece of me. I stood by the window to watch the pregame festivities.

"What's our bet today, Cookie?" Ryan asked. He put his arm around me. "You know, I did you a favor with our last bet by *letting* you wear my Bearcat jersey. My number on your back upped your street creds a few notches."

Don't bring up the jersey. "Ha, ha." I elbowed him in the side and walked away to pick up a water bottle. "What are the odds on the game, Boris?"

"Ravens by three, *Cookie.*"

"I hate the Ravens. Can't pull the trigger on that one. What do you think, Mr. Ivanov?"

He eyed me like a jungle cat that just heard a branch snap. "I don't gamble."

"Excuse me?" I put my hand on my hip and wrinkled my nose. He was as competitive as I was—maybe even worse.

"If you gamble, you set yourself up to lose."

I crossed my arms. "Then you can't win, either."

"I'm already a winner. Why would I want to be a loser?"

"Good point," Ryan said. "I'll take advice from the rich guy. No bets."

The men laughed. Ryan raised his Coke and cheered their drinks.

"Want a beer?" Boris was sure acting chummy toward my boyfriend.

"No, thank you, sir. I don't drink."

"Wait, wait." I held up my hands. "If you don't play, you can't win."

"You also can't lose," Boris said. "That's why I don't gamble, either."

I shook my head, unable to wrap my brain around that one. The real me, as opposed to the trembling nutcase I'd become over the weekend, would have grilled the Russians on their bullshit. "You make bets with me all the time. What about that?"

"I said I don't *gamble,* not that I don't make *bets.* Gambling is risky business. When I make a bet with you, it's a sure thing."

Ryan chuckled at my notoriously bad betting record.

I raised my empty water bottle. "Touché."

"I'll make a bet with you, babe, if it will make you feel better." He picked up my hand, pulled me over to his side, and plopped me down on his lap.

"I'm sure you will. I'm bleeding out over here." I stood and went to our private bar for another water.

Vladimir followed me. He wrapped his arm around me. "Did you rest well last night?"

I froze.

"I slept very deeply." He pushed my hair over my shoulder and ran his finger down my neck. "I'll make a wager with you. What do you want to win?"

I peeked over my shoulder to make sure Ryan didn't see us. Boris was pointing at the Ravens defense, and Ryan assessed the Bengals o-line.

"Nothing. I do it for fun. It's no big deal."

The bartender placed my ice water and a bottle of vodka with a round of shot glasses on the bar.

"I want to have fun, too."

Out of fear, I played along. "Okay. I'll try to think of something." No more mistakes, especially now that Ryan had become the *pakhan's* public enemy number one. We walked back to our seats as the Bengals managed an eleven-yard run, which earned them a fresh set of downs. The crowd cheered.

I tried to veer toward Ryan, but the boss caught my hand and set me down next to him. "I thought of a nice bet for you to win, Miss Cook."

I wiped off my mouth with the back of my hand. "Did you hear that? He has a nice bet for me to *win*," I said, trying to ward off the tension.

The guys laughed.

"I don't need your pity, boss—I mean, Mr. Ivanov. I can

take it." I leaned back in my swivel chair and took a sip of my water, trying my best to act casual. I didn't want Ryan to pick up on my apprehension; there was room for both of our bodies in the trunk of the Cadillac.

The Bengals ran in a touchdown and tied the game ten to ten in the last seconds of the first half. The stadium roared. Ryan leaned across the table, interlaced his fingers with mine, and smooched me on the lips. I shook my hands free and tucked them under my legs. I hoped he didn't get a whiff of the boss's aftershave on my skin.

Vladimir scooted my chair closer to him and farther away from Ryan. "You'll want to take this bet."

"Let's hear it," Ryan said.

"If Baltimore tries an onside kick, I win. If they don't, you win. Is it a bet?"

"Take it, babe. Trust me. There's no way—no way the Ravens will do it."

Vladimir extended his hand and waited for me to accept the deal.

"Hold on. What's the wager?" I held my hand back out of his reach.

"A new tennis racket for you—and if I win, you prepare dinner?"

"Hope you like peanut butter," Ryan said.

"First of all, I would never retire the Silver Bullet, and I already cook dinner for you."

Ryan wrinkled his brow. I had to be careful. No one knew about our arrangement. "You know, this weekend of course."

Ryan seemed satisfied with the explanation.

"She drives a hard bargain, boss. Better raise the stakes." Boris egged him on.

"Let me see. If I win, you must give me a private tennis lesson. How does that sound?"

"I can live with that."

"What do you want, Carter?" Vladimir asked.

"Really, I don't want—"

"Boris, help the poor girl."

Boris stroked his beard. "I got it, boss. Use of the private jet to take her and a friend anywhere in the world."

Ryan's brown eyes opened as wide as footballs. "Are you serious?"

"Mr. Ivanov, it's too much." I held up my hands. "I can't accept that."

Before I could protest further, Vladimir picked up my hand and shook it.

Of course, the Ravens didn't try to run a sneaky play. I had won the bet. My gut told me I might have won this round, but somehow the boss had stolen a little piece of me.

38

NINE LIVES

When we got home, I said goodbye to Ryan and hightailed it to my room to get out of sight. Before I had a chance to shut the door, Boris latched onto my shoulders. He pushed my body into the room and shut the door behind him. The Grandpa Boris façade he'd displayed at the game had subsided. The knuckle-busting mobster had returned. "You think I've forgotten about this morning?" He moved his hand down to his belt.

Oh, God. "Where's Vladimir?"

"He has some business to attend to. He'll be gone for a while." He unfastened the buckle and slid the black leather belt off his pants. "You and I need to get a few things straight about who's in charge around here."

My body trembled, overcome with fear of what was about to go down. He motioned for me to sit on the bed. I hesitated, but when his jaw clenched, and he looped the belt in his hand, I did what I was told. I prayed his intention was only to scare me.

"Good girl. You had a nice time as our guest? A relaxing holiday weekend?"

"Yes."

He circled in front of me. I curled my knees up to my chest. "Your boyfriend is a nice guy. Would be shame if he got into trouble."

My body stiffened. "Why do you say that?"

"Our friends out back planted evidence in his truck that will put him away until he's an old man. Speak of anything that happened here and police get an anonymous tip, understand?"

I couldn't breathe.

"Answer me." He shoved me down on the bed. With his buckle in hand, he pinned my forearms and yelled in my face. "*Otvet' mne.*"

"*Da, da,*" I squealed, not sure of the question but certain of the answer.

He yanked me back to my feet and cornered me against the wall. "You belong to boss now. This evening you will show your *appreciation* for his generosity."

Sweat trickled down my back. I could barely hold myself up.

A dirty smile crept across his face. "Anything I can do to help you get ready? Massage? Soft music? Red wine to get you in the mood?"

Feeling sick, I covered my mouth and shook my head.

His face flashed with anger. He lifted the belt. "No?"

Don't challenge him, Sophia said.

"No, I don't need anything," I whimpered.

He steered me toward the closet. "Let's get you changed for dinner, dear." He examined my expensive new wardrobe and selected a low-cut, honey-colored silk dress. "This one brings out the gold in your eyes." He unbuttoned my cardigan, slid it off, and dropped it to the floor.

I panted as he unbuttoned my jeans with his belt in hand. I prayed for a miracle. No more chances. If I resisted, he would whip me into submission. He lifted my t-shirt out of my pants and slid it over my head. My hair fell into my face. Gently, he pushed it out of my eyes and flipped it back over my shoulder, leaving me exposed in my bra and jeans.

When his fingers fumbled to unhook my front closure bra, I panicked. I folded my arms across my chest and hunched my shoulders forward. "Please don't. I'm sorry—"

"*Shush.* I'm trying to help you. Boss is angry with you. Don't make things harder on yourself." His tone was sincere like a father giving his daughter worldly advice. "Would you rather take it off yourself?"

I nodded, pulled all my hair forward to cover myself, and then slid off my bra. I reached for the dress, but he held it back.

"Not yet."

He pushed down on my shoulders and sat me on the edge of the bed, placed his arm under my knees, and flipped my legs on top of the covers. He slid off my boot, unfastened the Velcro on my cast, and tossed it aside. "Vladimir hasn't had a smile on his face in eight years. That changed the night he met you. All the money, the power that comes with his position, nothing has brought him happiness—except *you.*"

I closed my eyes to mask my terror when he sat next to me and rubbed his thick fingers across my stomach with the hand holding the belt. "You are going to want to please Boss tonight of your own free will. He deserves that much from you." He traced the lace around the top of my underwear. "Your bullshit ends now."

"He doesn't want me like this." My voice trembled. "I know he's mad, but he would never order you to hurt me. This is all your sick—"

"Keep talking." He raised the belt over his head.

Fight!

I thumped him in the chest with my fists and tried to roll off the opposite side of the bed, but he wouldn't relinquish his grip. All I had accomplished was to make him angrier. Out of patience, he growled and shoved me off the edge of the bed. I landed on my back with a thud. The force of my fall knocked the wind out of me, and the throbbing pain shooting up from my ankle paralyzed me.

While I caught my breath, Boris stalked around the bed and towered over me. "I'm wise to your game, girly. Bat your pretty eyes, flaunt your little body, cry your sad tears—boss gives you anything you want. Boss leaves his home, his family, his business, and drags me with him to America to rescue you. What does he get in return? Lies, deceit, and disrespect."

I sucked in a deep breath, rolled over on my stomach, but before I could stand, Boris held me down with his heavy boot like he was rubbing out a bug. "Want to leave? Go ahead."

My bare skin chafed against the carpet as I tried to squirm away. "The *pakhan* will kill you when he finds out what you're up to."

He removed his foot from my back, grabbed a fistful of my hair, and yanked me back to my feet. "What do you mean *when* he finds out?" His expression oozed with rage.

"I'm sorry. I won't say anything."

He caressed my cheek with the back of his prison-tatted hand. "Think of me as your coach, dear. I'm just getting you warmed up."

"No!" With the last reserve of courage I had left, I dug my fingernails into his hands and tried to pry him off me.

He flung me back onto the bed. Using one hand, he pinned me down, and with the other he wrapped the belt around my wrists. "Fight me again, and it goes around your neck."

"Get off me." I struggled to free my hands.

He twisted the skin on my torso in the same spot where I'd pinched Ryan to get his attention. "Is this how you get what you want, little tease?"

I begged him to stop, but he didn't let up.

"I tried the easy way, but you never learn, do you?" He unzipped my jeans, and as he slid them down, his phone rang. He retrieved his phone from his pocket.

I gasped for air.

He covered my mouth.

"*Da...da...*she'll be ready." He slipped the phone back in his pocket and seemed to be contemplating the most punishing way he could kill me. "You have nine lives, pussy cat. Your papa will be here to collect you in a half hour. Your family cut their trip short to spend Christmas with you." He lowered his hand, allowing me to breathe, and removed the belt from my wrists.

I closed my eyes and sucked in a deep breath. He yanked me to my feet, pinned me against the wall, and stuck his thick finger in my face. "Rule number one, you will act like nothing out of the ordinary happened here. Two, your work schedule will resume without interruption. Three, you will keep your bruises covered. I can make anyone disappear. You don't want anything to happen to your beautiful little sister, right?"

I shook my head.

"I see and hear everything, *Cookie*. Breathe a word about our secrets, and you put your family in the ground."

DAD'S happy face tanked as Vladimir walked me to the car. At Boris's insistence, I ditched the air cast and stuffed my swollen foot into my snow boot. With a limp in my step, dark circles under my eyes, and the fear of God on my face, the Russians returned me to my family. To an outsider, it would have looked like a P.O.W. exchange.

"What happened to you?" Dad stole me away from his boss.

"She didn't tell you?" Vladimir asked.

"Tell me what?"

I looked my dad in the eye and delivered my rehearsed response. "I got the flu. I've been so sick the last couple of days."

"Oh, sweetie. I wish you'd told me. I would've come home sooner."

"I didn't want to ruin your trip. Mr. Ivanov has been so sweet. He brought a doctor to the house and made sure I got plenty of liquids and saltines. I think the worst of it is over." I forced a smile. "Thank you for everything, Mr. Ivanov."

"Anything for you, Miss Cook."

"You're shaking. Let's get you out of the cold. Sorry to put you through this, Vladimir. I appreciate it."

My stomach churned.

Vladimir shot his icy blue gaze down on me. "My pleasure, Ricky. Your daughter is an angel."

39

BRAVE OR STUPID

On my first day back to work after D-Day, I crafted a plan and just had to summon the courage to go through with it. When I met Boris at our pickup spot, I got into the Caddy like it was any other day.

"Good to see you. We missed you. How was your Christmas?"

"Cut the bullshit," I said.

He cocked his head, stunned by my disrespectful tone.

"I know you'll hurt the people I love if I don't do what you say. You win."

"Are you wearing a wire?"

"No. This is between you and me."

It was clear in his face, in his posture, that he was skeptical of my surrender. I handed him a plain white envelope. He slid on his reading glasses and pulled out the paper—the rental agreement for our apartment. I had worked so hard, scrimped, saved, and sacrificed to finally bust down the door to adulthood, and there was no way I would let the Russians hijack my freedom.

He stuck the letter back in the envelope. "Congratulations."

"*Spasibo.* I have a problem, though. You get what you want from me, but what do I get in return?"

He seemed intrigued by my strength. After two days away—Dad wouldn't let me leave the house any sooner—I had color back in my face, the bags under my eyes were fading, and I'd wolfed down protein bars to gain back some weight. Over the last few weeks, the Russians had cranked me through the sausage grinder, but they failed to break me.

"Continue." The car was still in park.

"If I do what you say, everything is good. My friends and family stay safe, right?"

He glared at me and waited for me to continue.

"But statistically speaking, I screw up a lot. Then what? The next time I make a mistake, you'll kill my family? Game over? That doesn't work for me. I have no chance to win. I can only lose."

Boris tapped his fingers on his leg. "I'm a reasonable man, Carter. What do you want? Money? Car?"

"An exit strategy. Is it true Vladimir is going back to Russia soon?"

"You heard this from your papa?"

I nodded.

"*Da.*"

"Perfect. Here's the deal. I'll play along with this sick game. I'll be nice, wear beautiful clothes, and be a delightful young plaything. We'll reset the game clock and go back to the way it was before Christmas."

He rubbed his chin. "That's right." He put his hand on the shifter to put the car in reverse.

I wrapped my hand around his and stopped him. "In return, I want to walk free from this deal when the boss goes home. I've finally done something right," I pointed to the rental agreement, "and I am not going to mess it up this time. The boss can have me while he's here, my family and friends remain safe, and for my *participation,* we part ways for good when his business here is over."

When I dreamed up this plan, I'd imagined Boris leaning over and choking me to death, but instead, he seemed impressed that he hadn't extinguished my fire.

"I like it. That's a nice deal. Good girl."

I stared at his hand, waiting for him to pull back the shifter.

The weasel alarm sounded.

He tapped his rings on the steering wheel. "That's it?"

"That's it."

He turned off the car and set the keys on the dash. "We're not going to get any more unexpected visits from your boyfriend?"

"I broke up with him. Will you please undo whatever you did to his truck?"

"You are *willingly* going to spend time with the boss?"

I hesitated for a split second.

"What are you up to, weasel?"

"Nothing."

"Dear, I'll cut you a break because you are so young, but you do know what *part* of the body controls man's mind?"

I nodded.

"And you know men don't like to be teased by curious little blondes?"

I nodded again.

"And if you try to pull your bullshit—"

"I got it. Please don't hurt my family. I know what you expect me to do, but—"

"*But*?"

"I have one condition."

No more Mr. Nice Negotiator Guy. "Say that again?"

"I will be a fantastic girlfriend, curl up on the couch, drink, hug, and even make out with him if I have to, but I will not let him rob my virginity. And if you try to pull anything on me like you did on Christmas Eve, you will have your way with my cold, dead body."

He blinked his eyes like he was about to short-circuit. "You're giving *me* orders?"

"No. No way. Remember, you've already won. I'm here against my will. I know what you're capable of. I surrender." I raised my hands to drive the point home.

He leaned back in his seat, possibly turned on by my flattery.

"What I'm proposing is a different matter altogether. Ask yourself, which Carter do you want? The fun to be around Carter before Christmas? The happy, competitive, slightly problematic college girl? Or do you want the bruised and battered Corpse Bride you turned me into over the weekend?"

I took my jacket off to remind him of the damage inflicted on me during our Holiday Adventure. "It can't continue like this. My dad cornered me about my *condition*. He bought two at-home drug tests from the pharmacy. He made me pee into a cup to check for illegal substances. When that theory didn't pan out, he became convinced I have an eating disorder. He threatened to check me into a mental hospital."

Boris's gaze drifted to my battered arms.

"You think this is bad?" I lifted up the bottom of my shirt to show him the damage he left on my gut. "That's nothing. You should see your boot print on my back." I took a deep breath. "Someone will eventually figure out something is wrong. What if Dad finds out? Then what?"

I was right, and he knew it. He stroked his beard.

"Vladimir would *never* force me to be with him. Don't you think he'll be happy with the pleasure of my company without going all the way?"

"*Nyet.*"

"I think he'd be crushed to see me walking around his house like an alley cat maxed out on her ninth life. Everything will be fine as long as—"

"As long as what?"

Tell him, Sophia said.

"As long as he doesn't drink too much."

"You're a brave girl, Carter." He let out an exasperated sigh. "Brave or stupid. I'll see what I can do to *remedy* the situation." He lifted the keys off the dashboard and started the car.

I knew it was sick, but I was giddy Boris hadn't hog-tied me and dumped me face down in the trunk of the Caddy. If all I had to do was hang out with Vladimir, talk, eat, drink, and have fun, knowing it would end when he went home—I could live with that.

Just like old times, Boris turned on the Russian music, and I ate my almonds, trying to suppress a winner's grin.

40

BROKEN TOY

Back at the house, Boris guarded me in the kitchen as I worked. He questioned me relentlessly as I prepared dinner. “You have kept your mouth shut?”

I nodded.

“Eating well?”

I nodded.

“No one has seen your bruises?”

I shook my head.

“The football player doesn’t suspect anything?”

“I broke up with him, remember? I haven’t spoken to him outside of a few texts.”

He held out his hand. “Let me have your phone.”

I gave it to him.

He slid on a pair of reading glasses and ran his finger down my screen. “Your little friend is boy crazy.”

I sucked in my bottom lip. Kiki had been texting me pics from Florida of hot guys sunbathing on the beach, which prompted us to play a game we had made up a few years ago. *Why didn’t I delete our last conversation?*

Dirty blond surfer or stubbly lifeguard?

Beard burn.

Same.

"What does it mean?"

I stirred the sauce on the stove. "Um—" I felt my face flush. Boris knew he had me on something, but he hadn't figured it out yet. He studied my body language and then went back to reading our conversation.

Six-pack speedo or tattooed parolee?

Three-way.

"Explain."

My face was hotter than the tomato sauce simmering in the pan. The last thing I needed was to piss him off on an otherwise uneventful day. "It means what you think it means." I lifted my eyebrows. "The pics of the guys on the beach? Who would you rather?" I winced, waiting for him to finish the sentence.

The answer registered on his face. "Naughty game. Want to play with me?"

I couldn't say no. I wouldn't let him rattle me. Over the last two days, I've had time to regroup my game plan. I had come to the realization that their goal was to *not* hurt me, instead of the other way around. They wanted me to do what they said. When I resisted, I got hurt. If I could stay in their good graces until my newly renegotiated Indentured Servant Contract expired, I could come out of this ordeal with a pulse.

"Sure. It's fun. I'll teach you how to play the original

version instead of the abbreviated text version. We need some paper, a pencil, and a bottle of vodka."

Boris rounded up the supplies while I explained the rules. "Okay, so each of us calls out the names of two famous people. They can be sports figures, movie stars, politicians, etc. Past or present works, too. Like you could say Elvis Presley or Kurt Cobain, you know?

"*Da.*" He was radiant, knowing he had officially broken my will to fight him.

"After I say two names, you can either write one down, or you can put 'priest'—or in my case 'nun'—if you'd rather be celibate than have sex with either of them."

"*Humph.*"

"Oh, and you have one more choice. You can write down a 'three,' as in you would have a three-way with the two aforementioned hotties." I had officially lost my freaking mind.

"What's the vodka for?"

"This is a drinking game. If I correctly guess more of your answers, you have to drink. If you get more right than I do, I drink. Or, if you're the loser, you can pick truth or dare instead if you don't want to imbibe."

He tapped his pencil on the paper. "This is what college girls do for fun?" I had never seen him in such a good mood.

Aha! Suddenly, I understood. Boris liked the feisty me much better than the scaredy-cat version. Everyone feared him. He commanded respect and submission from his underlings, but from day one, I gave it back to him in a way no one else dared. I was *his* little plaything, too. I batted my eyelashes. "Only the sad, lonely ones who can't go out and play."

He chuckled and tipped the bottle to fill my glass.

I held my hand up in a stop motion. "*Nyet, spasibo.* I'll

take my chances with truth or dare. My body is still recovering from the long weekend."

Without a glint of remorse, he generously filled my glass anyway.

I slumped my shoulders and sighed. "Maria Sharapova or Anna Kournikova?"

He wrote down his answer and then asked, "Rafael Nadal or Roger Federer?"

Duh, remember my affinity for Spaniards? We went back and forth until we each had five answers on our papers.

"I'll go first. Nadal, Wilson, three, DeNiro-in-his-twenties, nun."

He showed me his paper. "Four out of five."

"Bravo. Nice job." *Jeez.* He was good at guessing my sexual preferences. "Your turn."

"Three, three, three, three, three."

"Um, you win." I crumbled up my sheet of paper and downed my vodka.

"Let me see," he said.

I got the angry eyes when I hesitated a split second before I tossed it to him. He uncrumpled my paper and smirked when he saw five consecutive threes written on my paper.

"Lucky guess."

"You won. Why lie? Are you not capable of telling the truth?" He downed his shot.

I lied because I was afraid he'd be angry. "Okay, I won. You drank your vodka. I need to finish dinner." I went to the stove.

He stood up. "Not yet, weasel."

I wrapped my fingers around the handle of the bubbling pasta sauce. If he came at me, I was ready to defend myself. I wouldn't go down without a fight. I was crazy to have willingly walked back into that death trap, but better to leave broken than in a body bag.

Don't challenge him, Sophia said.

I took her advice and changed up my losing game plan. "Sorry, I lied. I was embarrassed about the whole thing. I can't believe I let you talk me into that." I snorted. "Can you teach me how to play poker instead?"

I kept my focus on the simmering sauce. I couldn't handle seeing his angry black eyes that were surely bearing down on me like the Christmas Eve incident. But then I realized he was walking away—to the drawer where Vladimir kept his gun.

I held my breath.

He pulled out a deck of cards.

Thank heavens.

When Vladimir came home from work, his lips curled into a smile when he found Boris and me with a big pot of cash between us, heavily invested in a Texas Hold 'Em poker game. He had probably expected to find me rocking on the floor in the fetal position instead of partying down with my abusers. If I wanted The New Deal to work, I had to entertain them. The boss didn't want to play with a broken toy either.

I had my tennis visor down low, covering my eyes, while Boris sucked on an unlit stogie. I had synced my music to the sound system and was blasting my Dance Party playlist throughout the house—Boris's idea.

"You might have to toss in the Ferrari keys, boss. The stakes are high," Boris said over the music.

We were in the final round of our game. There were five

community cards on the table: two eights, a king, a three, and a nine. Boris had given me a quick rundown on what the hand rankings were, but I didn't remember what beat what. I just knew it was good to have high numbers and cards that matched.

Vladimir rubbed his hands together and laughed. We needed a distraction. Sophia was more powerful than the devil after all. She didn't leave me in my time of need; she just had to readjust her strategy. Brute strength-wise, she couldn't overpower him, but she did have the wits to outsmart the son of a bitch.

The boss poured himself a drink and refilled our shot glasses. He put his arm around me. "What are you getting yourself into, angel?" He rubbed my back and played with my ponytail as I rocked my shoulders to the beat of the music. His eyes were soft and loving—not angry like they were on Christmas Eve. I knew I could steal Vladimir away from the *pakhan*.

He checked out the pile. Among the bills was one piece of lined notebook paper with a handwritten wager on it. I had burned through the bank Boris had given me to start off with. To stay in the game, I had to add something to the pot.

"Oh, no. Our little gambler is out of control again." He picked up the paper . "Truth or dare."

"That's what he wanted. You know I can't back down."

Boris turned over his two cards. With the community cards, he had two pairs.

I glanced at my hand, then at his. "Does this beat?" I turned over two nines. That made three of a kind when added to the one already on the table.

"Double or nothing." Boris retrieved the cards.

"Wait. Did I win?"

Boris downed his drink.

Vladimir kissed me on the top of my head. "Yes, you little fox." He handed me a shot glass. We toasted, clinked, and downed.

"So, I should quit while I'm ahead, right?"

"Unless boss wants to take my place," Boris said.

He had to be the best wingman in the history of mankind.

41

FOREVER

Boris stood and gave his chair to Vladimir. "I'll deal." Boris collected the cards.

Sneaky little weasel that I am, I reached into the pot to retrieve my wager.

"Double or nothing means it all stays in," Boris said. "Now you have to add something. What do you want to put in, boss?" Boris shuffled the cards.

Worried he might toss in the car keys, I slid the notebook across the bar and rolled him a pencil. "Make it good." I stared him down and rocked to the beat.

"Hmm." Vladimir contemplated his next move, marked his wager, folded his paper into a square, and tossed it in the pile.

I twisted my ponytail. "What does it say?"

"You'll find out if you win," Boris said.

"Your turn, angel." Vladimir slid the pad of paper and the pencil back to me.

I rested my chin on my fist as I thought about what to write. I couldn't think of anything. I was wasted. I exhaled and sketched out a picture of a heart with angel wings. I drew an arrow through it and scribbled the word *forever* across it. He would take whatever he wanted from me anyway. Following Vladimir's lead, I folded it up and tossed it on the pile. "Deal."

As Boris dealt the hand, I tried to think two steps ahead as I bounced to the music. If I won, Vladimir would continue to raise the stakes until he came out ahead. I already had two wagers in the pot, which was enough. I would blow the game and let him win already, but I had no clue what I was doing.

I bobbed to the beat and peeked at my hand. Luckily, my cards were crap, a three and a five. Boris set out the community cards: a four, a six, and a two.

Shit. Cards in numerical order were good, too.

Vladimir slid the notebook to me.

I thought for a moment. "I fold."

"Are you sure? You'll lose everything." He nodded at the pot.

"I'm cooked anyway."

Vladimir picked out his wager from the pile, slid around the counter, and slipped the paper into my back pocket. "I'll share the winnings with you, angel." He kissed my cheek.

"Well, that figures." I threw back my vodka.

The guys laughed. I think we could all agree that Vladimir winning was the best possible outcome. He removed the sweat-stained visor from my head and tossed it on the counter.

"Now, to collect my prize." He left the thousands of dollars in cash on the table and went straight for my wagers. He flattened out my truth or dare paper and stroked it like a fine fur. He didn't open up the secret wager; rather, he slid it into his shirt pocket and patted it as if I had handed over an Imperial Faberge egg.

My belly fluttered. It wasn't butterflies per se, more like the sensation of bats *thunking* around in an empty bucket.

Boris went to the bar and came back with a new bottle to refresh our drinks.

"Truth or dare?" the boss asked.

"Should we eat dinner first?" I touched Vladimir's arm. "You must be starving. I don't want to make you wait."

He twisted his lips.

Oh, oops. That came out a bit skanky. How many shots had I downed? The vodka or maybe the music had me a little frisky. I covered my mouth and giggled.

He enjoyed my loose and playful alcohol-induced demeanor. "Truth or dare?"

Say truth, say truth, say truth, say truth, say truth—

"Dare."

Judging by their incredulous reactions, Dad was right. I belonged in a mental hospital. I bet Vladimir expected the wrong answer from his naughty, self-destructive little plaything. Boris shook his head and mumbled to the boss in Russian.

I downed my third or fourth or whatever shot of vodka and jammed my pointer finger into Boris's chest. "Zip it. You stay out of this. Vladimir won."

"I wouldn't dream of interfering, *lapsha*."

I tapped my hand on my leg in time to a hip-hop song. The thought of what he was going to make me do was exciting. If I survived the next few weeks, I was certain I would be strapped down and locked in a padded room.

The boss downed his drink and licked his lips. "Dance."

"What do you mean? That's not a dare."

Boris refilled our glasses.

"You've been swaying your body to the music since I got home. That's what you like to do with your friends, right?"

"*Da.*"

He picked up my hand and kissed the inside of my wrist. "I'm your friend. Dance with me."

I shot a stupefied look at Boris and then back at the boss. "That's it? Crank up the jams." I was fully expecting something like naked cartwheels or a striptease, but even though Vladimir was of questionable character, he was a gentleman.

Well, at least when he was relatively sober, and that battleship was about to sink. Maybe I was giving him too much credit. He still had the other wager to cash in, whatever the hell a winged heart with *forever* scribbled across it meant.

Vodka flowed like the river Styx in that house. Alcohol and music helped ease my tension and loosen up my body. I was sure these two fine gents already knew that. I would have to keep my mojo in check. I was rather notorious for my dirty dancing. Of course, after my Friday night blitz, they knew that, too.

I scrolled through my music. "Old school, country, pop, classic, oldies, Euro, grunge, disco, hip-hop, R&B, or Broadway?"

He tapped his fingers on the counter as he thought it over. "A love song."

I scanned my playlist and selected a song.

The boss whisked me away to the other room, but before I left the kitchen, I latched on to the doorframe and gave Boris a warning. "Dad will release the bloodhounds if I'm not home by ten o'clock. He has me on a short leash these days."

He checked his watch and nodded.

Vladimir had on a dark blue suit with a white shirt and a rich paisley tie. I couldn't figure out why he was chasing *me.*

He could have any woman he wanted. Why did he have to turn me to the dark side?

He squeezed my hand and twirled me around to face him. I caught him checking me out and covered my mouth to hide my embarrassment. Unashamed I'd busted him, he lifted his shoulders. "I'm just a man, Carter."

Part of me was ready to stop resisting. Vladimir was the hottest guy I have ever been in the same room with. Maybe I should give in.

Wait. Is this the devil talking? Is he on Vladimir's payroll? Where did Sophia fly off to? God must have fired her for doing a shitty job.

As the guitar intro played through the sound system, the boss hooked his arm around my waist and rested his hand on the small of my back. He led me to our makeshift dance floor in front of the glass doors that led to the back patio.

He spun me around, held up my right hand, and placed his other hand on my hip. He was so much taller than me, my head was level with his chest.

I settled in and inhaled his cologne like a junky huffing on a crack pipe. My brain knew he was bad for me, but my body couldn't resist him. We swayed to the rhythm of the sexy R&B song *I* had selected. By the time the chorus played, his neck was sweaty. I ran my finger around his collar and fingered the waves I had admired for so long.

My body trembled, but not from fear. He wrapped his arms around my waist and pulled my body into his. His erection poked against me as we rocked to the beat. My cheeks warmed, and I tried to blink away my embarrassment, but my body ached for him. I rubbed against him to encourage his arousal, and Vladimir loosened my ponytail and ran his fingers through my hair. I slid off his suit jacket, flung it on the floor, and wrapped my arms around his luscious body.

Sophia and the devil were officially at war.

Vladimir moaned a deep, primal sigh as I ran my hands across his backside. He kissed me so hard and deep, I thought the weight of our entangled bodies would drop us through the floor. He led us to the couch and lowered my body on top of his. I loosened his tie, unbuttoned his shirt, and admired star tats on his shoulders, and a bounty of religious icons inked on his chest and all the way down his tight abs. The devil above his pecs kept his eye on me the whole time I sexed up his host.

"Say something sexy in Russian, boss." I lined up our bodies and grooved my chest against his decorative torso. I moved my hips and moaned as his hands cruised around downtown. I slipped my hand inside his pants and ran my fingers along his length. I wanted him. I was ready to lose it tonight.

"I'm ready for you, boss. Take me to your bedroom." I nibbled on his ear. "Or we can go to your office." I traced one of the star tattoos on his shoulder with my fingernail.

"Vladimir." Boris towered over us. "Boss."

I stopped ravaging Vladimir and looked up to my keeper. "It's okay. I want to."

The boss reprimanded Boris in Russian.

He argued.

Vladimir patted my cheek. "My apologies, angel. Boris is going to take you home now."

"Why?"

"Your papa is here to see me. It's urgent."

Oh, shit. If he knew what I was up to—drinking, gambling, and stripping the suit off his boss—he would sprout dragon wings, fly over the castle, and burn the devil's den to the ground, with me in it.

42

PARTY FOUL

Boris drove me home, and I finger-combed my hair and tied it back into a spare ponytail holder from my bag. He sent me into Starbucks to get a Frap to sober me up before he dropped me off. Dad wouldn't be home—he had urgent business with Vladimir—but Karen probably had orders to give me a visual frisking when I walked in the door.

I slurped my drink, but otherwise the car was quiet.

"Want to listen to some music?" Boris asked.

Slowly, I turned my head and shot him the evil eye.

"My bad," he said.

"Do you know what my dad wanted? It's about me, isn't it?"

He tipped his head.

"What's going to happen now? Things have gone too far."

He didn't answer.

I felt sick. "Pull over."

He did. I got out of the car, dropped to my knees, and party fouled in the parking lot of a Burger King. I misfired and got it all over my shirtsleeve. I dragged myself to the curb and sat between the snow-covered landscape and the icy blacktop. Boris got out of the car and blanketed me with his long gray shadow.

"I can't cruise through the front door of my house reeking of vodka, Vladimir's after-shave, and vomit."

Boris drove us to a shady motel and got a room. "Clean up, and I will get you some fresh clothes. We still have time to make your curfew."

It was the fastest power shower of my life. When Boris returned, he tossed me a long-sleeved pink t-shirt, a pair of sweats, and a toothbrush. I closed the bathroom door, changed, brushed, and came out ready to dash back home.

Boris sat on the edge of the bed. "I have spoken to the boss."

"And?"

"Your papa went to the tennis club this evening. Your lies have caught up with you."

WHEN BORIS DROPPED ME OFF, Dad's car wasn't in the driveway, but the house was illuminated in full interrogation mode.

Karen met me in the foyer. "Are you all right, Carter?"

I acted surprised. "Of course. What's up?" My tone sounded a tad chirpy.

"Where have you been? Why is your hair wet?"

Lifting my wet ponytail, I answered, "At Kiki's. Is it a crime to take a shower after a workout? We did, like, an hour and a half of Zumba."

"Heads up, Carter. Your father called Kiki's dad, and he knows their family is still in Florida."

Shit. My dad's headlights flashed on the wall of the living room when the Camry turned into the driveway.

"Your father is worried sick about you. You have some explaining to do."

I sat on the couch with my head down, elbows on knees, and hands folded in the parental smack-down ready position. When the front door opened, it occurred to me Dad might not be okay—like Coach. He stepped into the living room looking messed up, not in a bloody or beaten kind of way, more like *deflated.*

"I went to Vladimir's house. He explained everything. Did that bastard hurt you?" Dad was so stressed, his right eye was twitching.

Say what? I blinked in confusion. "No, no. Of course not."

Karen put her hand on my dad's back and stared at him like he had ceremonial war paint smeared on his face.

Dad clutched my shoulders and eyed me in strict parental mode. "I know you've been lying to me about your whereabouts the last few weeks, but after speaking with Vladimir, I understand why."

I fluttered my eyes in mock confusion. "Why did you speak to Mr. Ivanov about me?"

"Rick?" Karen said.

"Let's talk in the kitchen. I need a beer."

Dad popped a cold one and sat next to me at the table. In case there were any more concerns about the eating disorder scenario, I munched on a big slice of cold cheese pizza and chugged a Gatorade. I was hungry and needed to eat anyway to soak up all the vodka still swimming through my bloodstream. Karen fingered the heart-shaped *Mom* pendant on her necklace, anxious to find out how bad her hot-tempered husband had messed up.

"Seeing you come home from Vladimir's over Christmas in your *fragile* condition, I had this crazy idea he had hurt you in some way."

Karen gasped.

I covered my mouth to keep from spewing all over his face.

"Are you joking?"

He lowered his head, took a deep breath, and raised his hands. "I know, I know. Vladimir had the same reaction. I'm lucky he didn't fire me or kick my ass or something."

I felt bad for lying to him. He'd just won the Best Dad in the World Award in my eyes. Confronting Vladimir took guts. He laid his job and his personal safety on the line for me. Not to mention, his instincts were dead on. *Way to go, Dad. I'm sorry you got saddled with such a horrible daughter.*

Karen put her hand on his back while he collected himself. "Vladimir didn't want to betray your confidence," he went on, "but under the circumstances of me accusing him of, well, you know—"

"Oh, Rick."

He sipped his beer. "He told me why you were such an emotional wreck and why you've been lying to us."

"Dad—"

"Enough. I know all about your older boyfriend. I know you've been pretending to be at work all the time because you want to be with him and you didn't think I would approve."

"Dad—"

He held up his hand. "I also know that fucking European meathead was pressuring you to take your relationship to the next level, and your refusal caused a big argument right before Christmas. Vladimir said it broke his heart to see you so upset. He wanted to hunt down that loser himself and teach him a lesson."

European meathead—Leonardo. "He told you that?" I covered my mouth with my hands.

"And Vladimir said you were afraid to come to me because you thought I'd be mad, so you sought his guidance. He said if I'd been a better father, then maybe you would've confided in me about your guy troubles rather than him."

My heart was officially broken. "Oh, Dad. It's not your fault."

Dad leaned over and hugged me so tight I felt like I might crack. Karen got up to get a box of tissues. "I'm sorry I work all the time. My family needs me, and I'm not here."

"No, no. It's my fault. I'm the one who lied. You're the best dad ever." My words came out a little slurry.

Dad pulled back. "Where were you tonight, Carter?"

Oh, shit. "I...I was at, ummm—"

"Have you been drinking?"

"Dad, just—"

"You were with that asshole again, weren't you?" Dad stood up and dragged his hand through his hair.

"Just to give him his stuff back, I swear."

"Why's your hair wet? Did you sleep with him?" His chest heaved, his face burned red.

"Rick, calm down." Karen stood next to him and put her arm around his waist.

"No. He smokes." I lifted my lanyard and shook it at him. "I have a key to Kiki's house. I went there to take a shower so I wouldn't stink when I got home."

Dad took a deep breath and held out his hands, trying to calm himself down. "Let me be clear, Carter. One, you are not to see him again. Two, if you lie to me again, you won't leave this house outside of school. Three—" He hesitated, overcome with a rush of sadness.

"I get it, Dad. I'm sorry."

"You've grown into a beautiful young woman. It kills me to see men staring at your body, objectifying you—"

"Dad, please."

"Let him finish," Karen said.

"Men will take advantage of your youth and vulnerability." Dad put his hands on my shoulders and looked me in the eye. "Don't let them, sweetheart. Save yourself for someone special who deserves your love and affection."

Tears dripped down my cheeks. Dad reeled me in for a hug. Karen joined in and rocked us side to side, kicking the parental awkwardness up a couple of notches.

"You and Ryan are just friends?" Dad asked.

"Yeah."

When our Blended Family Love Fest subsided, I ran upstairs and locked myself in my bedroom. I removed Vladimir's wager from my pocket and unfolded it. The note said:

Anything for you, angel

I wondered how he would react when he saw my winged *forever* heart. I clutched the note to my chest and placed the other on my belly to settle the bats.

43

WEASEL

After the vodka stopped talking the next day—and my hormones stopped raging—I had to figure out how to smooth over the fact I had straddled Vladimir and enthusiastically grinded my body all over him. Not to mention, I shoved my hand down his pants.

God, please tell me I didn't suggest we go to his office instead of the bedroom. Wasn't I the one who came up with the Purity Plan?

When I got into the car with Boris, he glared at me. "Everything okay at home?"

I nodded.

"Your papa is a brave man."

I nodded again.

"I see your friend came back from Florida today. You're spending the night with her?"

"Yep."

He relaxed his shoulders. "We're not going back to the house."

"Why? Where are you taking me?"

"It's a surprise. Text your friend and tell her you're not coming."

"Is this a sex thing?" I blurted out.

"What do you think, party girl?"

"No. Stop the car. Let me out, or I'll jump."

Boris clamped onto my arm and jammed his thumb into my bicep. "You want to go to war with me again?"

"Please stop. No more bruises," I whimpered.

Surprised by the desperation in my voice, he loosened his grip. "Enough with your bullshit. Take a sip of vodka and turn on the radio. You'll be right back where you left off."

I took a deep breath to calm myself down. "Last night was a mistake."

"No more mulligans."

"You poured me, like, four shots."

"No one made you drink."

I dropped my head in my hands and let the consequences of my actions settle in. "Are you going to kill me?"

Boris glared at me like he was offended by the notion. "Why would I do that?"

I ticked off my fingers as I listed my offenses. "Because you're sick of dealing with me. I can't do anything right. I make you mad every single day. I don't listen. I tease boys. My singing in the car is insanely annoying. I can't handle my alcohol. I get green tennis ball fuzz all over your seats. I come crawling to you every time I'm in trouble—which is a lot. Haven't I burned through my nine lives yet?"

He acted stunned. "You think I—" He shook his head and didn't finish.

"I know you've done it before. When you rolled up your sleeves, I saw your snaky chain tattoo. Each link represents someone you...*whacked*."

"You found this out on the Internet?"

"You ink it, you own it," I said.

Instead of being pissed, he chuckled. "You don't know anything, stupid girl."

I guess humping the boss was good for our relationship. *Ugh. What a sick thought.* "Please tell me where you're taking me."

"It's nice. You'll have good time."

If Vladimir told him not to tell, that was the end of it.

Boris stopped at the gas station to fill up. Pushing my luck, I asked if I could go inside to grab some snacks for the road. He flipped me a hundred-dollar bill and told me to get him a Coke. Subconsciously, I must have asked myself, W.W.W.D.? *What Would a Weasel Do?*

I snagged some Corn Nuts, a sleeve of peanuts, an orange juice, a Coke, and a pack of condoms. At the checkout counter, the grandma-aged clerk raised an eyebrow when she scanned the dirty stuff. Her gaze drifted outside, and she sized up Boris pumping gas.

Her face blanched as she counted back change from a hundred. I wanted to say something snarky like, "Not unless he put a gun to my head," but I kept my mouth shut, slid the condoms into my back pocket, and then marched back to the car.

When we got on the road, I sipped the OJ and ate my peanuts. Boris glanced in the rearview mirror and then veered off to the median. "What did you do?"

"Nothing." I peeked behind and saw the blue lights of a police car flashing behind us. "I swear I have no idea." I recognized the officer as she walked toward the Cadillac. "Oh shit, it's Officer Montgomery."

Boris slid on a pair of gloves and gave me the low-down on our agenda so we had our stories straight. "If I find out you pulled something—"

Officer Montgomery leaned in the car and smirked when she recognized me.

"Hello again, officer. What's the problem?" I asked.

"May I see your license, sir?" Boris handed it to her.

She shook her head. "I would say I'm surprised to see you, but, sadly, I'm not. Out of the car, Miss Cook. You and I need to talk." The officer walked me back to her cruiser and told me to get in the front seat. As she ran Boris's license—which I assumed would show a spotless record—she took off her sunglasses. "Know why I pulled the car over?"

I wiped my sweaty palms on my jeggings. "No idea, ma'am."

"Where are you going?"

I gave her a puzzled look. "He's taking me to my cousin's house. He bought us concert tickets for Christmas. Why?"

The officer scanned her screen. "Mr. Chuchin is your grandfather, right?"

I was sure *Gramps* was an upstanding citizen. "Yeah, by marriage. He's my stepmom's dad."

"A concerned citizen called in worried about an older gentleman and a pretty young girl buying condoms at the gas station."

I put my hands over my face and slid down in the seat. "Oh, my God. That old lady narked me out? Please don't say anything to him. I'm begging you. He'll die of embarrassment."

She held her hand up to stop my rambling. "If there is anything you want to tell me, now is the time. I can help you. You're safe with me. Is this man hurting you in any way?"

I shook my head. "I took to heart what you said the other day about alcohol and boys. I was trying to be prepared—just in case."

"Let me go talk to your grandfather. You'll need to get into the back until I can corroborate your story."

I got out of the car and let her shut me into the back of the patrol car. *Will Boris kill her if he thinks she's busted us?*

She leaned over and questioned the Russian mobster pretending to be my grandfather. I prayed for her. Boris reached into his coat pocket and pulled something out. The officer held out her hand and inspected what appeared to be a pair of concert tickets.

She smiled and tapped the tickets in her hand.

I exhaled. The officer came back to the car and released me from the backseat. "You are lucky to have such a sweet grandpa. Have a nice time."

"Did you say anything to him about the *you-know-whats*?"

"No, I didn't. You're an adult. No crime has been committed." She patted me on the back. "Make good choices, Carter, and stay out of trouble for a couple of days."

"Thanks." I slunk back to the car, mentally preparing for the bullshit storm. We got back on the road. Boris didn't talk. I didn't either. The silence was terrifying.

Is he mad? Happy he didn't have to shoot the cop? Is he mad?

I turned on my side and closed my eyes. He plucked the condom pack out of my back pocket, shoved me down in the seat, and bore down on my chest. The car swerved over the double yellow line, then back into the right lane. "You know what I would've done if she suspected anything?"

"I'm so sorry. I wasn't thinking."

He was pushing down on me so hard I thought I would snap. I gasped for air, and he let me go. I turned over and curled into a ball.

He rolled down the window and tossed the contraband

in the median. "Get your rest, weasel. You'll be up late tonight."

Asking for another punishment, I asked, "Will you warn me before you pull the trigger? I don't want it to be a surprise."

I thought he was ignoring me, but before I fell asleep, he answered, "*Da*."

44

SWINGING

Boris opened my car door and woke me up. As I blinked my eyes open, I saw an airplane. We were at a goddamn airport. "What the hell, man? I thought we were going to a concert. Where are you taking me?" My blabbering questions went unanswered.

Boris popped the trunk, lifted out a Louis Vuitton suitcase, and escorted me down the runway. I had to get my game face on. Like before a match, I cleared my mind of distractions and shut out everything except my Coach's words of wisdom:

Come out strong. Make them play your game. Be aggressive. Even if you make a mistake, they'll be afraid of what you'll do next time. Go for high percentage shots, and keep the ball in play until you can put away a clean winner. And most important of all: Don't back off if you're losing. Make your opponent beat you. If you're going down, go down swinging.

Boris ushered me to the airplane, and I clutched Vladimir's wager inside my jacket pocket. As we stood at the bottom of the stairs, Boris put his big hands on my shoulders. "Don't mess this up. I'm going back to the house now. You're on your own, understand?"

I nodded.

"Good girl." Before he handed me over, he issued a warning. "Do yourself a favor and don't bring up alcohol—I mean it." He patted my cheek and waited for the boss to collect me.

Vladimir padded down the stairs wearing a short-sleeved blue silk shirt, casual pants, and leather loafers. It was about thirty degrees outside. He greeted me with kisses. "Let's get you out of the cold."

I was down, and it was time to start swinging.

As the plane headed south, Vladimir popped a bottle of champagne and poured two glasses of Cristal. He picked up my hand, kissed it, and wrapped my fingers around the champagne flute. "To you, my angel." We clinked and sipped.

The plane cut through the clouds. Vladimir set down our drinks, swept my hair off my shoulders, and kissed my neck. He unzipped my jacket and tried to slide it off.

I held my arms at my sides, not allowing him to undress me. I wondered how he would react when he saw my bruises. Did he even remember *he* had hurt me over the weekend?

"What's wrong?"

Summoning all the courage I had left, I said, "Last night was a mistake. It was a blessing Dad came to the house when he did."

The boss didn't look happy. I could see the crazy bubbling

in his eyes, so I spoke my mind quickly. "What I mean is, I want you. Your bod makes me hot." I reached up and rested my hands around his neck and twisted one of his blonde waves around my finger. "No one has ever made me feel so—if we hadn't been interrupted, I would've been yours."

"We have tonight, beautiful. No interruptions."

I lifted his hand up to my chest to feel my pounding heartbeat. "See what you do to me? I've never been with a man before."

"I celebrate your choices."

I slipped his wager out of my pocket and pressed it into his palm.

He unfolded the paper. "Ready to cash in your wager?"

"Can I talk to you about something?"

He led me to a seat by the window and sat me down on his lap. With the reflection of the sky behind him, his vibrant blue eyes glowed in the sunlight.

"If I'm being honest, I've thought about us *together*." I turned away, embarrassed.

He stroked my hair. "Really? I had no idea," he teased.

I shoved him in the chest. "Surprise." I laughed with him, and then I tried to get back to the point. "But I want my first time to be special."

"Making love is an expression of our commitment to one another. Don't worry, sweetheart. I'll make sure it's a night we'll never forget."

I knew he wanted me right then and there. I had to swing higher. "By *special,* I mean I'm saving myself for my wedding night. I know I led you on last night. I'm sorry."

"Just when I think I have you figured out, you blow my mind once again. Your future husband is the luckiest man in the world."

Under his spell, and totally turned on, I wanted to take all my words back and pick up where we'd left off last night.

Vladimir peeled me off his lap, leaned over, and snagged the suitcase. "Let's see if we can find something for you to wear this evening." He turned it around so I couldn't see. "Ah, this is perfect." He revealed a sexy little red dress.

"Where are we going?"

"Dancing...in South Beach."

"Ah, that's sweet, boss." I was honestly touched by his thoughtfulness.

Vladimir may have had his share of faults, but one thing about him was undeniable: he loved to make me happy. And at that moment, he was checking every box on my sexiest-man-alive score sheet.

When we arrived at the hotel, I took a solid hour and fifteen minutes to get ready for our hot date. Boris had packed everything I needed: a strapless bra, a clean ace bandage for my ankle, open-back pumps, and a long-sleeved shrug to cover up the thumb bruises on my collarbone, the hoof mark on my back, and the plethora of imprints up and down my arms.

When I emerged from the bathroom ready to go, Vladimir was waiting for me with a single red and pink rose in his hand. He had on slick black pants, Bally shoes, and a red shirt unbuttoned a few notches. His devil tat peeked at me from behind the fabric.

Vladimir was a bad guy in some respects, but he wasn't *all bad*. He would move heaven to hell if it would make me happy. And I knew he would never order his *sovietnik* to coerce me into having sex with him. That was all Boris's fucked-up idea. If it was just my body Vladimir wanted, he had plenty of chances; the boss was after my heart.

"What are you doing to me?" I giggled at my sophomoric reaction to his hotness. "*Buenmozo.*" I fanned my face.

He spun me around and admired my body. "You are the most beautiful young woman in the world, Carter. You take my breath away."

I bit my lip and looked away, embarrassed by his unjust flattery. "Oh, please."

"I mean it, angel. I cherish every moment we spend together." He lifted my chin, trailed kisses down my neck, and teased me in Russian.

Breathe, breathe, breathe...

45

AN IMAGINARY LINE

On the rooftop of our hotel, which doubled as one of Miami's top nightclubs, I could barely stomach more than a couple of bites of the amazing Cuban appetizers we shared for dinner. The scene the boss had set up was ground zero for my erogenous zone: live Latin music, a packed dance floor, and a devilishly romantic companion.

I rocked my shoulders to the beat of the bongos and sipped my mojito. I'd ordered one for both of us to keep a bottle of vodka from joining the party.

"Ready to dance?" Vladimir asked.

"Sí, estoy lista para divertirme contigo, mi amor."

He licked his lips. "What does it mean?"

"Something good."

Vladimir guided me to the dance floor and planted his hands on my hips. I snaked my body around my host and snuffed out my brain under a pile of humidified, beachy blonde waves.

As I shook it, I leaned back against Vladimir's chest and wrapped his arms around my waist to incorporate him into my forbidden dance. I sang along *en español.* He clung to me and swayed to the beat. His skin felt warm and moist from the humid evening air, and his masculine scent, coupled with his wandering hands, made it impossible for me to think about anything except—*us.*

After hours on the dance floor, I was a hot and sweaty mess. I'd only had one drink all night, but my energy was zapped. I rested my cheek on his chest and yawned.

He lifted my hair and blew on my neck. "Let's get you to bed."

When we got back to our suite, the room was filled with dozens of Vladimir's trademark roses. Trays of chocolates, cheeses, and breads were spread out on the dining table, and there was a bottle of vodka in an ice bucket on the bar.

"You're too good to me, boss."

"You deserve it all and more." Vladimir held my hand and guided me to the bar. He turned over two shot glasses and picked up the vodka bottle.

I flipped one of the shot glasses upside down. "None for me tonight. I'm exhausted."

"You don't expect me to drink alone, do you?"

I lifted my shoulders. If he got angry, and Boris wasn't here to help me, I would be at his mercy. Sober, Vladimir would never hurt me, but an intoxicated *pakhan* was merciless. My hands trembled. I balled them up into fists and hid them behind my back.

Vladimir set down the bottle and flipped over his glass, too. "Then we won't drink."

"I'm sorry—"

"Don't be." Vladimir picked up a mini key lime cheesecake and fed it to me. As we noshed on sweets and savories, Vladimir unpacked the suitcase and laid out all the stuff I needed to get ready for bed. Instead of my usual cotton jammies, I got upgraded to a silky white nightie with matching lace panties.

"Need any help?" he asked.

I bit my lip and shook my head, sizing up the king-sized elephant in the room.

His gaze followed mine to the bed. "Don't worry, angel. A Russian never goes back on a deal. I gave you my word, right?"

The fine upstanding crime boss was going to honor my purity plan? Even after I was all over him for, like, the last six hours? Not to mention, his body had been ready for me since we boarded the plane. He'd also nixed the vodka, which had to be difficult. He honestly was trying his best to make me happy—and he respected me, too.

"It's not *you* I'm worried about." I twisted my lips and peeked up at him.

"Don't worry. I can fight off your advances."

"That's big talk. Sure you can take me?" I tugged on his belt playfully, but I flinched when the touch of a man's belt forced back memories of Boris's Christmas Eve *coaching* session.

"You're a naughty girl, Carter." He steered me into the bathroom and gave me some privacy.

After I washed up, I emerged in my sexy gown, sporting fresh breath and a clean face. Vladimir was waiting for me on top of the covers. He had changed into a white tank and black silk pajama bottoms. He always wore long pants, never shorts—even when he played tennis. Maybe he was worried his weird tats would freak me out. *Wrong.*

He rested his chin on his fist and admired my upgraded nightie. I had strategically placed my hair over my bruised arms to avoid an issue, if there even was one. I got the sense, though, that in the Russian Criminal Code of Ethics, the lying little weasel in me probably deserved the *lessons* imprinted on my skin.

He drew back the covers and smoothed his hand over the crisp white cotton sheets. "Come to bed."

I snuggled in, and he adjusted the pillows under my head in the perfect comfy spot. His sexy bedroom eyes melted my resolve. I had zero faith in my ability to resist his charms.

He held up his finger and drew an imaginary line down the center of the bed. "We have a deal, Miss Cook. No crossing the line," he teased. "Get some rest."

"I'm not sleepy," I said before he had a chance to turn off the light.

He sighed and rested his head on the pillow on the edge of our boundary. I imagined how awesome it would be to cross the border and cruise into enemy territory. *Skin on skin, soft lips kissing my neck, wrapped in his strong embrace...*

I scooted to the line and snuggled the sheet up to my neck. "Why are *you* the boss? Why not Boris?"

"My papa was the *pakhan*. In my world, it's like being born into royalty." He studied my expression. "Do you think I'm a bad guy?"

"Part of you is bad, but you have a brilliant mind and a generous heart." I eyed the watch tattoo on his wrist. "So why be bad? Why not be good?"

"That's it? Good or bad, black or white? I grew up in Soviet Russia. My grandfather, papa, brothers—my family was no worse, no less ruthless, than the government that controlled us. My *babushka* served three years of hard labor in the gulag for simply speaking her mind."

"That's awful. Does your family still live in Russia?"

He crossed the line and smoothed my hair out of my

eyes. "My blood relatives are all gone. Boris and the *Bratva* are my only family."

"I'm sorry."

He rubbed my arm over the sheet. "Are you cold?"

"A little. How long have you known Boris?"

"From the day I was born. He and my papa were like brothers." He covered me with the throw blanket from the end of the bed.

"Was prison scary? Did you ever see one of those bear-sized Siberian guard dogs up close? Do you have cathedral tattoos on your back, or did they only do that during the Soviet—"

He pressed his finger against my lips to silence me. "My turn."

I lowered his hand. "You already know stuff about me. I hardly know anything about you."

"Tell me a secret."

"No way," I said.

"You have plenty. Give me one."

"Fine. Kiki and I are getting an apartment in Clifton. We're moving into our new place in two weeks. I haven't told Dad yet. Surprise."

Vladimir tapped his fingers on his leg as he processed my confession. I thought for sure Boris had already ratted me out, but he had kept his share of secrets from the boss, too.

"I'm a grown woman, but Dad still treats me like a kid. I'm ready to move on."

He flashed a naughty grin. "Anything I can do to help you move on to womanhood?"

I cracked up. He was so relaxed and *cute* when he was sober. "You promised, boss." I crossed the line and shoved him playfully. "I need you to be my 'Just Say No to the Sexy Russian' buddy."

His bedroom eyes lit up, and he smoothed his hand over my silhouette. "I can do things for you, angel. We can enjoy ourselves without going all the way. I'll protect your virginity with my life. Trust me."

His seductive smile and practiced hand dissolved my Purity Plan like acid rain on a paper umbrella. I tried to resist him for, like, two seconds, but the fire burning *down there* had tipped over into Inferno Mode. "Turn off the lights," I said.

He did, leaving only a sliver of moonlight to light the room. Vladimir tossed his clothes on the floor and slid under the sheets. When he lay on top of me, the heat emanating from his strong body ignited the sexual tension that had been smoldering between us since the first night we met. He hardened as I ran my fingers through his hair and sloppy-kissed his face and neck.

He slid my nightgown off, trailed kisses down my neck, and ran his tongue across my nipples. "Your body is perfection, Carter." He exhaled a deep, pleasurable growl and teased me with Russian words as he sucked on my breasts.

I groaned and swiveled my hips, enjoying his kisses yet longing for him to move his attention further down my body. He understood my need and slid his tongue across my six-pack on his way downtown. Once he landed in the zone, I gasped at the sensual arousal of his oral pleasure. He circled his tongue over me until the warmth and wetness kicked my excitement over to a new level.

"You want me to take you there, angel?"

I hummed an affirmative *mm-hm,* and he brought his fingers to his mouth and wet them. He slid one inside me and massaged me gently. "You're so wet."

My body stiffened, unaccustomed to the new sensation.

"Want me to stop?" he whispered, withdrawing.

"I like your *mouth.*"

Vladimir spread me apart and kissed me passionately between my legs. He swirled his tongue and rubbed me in the zone over and over and over. My excitement escalated, and I thrust my hips against him to increase my pleasure. When I thought I couldn't possibly feel any better, my body stiffened, and I groaned as I climaxed for the first time.

"Oh, Vladimir." As I came down from my release, I exhaled a sigh of relief as the pleasure he gave me pulsed through my sex. My body relaxed, and while my excitement subsided, he nuzzled my virgin skin.

"Your taste is so sweet, angel. Your body is heaven."

"Thank you for...*that.*" I draped my hand across my forehead as I caught my breath.

"So happy I could please you." He cuddled up beside.

"Yeah, me too." I opened my eyes and met Vladimir's smug expression. "You're proud of yourself, aren't you?" I shoved him in the chest. "Now it's your turn." I placed my hands on his shoulders and pushed him back toward the foot of the bed. Unsure *exactly* how to return the favor, I lay across his chest and stroked him. When I got into a rhythm, it pulsed and grew stronger.

At the risk of sounding completely lame, I whispered, "What do I do now?"

"I like what you're doing, angel."

"How do I...*make it happen*?"

Vladimir took my hand and schooled me in the ways of how to make a man feel good. Once I felt confident, I teased him with my tongue and moved my hand up and down his length until his excitement peaked. He moaned and panted, even more dramatically than I did, and when he recovered, he pulled my body into his and tucked me into the contours of his body.

Naked and intertwined under the sheets, we bonded in a way we never had before. Of course, I was attracted to him, but I felt *connected* to him.

In that moment, I knew Vladimir and I were destined to be together—forever. I rolled over and rested my head on his shoulder so that I could see his eyes. "I love you, Vladimir."

With an expression of uncertainty, he placed his hands on my cheeks. "I love you too. More than anything in the world."

My eyes welled up. He wiped away my tears and with them all the negativity about my self-worth I had bottled up for so long. This man, this gorgeous, powerful man, loved *me*.

"Oh, Carter. You are the reason I breathe." He rolled on top of me and kissed me so passionately, I had to fight for air between gasps. I clung to him, trusting my sexy Russian not to take more than I was willing to give. For better or worse, it was our moment, our time, our Day of Infamy.

46

AFTERGLOW

The morning after, we shared an intimate breakfast on the balcony and noshed on fresh local fruit, steel-cut oats with warm milk, yogurt and honey, and fresh-squeezed orange juice. Seagulls stalked our mini buffet from the sky, and Vladimir's eyes sparkled in the Florida sunshine as we talked, laughed, and enjoyed our private getaway. In the weeks I had known him, I had never seen him so relaxed and *happy*.

He leaned over and kissed my cheek. "*Ya lyublyu tebya.*"

His unshaven cheeks felt sandpapery against my skin. "What does it mean?"

"I love you."

I curled my finger around one of his ringlets. "*Ya lyublyu tebya.*"

As we enjoyed the sunshine and salty ocean air, I couldn't ignore Boris calling me on the special phone. I'd heard it going off in my purse for, like, the billionth time. "I'd better get that. It might be important."

"My phone has been going off all morning, too."

I could tell by his expression he was amused, rather than

alarmed, but nonetheless, I was nervous considering I had lied to everyone and jetted off to Miami Beach with my dad's boss. Maybe someone had found out, and Boris was trying to warn me.

I ran inside and lifted the ringing phone. "What's wrong?"

"*Dobroye utro*. Good morning." Boris sounded relieved. "Everything okay?"

I glanced outside. Vladimir motioned for me to join him. "I'm *khorosho*." I went back outside and curled up on his lap. He wrapped his arms around my belly. His touch excited me. I sucked in a deep breath.

"What's wrong? Is boss there?"

"I'm with Vladimir now." I turned my head and smooched his lips. "Vladimir is *khorosho*, too."

"I take it you and Vladimir had a *khoroshiy* evening together?"

"*Da*."

"Good girl. Call if you need anything."

After breakfast, I went to the bathroom to get changed for the beach. I slipped out of my robe and slid on a super cute fringy white and gold bikini. As I checked my reflection in the mirror, a bony, battered, bruised young woman with bags under her eyes and sallow cheeks stared back.

If I set foot on the beach with my older, prison-tatted Russian boyfriend looking like I got my ass beat daily, someone would call the cops. Up until that point, I'd kept my bruises hidden from everyone—including Vladimir. When we were naked, the lights were off, and my body was hidden under the sheets.

"How does it look? You like it?" he asked from the other side of the door.

"Love it. I'll model it for you after I finish getting ready."

Shit. He would be mad for sure—either at me for *deserving* the marks he had left on my skin, or he'd be pissed at Boris for hurting me. Or he'd interrogate me about what *I* did that made Boris so mad, and then I'd have to cop to the Leonardo Examination Incident. If I ratted out Boris, I would have hell to pay with him all over again.

Secrets or lies? Neither option ended with us happily frolicking on the beach. I had to call for backup. I picked up my special phone and turned on the shower to mask my voice.

Boris picked up on the first ring. "What's wrong?"

"I don't look good in my bikini. I'm afraid to go to the beach."

"You have a nice figure, *lapsha*, get over—"

"That's not what I mean."

"I packed a long-sleeved swim shirt. One for boss, too."

I heard a knock at the door. "May I come in?"

"Of course." I tapped the screen and hung up on Boris.

I pulled my hair forward to cover my arms, leaving only the good parts from the neck down visible. I put my hand over my side to cover the yellowing bruises on my stomach where Boris had pinched my skin. "What do you think?" I turned to give him a good view.

He leaned in for a smooch. "Amazing. Who were you talking to?"

"Boris called to remind us to wear the swim shirts he packed. I guess coming home with matching sunburns might raise a few eyebrows."

He took the phone from my hand to check the call log. "You said Boris called you, but *you* are the one who called him."

I dismissed his objection with a wave of my hand. "Um, he called me, and then I called him back. Are you ready to hit the beach?"

He checked the call list again and shot me an accusing glare.

Don't lie, don't lie, don't lie...

"I needed his advice. He's my *sovietnik*, too."

"What do you need? Why not come to me?"

I pushed my hair over my shoulders and exposed my secret.

Vladimir ran his fingers down my arms and assessed the damage. The bruises on my body told a story on my skin, just as his Russian tattoos revealed his crimes and time served behind bars. He lined up his fingers over the marks he'd imprinted on my arms. Judging by his pained expression, he had no memory of hurting me.

"This happened while you were a guest in my house?"

"Saturday night after you—"

My phone rang in the palm of Vladimir's hand. I shut my mouth, remembering Boris had warned me not to bring up alcohol.

His jaw clenched. "After I what?"

I hesitated. The phone continued to ring.

"Tell me."

"After you had a lot to drink."

His eyes dulled, and his expression went blank as if the truth had planted a bullet in his brain. He reeled me in for a hug. "Never again." He rubbed circles on my back, kissed the top of my head, and rocked me side to side. "I swear to God, I'll never lose control around you as long as I live. I'll never have a sip of alcohol in your presence again. I love you, Carter. More than anything in the world."

I burrowed inside his robe and buried my head against his bare chest. He let out a mournful sigh when my tears wet his skin. "*Moy slomonnyy angel.*" He hugged me so tightly, I could feel his heart beating against my cheek. "Say you forgive me."

I could tell he felt horrible for hurting me, and I believed that if he didn't drink, he would never become violent. He loved me, and I loved him. "I forgive you." My words caught in my throat.

The ringing stopped.

47

HOUSE RULES

We skipped the beach and flew back home in case Dad tried to reach me. Once we landed in Cincinnati, Vladimir pulled into the church by my house and parked the car. He took off his seat belt, unfastened mine, and leaned over to kiss me. "Come with me. The house is empty without you. Boris misses you, too."

"I need to check in with Dad." I finger-combed his hair.

"Let me go back with you. We'll tell your papa right now."

I shook my head.

"We're in love. Why hide our affection?"

"Let's take our time and do this right—and I'm sure Boris doesn't miss me." I laughed.

"You're wrong about that. He said you remind him of his daughter."

"Wait. Boris has a daughter? Does she live here or in Russia?"

"Sadly, Katia died when she was a young girl. He's left with two sons."

Why are so many of their family members dead? "That's so sad."

"Life is precious. We must cherish every moment we have together."

Vladimir let me go but made me promise I would call when I got to Dad's to make plans for the rest of the weekend. When I walked in the door, I was surprised to find a house full of guests. Karen's family had stopped by to visit, and Ryan and his dad were there to watch a bowl game with Dad and a bunch of his Ohio State buddies.

I was so distracted by all the guests, especially my aunt's six-month-old baby boy, that I didn't immediately call Vladimir back like I said I would. As I held the blue-eyed cutie in my arms, someone knocked on the front door. My hands were full, so Ryan answered it.

"Good to see you, sir," Ryan said. "Here to join us for the game?"

I turned to see who he was talking to: Vladimir. He wore his sexy glasses and held a computer bag in his hand. He stepped inside and shook Ryan's hand. "No, just a quick question for my star employee." I thought he would be pissed to find Ryan at the house, but he was delighted to see my cooing cousin perched on my hip.

Ryan noticed Vladimir's quizzical expression. "Carter didn't tell you she had a baby?"

"Ryan!"

He laughed and jogged downstairs to watch the game. Things were back to normal between us as if our flash romance had never happened. He was hurt when I told him I only wanted to be friends, but after a few days, he started texting me his lame jokes again—and Kiki said he'd gotten back together with his ex-girlfriend Jessica.

The baby clung to me with a big smile on his angelic

face. Vladimir's complexion shone with adoration. The little guy bounced with joy, clutched a fistful of my hair in his tiny hand, and babbled in baby talk.

"Who is your friend, Carter?"

"This is my cousin, Christopher."

Dad walked in from the kitchen, in head-to-toe Ohio State garb, with a beer in his hand. "Vladimir, what a surprise. Want to join us for the game? It's about to start."

"No, I don't want to intrude, but I have a question about the claims billing system."

I jumped in for the save. "Sorry, Mr. Ivanov. There's no working during OSU games, right, Dad?"

Dad shrugged apologetically. "House rules. Can I talk you into a beer instead?"

Vladimir's gaze flashed to mine, then to the baby's, then back to Dad. "I would hate to break a house rule."

Dad patted him on the back, told him to make himself at home, and then went downstairs to join the guys in the middle-aged-frat-boy cave. Karen and her sister were in the kitchen whirling up margaritas and yowling like hyenas, and while we were alone, Vladimir kissed me.

The baby fussed.

"It's time to feed him." I motioned for Vladimir to sit in the recliner. He took off his coat, and I draped a burp cloth over his shoulder, placed Christopher in his arms, and handed him the bottle. Vladimir's complexion glowed as the hungry baby sucked down the milk.

I sat beside him on the arm of the chair. "You're a natural," I whispered.

"He's beautiful." When Vladimir spoke, Christopher smiled.

We laughed at the unexpected joy the baby brought us. "Wish you had one?" I teased.

"Carter, my dear, you have no idea."

The second the words came out of my mouth, the answer registered on his face. It was the same reason Boris wasn't concerned over my birth control crisis: it wasn't by *choice* he'd never fathered a child. I felt horrible. Had I just rubbed it in?

He read my tortured face.

The baby coughed.

I readjusted his position in Vladimir's arms.

"It wasn't meant to be, angel."

48

NAUGHTY

The next morning was New Year's Eve, one of the most celebrated Russian holidays. Vladimir and I made plans for me to meet Boris at nine-thirty a.m. at our usual spot. I told Dad I was going to spend the night with Kiki and headed to the club. I hadn't seen Boris since he had dropped me off at the airport. So much had changed since then.

When I plopped down in the Caddy, I caught a glimpse of Boris's expression. His eyes were locked and loaded in lie detector mode. Always on duty. I suspected he wanted to find out if I was pulling some weasel move on the boss.

I covered my mouth with my scarf to hide my telling grin. Even Dad noticed I had miraculously bounced back from my lingering *illness* when I came home the morning after.

"You had a nice weekend?" Boris asked.

I kept my gaze out the window. "*Da*."

"Everything okay at home?" He tapped his rings on the steering wheel. "Got some sunshine? You have a healthy glow—matches the one boss has."

I snuck a sideways glance at him.

"Over your contraception problem?"

"Mm-hm. Wasn't an issue."

He blinked in confusion. "*Because*?"

"Um—"

He had that murderous look in his eye. "You weaseled out of it?"

"Well, uh, remember the wagers we made the night we played poker?"

The veins popped.

I twisted my ponytail around my hand. "His note said *'anything,'* so I cashed it in on, you know...*that*." I held out my hand and continued. "He respects my decision. Does he look unhappy to you?"

My keeper was ready to blow. "You're a lucky girl, Carter. If you pulled that bullshit on me, I would've—"

"It's not bullshit."

His knuckles were white. He didn't speak to me the rest of the way home. When we got to the house, I jumped out of the Cadillac like it had a bomb strapped underneath it. I ran inside and crashed into my sexy boyfriend's waiting arms.

He lifted me up.

I wrapped my legs around his body.

He sat me down on the kitchen counter.

We made out like we had guns to our heads.

Boris walked in the door, grumbling in Russian.

"Did you miss me, Vladimir?" I asked.

"No." He flashed his crooked smile.

I shoved him in the chest.

"I couldn't breathe the whole time we were apart," he amended. "Isn't that right, Boris?"

"*Da.* His lips were blue." Boris shook his head, wanting

nothing to do with our gooey love fest. "Thank heavens you came back to resuscitate him, Carter."

"Let me make sure he's okay." I ran my fingers through his wavy hair and kissed him again, louder and sloppier that time. Vladimir liked it. He flung off my hat and scarf, unzipped my coat, and tossed it on the floor. "I think he's okay now, Boris. I saved him."

We laughed.

Boris mumbled in Russian and left the house.

Vladimir noticed what I was wearing and grinned. I had on a red, Christmas-themed t-shirt that I borrowed from Kiki with 'naughty' scrolled across the front in sparkle letters. It was too short, too tight, and I hadn't bothered to wear a bra.

He licked his lips and lifted my shirt, but I stopped him from taking it off. From my perch on the counter, I had a perfect view of the white murderer van parked by the basketball court. "Not here." I closed my hands around his. "Show me your bedroom."

He scooped me up and swept me away. I had never been in there before—never even snuck a peek inside. I thought it would look like the rest of the house, decorated with a designer's touch but not too personal. I was wrong. I spied a soccer ball on the floor, a collection of egg-shaped music boxes on the dresser, and photos of his family lined the walls.

Vladimir enjoyed seeing my reaction to the side of him I'd yet to know. A vintage photo of a handsome young man caught my eye. "That's your papa? What's his name?"

"Victor."

"I see where you get your blue eyes. Do you have a picture of your mama?"

He carried me to the other side of the wall and stopped

in front of a photo of a beautiful young woman holding an infant in her arms, and two little boys sat next to her on the front stoop of an apartment building.

"You're the baby? And they're your big brothers?" I slid my legs down and stood next to him. "You seem like you'd be the oldest, personality-wise."

"Interesting observation. The oldest was Mischa, and the middle boy was Alexei."

I curled my finger around his belt loop. "Your mama was lovely. What's her name?"

"Irina. According to my papa, she was the most beautiful woman in all of Ekaterinburg." He smiled with a glint of sadness in his eyes.

"I'm sorry you lost them." I wanted to ask how they all died, but I didn't want to upset him.

He squeezed my hand and pointed to a picture of him, around age twelve, next to a robust dark-haired boy and a younger boy with a round belly. The youngest one had a stick in his hand, and the older boy held a cap gun aimed at a shirtless Vladimir, who was flinging a rope at him like a lion tamer. At first, I couldn't figure out who they were. Then I spotted a much younger Boris in the background, looking pissed off at the antics of three young boys.

I covered my mouth to stifle my laughter as the scenes of growing up Russian gangster-style played out in pictures. "No wonder Boris has zero patience. You guys destroyed him." I pointed at Vladimir's picture. "Hey, you were skinny, too." I tickled his ribs.

"Of course, I was skin and bones. Look at my brothers. I had to fight for every scrap of food I got."

"What about the little guy? You didn't fight with him, did you?"

Vladimir touched his brother's image through the glass.

"Never. Pasha has the heart of a saint. Anybody who said a cross word or laid a hand on him had to deal with me." His finger slid across the picture and tapped the big boy's image. "This one, on the other hand," he shook his head, "Yuri and I would go to war over a stick of bubble gum."

As I examined the picture more closely, I noticed the youngest boy had tears in his big brown eyes, the oldest of Boris's brood had a ripped shirt, and Vladimir had a welt across his side like he'd been whipped with a *belt*. I wrapped my arms across my body. "Boris took care of you after you lost your parents?"

"In his own way, he looked after me." He kissed me on top of the head. "Everything we experience happens for a reason, like us. I traveled halfway around the world to help a young woman. And *she* is the one who saved me." He kissed my lips. "I thank God every day for bringing us together. You are my world."

If I had to describe to my shrink how our relationship evolved, *dysfunctional* would be the politest possible description of our love affair. But despite the messed-up stuff, where we were at that moment was a magical place. He loved me, and I loved him. What did it matter how black and blue, broken, and busted-up the road was that brought us together?

"We have all day and night. How do you want to pass the time, angel?"

"I have a present for you," I said. "I was going to give it to you tonight, in the Russian tradition, but I can't wait. I'll be right back."

I retrieved his gift from my purse and hurried back to the bedroom. I placed it in his hands, and he sat on the edge of the bed and pulled me down on his lap. Then he untied the bow and ripped off the paper.

"Oh, Carter."

It was a two-sided frame hinged down the middle. On the left half was a picture of me cuddling my toy poodle twins in my arms. On the right half, I placed a selfie of the real poodles and me. I printed a caption under the photos that read:

My dreams came true when I met you.
Love, Carter

Vladimir's eyes were bright and wet. "This is the most thoughtful gift anyone has ever given me." He kissed me and then set the picture on his nightstand. The reality was, in order to leave the house, we would have to unwind ourselves from each other's arms—and that wasn't going to happen.

"I have a gift for you, too, but *you* must wait," he teased. He leaned me back on the bed and slid off my naughty shirt.

I unbuttoned his shirt and tried to take it off, but he kept his arms stiff. I had only seen the front of his body, never his back. He was self-conscious about something. Maybe he had a stab wound or a gruesome scar or something unsettling like a tattoo of Stalin he didn't want me to see. I slid off his pants and finally saw his bare legs in the light of day. He had star tats on his knees.

The meaning: I bow down to no one.

He lay on top of me and kissed my breasts, slid off my jeans, and rubbed me between my legs. I'd pledged not to lose my virginity until my wedding night, but my willpower was dissolving. Sticking to my virtues when I was single was easy, but thwarting the advances of my incredibly sexy Russian would require a completely different game plan.

To hell with virtue! The devil chided.

I couldn't agree more. I rolled over and straddled my man—underwear still on—and rubbed against him while my blonde locks rained over his face. It was a powerful feeling knowing Vladimir could have any woman he wanted—and he chose me. I ran my fingers along the muscles of his abdomen and admired the results of his early morning workouts. "What does this say?" I drew an imaginary line with my finger around a Russian phrase inked on his side.

He answered in Russian.

I shoved him in the chest. "What does it say in *English*?"

"It says, 'My girlfriend asks too many questions.' "

I kissed the devil on his chest. "Why did you get this ugly guy?"

He exaggerated a long, drawn-out groan. "When will this interrogation end?"

I pinned his wrists and held him down. "It will end when I say it ends."

"Is that so?" He smiled seductively, turned on by my inner dominatrix.

I squeezed his wrists. "Mm-hm. You're my prisoner now."

"Well then, I'll have to escape." He sat up, flipped me on my back, and had me pinned underneath him before I even knew what happened. I yelped, and we were both laughing so hard we could barely catch our breath. The weight of his strong body was a total turn on. "Now you're my prisoner." Vladimir kissed my cheeks, my neck, my breasts...

He cruised down my body and teased me in Russian. He slid off my panties, slipped his tongue inside me, and swirled and sucked my sweet spot. My arousal was coming on fast, and I swiveled my hips, syncing up with his rhythm. The intensity grew, and I panted and groaned my satisfaction as he nuzzled my sex and savored my release.

He inhaled my scent and rubbed his cheeks against my delicate skin, then cuddled up next to me. "You are more important to me than anything else in the world."

I curled beside him and nestled my face in the crook of his neck. "When are you going back to Russia?"

His body tensed. "I've been meaning to talk to you about that."

"When?"

"In a few days."

Days? I rolled off him and dug my thumbnails into the tops of my fingers to calm myself down, but the tears were coming despite my effort to stop the drama. "So, what was the plan? You were going to send me a postcard?"

"No, angel. Let's not ruin our perfect day. We'll talk about it later." He cupped my chin in his hands and kissed me on the lips. I wanted to shove him off the bed, but instead, I gave in and kissed him back. I was in shock, and at the same time humiliated about how much he meant to me, and how insignificant I was to him.

Boris was right. I am *stupid girl.*

49

MOTHER RUSSIA

Vladimir drew a bath in the whirlpool, filled the tub with bubbles, and added a few drops of lavender essential oil to the warm, sensual water. I was shell-shocked, but I tried to live in the moment and not be a killjoy over the fact he was leaving—forever. Still, I couldn't help questioning why he had tried so hard to win me over, only to dump me as soon as he got a little piece of my puzzle.

"Relax, angel. I'll wash you." He turned me around so my back was to him, took off his shirt, and sank us in the tub. He wet my hair and massaged a big glob of shampoo through my waves. Once he worked up a lather, he rinsed it off, ran a silky seaweed-colored conditioner through my hair, and then stacked my locks on top of my head in a freestyle bun.

With my hair up, he had a perfect view of my Christmas Eve bullshit Boris had imprinted on me after the football game. He drove a bar of soap back and forth over the foot-stomp impression still visible between my shoulder blades.

It was as if he thought he could magically erase it—or maybe he was rubbing it in.

While the conditioner set in, he scooted my body back and rested my head on his chest. He lifted my left leg, lathered it with soap, and commenced shaving. After both my legs were smooth, he ran a washcloth down my body, starting at my neck and working his way down to my feet, stopping at all stops on the journey south.

After he polished my body, he rinsed my hair and washed my face. Neither one of us said a word. I understood: I was disgusting. In his mind, the game was over. He had won. What use was I to him anymore? Now that the skank was clean enough to sit in one of his fancy cars, he could send me back home to my papa dirtier than I was before I left the house.

Bravo. Well done, Vladimir. It must feel awesome to con a virgin into letting you work your magic down there. Is there a special tattoo for that achievement?

Sophia huffed.

The devil pumped his fist.

I stood up and got out of the tub. Dirty gray suds clung to my body. I covered myself with a towel, collected my rumpled clothes off the floor, and scurried back to my bedroom to shower off the grime. I sent Boris a text and asked him to take me home. He would be giddy knowing he was rid of me once and for all.

I put myself back together, slid on my coat, and braided my wet hair as I waited in the kitchen for my keeper to show up. When Vladimir found me, I wouldn't look at him.

"What's wrong?"

"Boris is coming to get me. I asked him to take me home." I hid my hands in my pockets. They were shaking like rattlesnake tails.

"Why?"

I sucked in a deep breath. "Stop pretending. You got what you wanted. Leave me alone and go back to Russia."

God, I hate myself. He tried to put his arms around me, but I shoved him off. "Just open the gate. I'll walk home." I ran to the kitchen door.

He bear-hugged me from behind, pinning my arms at my side. "I don't understand. What did I do?" He dragged me away from the door.

"Cut the shit. Let me go."

"Talk to me. I honestly have no idea why you're so upset."

I struggled to get free, which only made him squeeze me tighter. "You won, okay? Let me go." I rocked my body side to side, trying to throw him off balance—no luck.

"You think I'm leaving you?"

Resilient and still high on the idea that I could out-muscle him, I tried to weasel my way out of his arms. "Duh, genius. You *are* leaving me."

He exhaled, his body lightening like all the air had been let out of his soul. "*Moy slomonnyy angel.*"

"Don't call me that. I looked it up, you jerk. I'm not 'broken,' and I'm not your 'angel.' Get off me. Let me go!"

He loosened his grip, and at the same time, I lunged forward, lost my balance, and crash-landed on the kitchen floor. Vladimir knelt beside me, scooped up my deflated body, and cradled me in his arms. I buried my face in his chest, hating myself for craving the warmth and comfort I felt cocooned in his arms.

"You are my world, Carter." Vladimir picked up my right hand and kissed my knuckle. "I planned to do this in a more romantic way this evening, but you leave me no choice." He pulled a gold ring with a huge blue-green stone out of his pocket and slid it on my finger. "This belonged to my mama. She'd want you to have it."

My face was wet with tears, snot, and sweat. "Why?"

He studied my bewildered expression. "I want to spend the rest of my life with you, Carter. Marry me."

I blinked at the exquisite engagement ring on my finger. "You want me to go back to Russia *with you?*"

Vladimir blotted my face with the sleeve of his starched shirt. "We have fine colleges in Russia—tennis courts, too. I'll hire the best coaches to train you."

As I considered Vladimir's proposal, still curled up on his lap on the floor, the kitchen door opened. Boris towered over us with his arms crossed, stance wide, eyes narrowed. Nothing fazed the big guy.

"What do you say, angel?"

I couldn't imagine living my life without Vladimir by my side. I needed him. I loved him. "*Da*," I answered.

"*Da*?"

"*Da*, I'll marry you."

Boris exhaled, mentally exhausted by our crazy. Apparently, the *pakhan* hadn't consulted with his *sovietnik* about his marital plans—or our future together back home in Mother Russia.

Vladimir and I stood up.

"Surprise." I held out my hand to show Boris Irina's ring.

Boris patted Vladimir on the back, clutched his shoulders, and said something encouraging in Russian that made Vladimir smile. It looked like an endearing father-son kind of moment. Boris even called him "Vova," which must be an affectionate nickname.

Boris turned to me. "Welcome to the family, *lapsha*." My future papa-in-law of sorts pulled me in for a hug and kisses on my cheeks. He held out his fist for a celebratory bump. I lifted my hand, made a fist, and squinted in anticipation of the customary way-too-hard knuckle-knock. Boris lightly bumped my hand and gave me a tiny smile. “You’ll make a fine Russian.”

50

PLAN OF ATTACK

From that point on, our *sovietnik* insisted on being involved in every endeavor. We huddled around the bar, an unopened bottle of vodka between us, and devised a plan that seemed as complicated as overthrowing the Kremlin. The demands of Vladimir's position were heating up in Russia. He and Boris would leave the States in three days to settle a rival conflict that had escalated back home.

Of course, Vladimir wanted me to drop everything, ditch life as I knew it, and board his private jet. That game plan only compounded the problems. Small detail, but I didn't have a passport. Vladimir scoffed and said he could get me one in five minutes, but Boris intervened on my behalf and denied him. I was an adult, and there was no need to leave the country illegally—or against my papa's wishes. Boris sealed the deal by adding that it was best to handle the *conflict* before introducing me to the life.

Vladimir held out a moment more, until Boris flashed the For Her Own Safety card. I'd stay here, waiting.

Their world was fascinating, really. I wondered if *rival*

conflict translated to *mafia war*, but I didn't push for details. I got the sense this was the "minor issue" back home that had him all fired up on my first day of work.

The Official Game Plan:

Vladimir and Boris would go back to Russia in three days.

I would apply for a passport and have it in hand in time for spring break.

Vladimir would fly back from Russia, and together we would confess our love and marriage plans to Dad.

I would fly back to Russia with Vladimir. We would spend spring break at his *dacha*, his summer home, and plan our June wedding.

These things were decided, but the last piece of the equation—whether I'd return to America after spring break to finish the semester and reach a peace agreement with Dad—was still under negotiation.

"Vladimir, we're going to spend the rest of our lives together. I need time to ease out of my life here. If I drop out, it won't look good on my record when I apply to colleges in Russia."

"You'll go to any college you want. I'll see to it personally."

"Newsflash: I don't need *you* to see to it. I earned my way. I'm not going to throw away everything I worked so hard for." *He's like me; he has to understand that.*

Vladimir tapped the tips of his fingers together and eyed the vodka bottle. "As my *wife*, you'll enjoy the privileges that come with being married to a man of a certain influence, understand?" His cheeks were red, jaw clenched.

"She understands, boss." Boris reached for the bottle.

Vladimir held up his hand to Boris like a stop sign and took a deep breath. "Let's do this. We'll stick to the plan as it is, and you will decide when or if you go home after spring break. You might love your new country so much that you may never want to return to America." He picked up my hand and kissed the inside of my wrist. "Your happiness is my only concern."

"Perfect. *Spasibo.*" I stood on my toes and kissed him. He ran his fingers through my hair with one hand, and with the other, he squeezed his arm around my back. He was a different person without the vodka, and he was willing to give up drinking—for *me*. In return, I would give up my family, friends, and country to spend my life with him in Russia.

When you love someone, you make sacrifices.

Our make-out session was getting a little sloppy. I could tell he was excited when he whispered in Russian and nibbled on my ear. I cracked up, embarrassed that the juicy love fest was going down in front of Boris.

"There you go, boss." Boris patted him on the back. "Now, let's talk about the wedding. Russians believe in elaborate celebrations. My mama will spoil you rotten, *lapsha*."

"I can't wait to meet your family, *Vova*."

"My family can't wait to meet *you*, angel."

51

IZVINITE

When Boris drove me home, the car was silent except for the sound of his gold rings tapping on the steering wheel.

"You have your *sovietnik* face on," I said. "Is something wrong?"

He glanced my way as he drove down the winding road. "Why do you say that?"

"You look deep in thought," I said, pointing at his hands. "And you do that tapping thing when things are messed up."

He thought a moment before he responded. "I don't like surprises."

"You're surprised Vladimir wants to marry *me*?"

"I'm surprised you want to marry *him*."

I scoffed. "Why?"

By the incredulous look on his face, it had appeared my Stupid Girl meter had tipped over into the red zone. "You do know what we do for a living, right?"

I nodded.

Tap, tap, tap, tap...

"You're a nice girl, Carter, with a bright future. You can handle being married to the *pakhan*?"

"Well, he's not bad. Like you." I peeked over at him. "He does the cyber stuff, and you handle the *other* side of the business."

"Ah, now I understand. He's the good kind of bad guy." He chuckled. "What he does is okay as long as no one gets hurt, right?"

"I know he had a hard life growing up behind the Iron Curtain—not to mention he lost his entire family, and went to prison," I said. "After all he's been through, how can I judge him?"

"You're a very understanding young lady, Carter." He pulled into our meeting spot. I opened the door to get out of the car, but Boris held my arm. "Once you're in the family, there's no getting out. If you have any reservations—"

"I love him."

Tap, tap, tap, tap...

"There's nothing to worry about, Boris."

Tap, tap, tap, tap...

"The boss is a lucky man."

"*Spasibo*. I'm lucky, too."

Tap, tap, tap, tap...

THAT NIGHT, Vladimir invited the family to a Middle Eastern restaurant for a going-away party. Bongos, belly dancing, and falafel balls would have been fantastic under different circumstances, but my fiancé was going back to Russia without me in two days.

When Dad, Karen, Megan, and I arrived at the restaurant, Boris greeted us at the door. I didn't know how

Vladimir and I were going to hide our feelings for each other in front of Dad, but knowing Boris was there to keep us in line eased my stress.

"Ded!" Megan bounced over to Boris, holding a fuzzy black kitty in one hand and a lanky white beanbag cat with blue eyes in the other. "This one is you." She held up the black one. "And this is *Dyadya*." She held up the white one. "Santa put them in my stocking."

Boris studied his feline representative. "Too fat."

"He's not fat, his fur is fluffy."

"If you say so, dear." Boris patted her on the head and handed her a chocolate bar.

"I hope I don't cry," Karen said. "I can't believe you two are leaving us. Wouldn't you rather stay in America?"

"*Nyet*. I miss my wife. My family."

"You're married?" Karen and I said in unison.

"Thirty-two years."

I knew he had kids and his mama back home, but he'd never mentioned his wife. "What's her name?"

"Anya."

I smiled. "Pretty."

"Vladimir and his guest will join us momentarily," Boris said to Dad and Karen.

Guest?

While the hostess collected our coats, Boris emblazoned a mind-melting warning directly onto my corneas. After that non-verbal assault, I decided to keep my coat on—my wardrobe choice was a tad questionable.

Mystery Guest: Vladimir arrived fashionably late with a green-eyed redhead with cascading curls, huge boobs, and legs longer than a camel's. He introduced everyone to his 'girlfriend,' Svetlana, adding that she only spoke Russian.

My mouth gaped. *What the hell was he trying to pull?*

"Good to see you again, Miss Cook. You look well. Over your boy troubles?"

"*Da.*" I evil-eyed the bombshell. "*Do svidaniya.*" I extended my hand to her.

"You mean *privet*?" Vladimir laughed. "*Do svidaniya* means goodbye."

"My bad."

Karen and Dad exchanged glances. "You picked up some Russian over Christmas break, sweetie?"

"*Da, Papa.*"

Vladimir laughed and patted me on the head like a child. I wanted to smack his hand away, but I had to keep it together in front of my family.

"Let's have a seat, shall we?" Vladimir asked.

Dad and Karen walked ahead of me, Vladimir behind. I unzipped my coat, slid it off, and peeked over my shoulder to gauge his reaction to my sexy duds. I had on low-rise jeans and a curve-hugging sequined top, with a matching shrug, a belly chain, and a rose-gold choker in the shape of a tigress chasing her tail.

I wore my hair down in a messy, wavy, sexy do and turned up the heat a bit by tracing black eyeliner around my eyes like a cat to accentuate my fiancé's favorite feature of mine. He bit his lip and chuckled at my crazy.

"Whoa," Dad said when he caught an eyeful of my dinner attire.

"What? I was going with a themed outfit. Too much?"

He gave me *the look*.

"*Izvinite.*" I apologized for my bad choice.

"You sure picked up a lot of Russian in two and a half days," Dad mumbled.

Vladimir motioned for everyone to have a seat. I headed for the chair next to him, but Boris caught my elbow and pointed to the other side of the table. Karen and Dad settled in seats across from Vladimir and his date, and I got marooned next to Boris.

Megan pulled her doppelgänger cat family out of her backpack and set up a nest for them using starched white napkins from the table.

A text came in from Boris on my special phone:

My idea. Relax.

THE BAND BEGAN WARMING up as the server brought pita bread, tabouli, and a pitcher of margaritas to the table. Vladimir poured the drinks and handed one to Karen, one to Svetlana. He said something to her in Russian that made her giggle.

I swayed and bounced to the beat of the drums, completely ignoring him. It may have been Boris's idea to bring Miss Moscow, but Vladimir didn't need to enjoy it so much.

A foursome of dancers, two ladies in belly dancer costumes, and two dudes—one hot, one not—in turbans, stretched out in the corner by the band. The hot guy busted me staring and swished a scarf at me. I turned away and pretended I hadn't noticed. I could feel Vladimir glaring at me, but I wouldn't look at him. He sent a margarita down to me. Apparently, the rules of underage drinking didn't apply to him *anywhere*, but I held up my hand and refused. "I'm going to stick with water tonight. Thanks anyway, *Vlad*—Mr. Ivanov."

"Good choice, Carter. You can be the designated driver."

Karen sucked down half of her drink and then turned and smooched Dad on the lips. They had already had a few beers before we left the house.

This could get interesting.

I got up and excused myself. I walked past Vladimir and 'accidentally' bumped his chair. When I came out of the bathroom, he pulled me into the kitchen. I tried to slap him, but he caught my hand and trapped me against the wall.

"Nice girlfriend, you jerk. You two make a charming couple."

He put his finger to my lips to shush me. "It's for appearances, angel. Svetlana is one of Boris's girls. No one could ever take your place."

"If she belongs to Boris, then give her back."

"How else can I mask my attraction, angel? I'm doing this for you."

Satisfied with his explanation, I stood on my toes and kissed him. Our public display of affection in front of the staff was getting a little sloppy. The owner came over and asked us to go back to our table, under the guise that our appetizer course was being served.

Back in our private room, Vladimir and Dad dove into a conversation about some technology thing. Dad had bought out Vladimir's shares of the company and was taking over as CEO. There was no way Dad could've afforded it without financial help. I knew without asking that Vladimir had made it possible. Boris had told me the truth when he said the business was legit, and Vladimir meant what he said about coming to America to help my family.

Svetlana sat quietly, drinking her margarita with my fiancé's arm around her narrow waist. She was a distraction for him, but what about me?

"Want to dance, Karen? Looks like the guys are talking shop."

"Sure. I've been dying to get out there." She sucked down the rest of her drink. "I think the cute one likes you."

When we stood up, I motioned to Svetlana to join us. She looked at Vladimir to check if it was okay. *Jeez. What a tool.*

He said something in Russian, kissed her hand, and she stayed at his side.

Whatever. When we joined the dancers, they wrapped scarves around our waists and showed us how to swing our hips like belly dancers. Karen busted out some dirty dancing moves with the twenty-something-year-old, but I turned my back on the male dancers and shook it with the ladies. Dad looked like he wanted to stab his eyes out with kabob skewers as he watched his wife dancing with a much younger, hotter dude with a full head of dark, wavy hair.

I knew better than to make my man jealous.

"Karen, why don't you come back to the table now? They're serving the appetizers," Dad said. His face was burning red.

I stepped in and tried to pull Karen away, but she didn't take the hint.

Karen raised her hands over her head and shook her booty dangerously close to the dancer's crotch. Dad chugged a glass of water and dabbed the sweat off his forehead with a napkin. I couldn't tell if he was more pissed or humiliated by his wife's behavior—and it was all going down in front of the manly Russians.

Dad dropped a stack of pita bread on Karen's plate and dumped a big scoop of hummus next to it. "Try this, honey. You'll love it."

Translation: *Down, girl.*

The dancer swished the scarf at Karen's behind, totally digging her sloppy, flirty cougar drunkenness. Poor Dad looked like he was about to go medieval on the dude. *Enough.* I tugged on Karen's arm and took her spot. "Sorry, my turn." I kept the beat with the dude to deter her from cutting back in.

"You can have him, Carter. I've got my man." She plopped down in the chair next to Dad and tried to kiss him, but he turned his cheek.

I glanced over at my dance partner. He looked jazzed at my enthusiasm to fight off my stepmom so I could have a run with him. He clapped in time with the beat and eyed my body as I danced. I turned my back to go back to the table, but the dude caught my arm and pulled me back. I prayed the Russians missed the fact that he'd touched me.

To mask his dangerous faux pas, I danced until the music ended. Then I went back to the table without making eye contact.

Vladimir will understand why I stepped in, right?

As everyone filled his or her plates from the family-style platters, a text came in on my special phone from Vladimir. I couldn't tell what it said, because the words were in Russian.

I snuck a peek at him and laughed.

The *pakhan* didn't see the humor.

52

SHARK BAIT

The next day, Vladimir wouldn't return my calls or texts. I stayed in my room and started packing. I had a feeling he would nix my apartment plans, but he hadn't brought it up yet. If he asked me not to move, I would oblige. I was already nervous about the dancing incident.

Before I was due to meet Boris, I went to the cemetery to visit Sophia—something I hadn't done in years. I needed her guidance, and I couldn't confide in anyone among the living about the Russians.

I loved Vladimir, but I feared him too. I stewed all night over the dancer, and now he was giving me the silent treatment. I had to admit doubts were creeping in about marrying him. Nobody said relationships are supposed to be easy, but where was the line? Love is love—when you have it, when someone cherishes you like Vladimir cherishes me, when all you can think about is the next time you'll see him, it's worth fighting for...right?

It was all so confusing. I thought about doing the right thing for once and confiding in my dad, but I couldn't risk it.

I needed Sophia's angel wisdom, but I could no longer distinguish between her voice and the devil's anymore.

I shuffled through the church parking lot and trekked through the snow to her gravesite. I spread out a stadium blanket, sat next to her memorial, and spilled the secrets I'd been hiding from my friends and family. I lifted my engagement ring from my pocket and held it up.

Should I call off the engagement?

Nothing.

I jumped when I heard a car door slam. Boris was leaning against the Caddy, watching me from the parking lot. If I married Vladimir and moved to Russia, Boris and the *Bratva* would become my new family. Dad, Karen, Megan, and Kiki would be out of my life.

I was in with the Russians, and there was no way out.

I slid my engagement back onto my finger, folded up the blanket, and said goodbye to Sophia. I got into the car with Boris and left my sister behind.

Neither one of us spoke until we neared the house. "I only danced with that guy to get Karen away from him. Did you see Dad's face?"

"Wasn't your problem to solve."

When we got home, Vladimir was leaning against the bar, his eyes rimmed in red. I crashed into him and swung my arms around his waist. A thick, bloody steak sat soaking in marinade on the counter.

"You're late."

Shit. I squeezed him tight. "I'm so sorry about last night. Forgive me?"

He went to the bar, tipped the vodka bottle, and poured himself a generous shot. The sun hadn't gone down yet, and he was already smashed. "Of course, angel." The seething tone of his voice didn't match the sincerity of his words.

I glanced down at my engagement ring. The once bluish-green stone had turned a dark, ruby red. I turned my hand to see if it was a trick from the light. "What happened to my ring? It changed color."

Vladimir picked up my hand. "It's the nature of the stone. Alexandrite from the Ural Mountains near my home. In the sunlight, it reflects the cool and vibrant colors, but at night, when the sun goes down, it shines blood red." Vladimir lowered my hand and looked out the window. "But the sun hasn't gone down yet. Perhaps you've done something to anger the stone?" He went to the bar for another shot.

When Vladimir's back was turned, I looked to Boris for guidance. He wouldn't make eye contact. Boris spoke to the boss in Russian. I forced myself to breathe so I wouldn't pass out.

Vladimir didn't like whatever it was Boris had said. "Take the night off. I want to spend the evening alone with my bride-to-be."

Boris glared at me as he passed by on his way to the mudroom.

Holy shit. I thought it best to keep my mouth shut and make him something to eat to try to absorb the alcohol he was drowning in. I tried to keep my hands steady as I sliced into a block of cheese. He watched me work but didn't speak. In a hurry, I carelessly sliced the top of my index finger. I turned my back and cupped my hand to inspect the damage. Blood dripped down into my palm. My stomach turned.

Careful not to make a big deal out of it, I wrapped a towel around my finger to stop the bleeding. It soaked right through. I jumped when I felt Vladimir standing right behind me. He had a sense for blood like a damn shark—and I was chum bobbing in the ocean.

Shark bait.

He picked up my hand and unwrapped my makeshift bandage. Blood oozed from the cut when the pressure was removed. I felt lightheaded. He lifted my hand, stuck my finger in his mouth, and sucked the blood that pulsed from the wound. I leaned against him to stay upright and fought the urge to scream, gag, or pass out.

Boris returned to the kitchen, and his gaze darted from my limp body to the knife to the bloody towel on the counter. Vladimir removed my finger from his mouth and checked the bleeding. He spoke to Boris in Russian, licked the fresh stream of blood that had tried to escape down my hand, and sat me down in the chair.

From experience, I knew when they spoke in their native tongue, it was because they didn't want me to understand. Boris got a first aid kit out of a drawer and set it down in front of Vladimir. I gasped when he pulled out a suture needle and thread.

"It's not that bad. I don't need stitches." I hopped to my feet.

"Hold her still." He held a towel under my hand and doused my wound with vodka.

I winced from the sting of the alcohol. Boris sat me back down. With steady hands, Vladimir pierced my finger with the needle and threaded the black plastic through my skin until the wound was stitched closed. It was over in a flash. I'd barely felt it.

"Thanks, babe. That wasn't bad at all." I reverted to damage-control mode.

"You doubted me?" he hissed. His eyes were distant and

cold, angry and murderous. The man I loved—the man who claimed to love me—had left me to the mercy of the *pakhan*.

I shook my head, slid off the chair, and got back to work on the *zakuski* while the Russians engaged in a heated conversation—an argument, judging by the volume. Boris held out his hands and spoke calmly to diffuse the situation.

In my gut, I knew what the argument was about. Boris was trying to talk my fiancé out of killing me. *Would Boris let him do it? Would he help?* By the looks of things, Vladimir had pulled rank, and Boris had no choice but to stand down. My only hope lost the argument, put on his hat and coat, and walked out.

I was alone with my killer.

53

TOSSED

To survive, I had to steal Vladimir away from the *pakhan*. Keeping up the pretense that everything was cool, I peeled an avocado, smashed it in a bowl, added cayenne pepper, and went to the pantry to get some tortilla chips. When I turned back around, he had vanished. I felt nauseous, but I carried on like everything was okay. Vladimir loved me, and I would go to war with the *pakhan* to bring him back.

I transferred the snacks to a tray and made a pitcher of ice water with lemon and lime wedges. I believed Boris would stop the boss if he tried to hurt me again. He probably didn't go far. I changed into sexy lingerie, slid on jeans and low heels, zipped up a jacket, and carried the tray and pitcher outside.

The *pakhan* sat beside the fire, bouncing a tennis ball for the poodles.

"Here you go, babe. Sorry it took so long." I picked up a chip, dipped it in guacamole, and lifted it to his mouth. "I made it spicy this time."

He took a bite, chewed, and swallowed. "I like it better the old way."

"Want me to make it over?"

He dismissed me with a wave of his hand.

Gustav trotted back with the ball and nudged me.

"Thank you, precious." I retrieved the wet ball from his mouth. "Mama loves you, Goosey." I kissed his long snout and patted his head.

"You are a lucky guy, my friend," he said to the dog. "You give my love a filthy tennis ball, she treats you like a king. I give her the world, and I get disrespect."

I glanced inside to see if Boris had returned. *Nyet.* I went back to the kitchen under the guise of getting dinner started and hustled to get my special phone. Our messed-up relationship had reached its tipping point. The *pakhan* was waiting for the right moment to kill me. I could see it in his crazy eyes.

Inside, I turned on the stove, slid an iron skillet over the flame, added olive oil, and plopped the bloody meat in the pan. While the steak cooked, I slid over to the drawer where Vladimir kept the car keys and his gun and peeked inside. The keys were there. The gun was not.

I shuffled back to the stove and flipped over the meat. The pink flesh sizzled in the iron skillet, and droplets of hot grease spat on my hand. Out back, Playboy was smoking a cigarette, stalking me from the basketball court. I retrieved my phone and tapped Boris's number, then the door swung open behind me.

"Making something good?" the *pakhan* asked.

I casually slid my phone back into my pocket. "Of course, babe."

He hugged me from behind and kissed my neck. His gun

was tucked in his pants and poked me in the back. "I like it pink and bloody."

I slid the rare steak onto a plate. He lifted a fork from the utensil drawer and pulled a long chef's knife from the wooden butcher's block. Blood oozed from the meat when he cut into it. He glared at me as he put it in his mouth.

"You like it?" I asked.

He chewed and swallowed, set down the utensils, and leaned in for a smooch. "Love it." I tasted raw meat on his breath. "Who were you calling?" He lifted my phone from my pocket and scanned my calls.

"Um—"

He wrapped his hand around my throat and shoved me against the wall. "Every time I turn my back, you sneak off to call my right-hand man. If I were the *jealous* type, I might think the two of you have something going on." He slammed my special phone against the wall.

I sucked in a deep breath. "Please stop. I'm so sorry about yesterday. I don't know how to make it right." *He loves you, he loves you, he loves you...*"I did a stupid thing. It won't happen again." My knees buckled.

He let go of my neck and held me up by my arms.

My gaze drifted to the knife resting on the plate behind him.

He turned to see what had caught my attention. "Do it." He released me and stepped back.

I caught my balance against the counter. It was him or me. One of us would leave in a body bag. When I didn't have the guts to go for it, he slapped the handle of the knife into my palm and held out his arms to give me a clean shot. "*Davai*!"

For a moment, I considered it. "Don't be ridiculous." I

kissed his stone face and set the knife down. "I love you, Vladimir." I prayed Boris would come back to rescue me.

He laughed, put his arm around my shoulder, and pushed me back outside. I turned on my Fiesta playlist to lighten the mood and to remind him of our time together in Florida. I needed to make a comeback before the buzzer sounded. I swayed to the sound of Latin music and sang along quietly *en español* while the *pakhan* gathered up a couple of empty vodka bottles, some Coke cans, and a wine bottle. He lined them up on the wall at the edge of the patio.

What was he up to? When he turned around, I unzipped my jacket to distract him with my sexy, baby doll teddy. He pulled my body into his. I knew I could win Vladimir back. I wrapped my arms around his waist. My elbow knocked into his gun. I jumped.

He clicked his tongue. "As my wife, you must get used to having these around." He slipped the blue steel pistol out of his pants. "They're part of the family, like you."

"Please, put it away. I'll get used to it when I get to Russia."

"I want you to learn now." He placed his left hand on top of the gun and pulled back, causing the gun to make a *click-click* sound. Then, with one arm around my waist, he aimed his weapon at the makeshift firing range he'd set up on the railing.

"Cover your ears." I did. He fired his weapon and shattered a vodka bottle into a million shiny pieces. He moved down the row and sent the wine bottle and cans into oblivion, too. As he fired, spent bullet casings popped up and then danced on the floor. He hit every mark with precision and didn't stop until he ran out of targets—six shots to be exact.

I lowered my hands from my ears. "Wow. You're a good

shot." Expelling bullets was a good thing under the circumstances, but the *pakhan* was lethal enough without a loaded gun in his hand. "How many bullets does it hold?"

He clicked on the safety. "Seven. It's more challenging to fire at *moving* targets."

One bullet remained in the chamber.

"Hmm, what shall we shoot next?"

Gustav trotted up to us with a tennis ball in his mouth and dropped it at our feet. Anastasia was curled up on the rug by the door, nervous about the noisy gunfire. "Good boy." He picked up the tennis ball and bounced it. Gustav tried to snatch it, but the boss intercepted.

He spoke to the dog in Russian, and Gustav sat up straight and obedient, eager to please his papa. "Your *precious* boy wants to play a game, Mama."

"Vladimir, please—"

"I'm going to bounce the ball like this." He pounded the ball on the concrete, and it bounced about eight feet. When it came down, Gustav leapt into the air and caught it. He took the ball back and patted his back. "*Khoroshaya sobaka.*"

He lifted his gun and unlocked the safety. "This time, we're both going to go for the ball. The winner gets a kiss from Mama."

I clutched his forearm and tried to lower his hand, but I wasn't strong enough. "Please, don't."

"*Odin.*" He bounced the ball once. "*Dva.*" He bounced it again. "*Tri.*" He bounced it harder the third time, and the height of the ball peaked a couple of feet over his head.

I had two choices: Crash into him to try to knock him off balance, which could backfire and get Goosey killed, or do nothing and hope he was only trying to scare me. I crouched down, covered my ears, and prayed Sophia would wrap her wings around Goosey to protect him from the monster who claimed to love him.

Gustav jumped up to catch the ball.

The *pakhan* took aim.

Bang!

He fired and hit his target—the ball.

I covered my mouth and nose to mask my scream and the insidious odor of burnt rubber.

Gustav learned his lesson and trotted off to find solace next to his more intelligent half, Anastasia.

"I win." The boss set his gun on the table and moved into my personal space to collect his prize. When his lips touched mine, I opened my mouth and let him in—not out of love or passion, but fear.

His lips trailed down my neck, and I swayed to the music to calm him and to extinguish the unsettling rush of bad boy adrenaline emanating from his body.

He held me tight and synced the rhythm of his body with mine. "You like to *dance*?" He emphasized the word *dance* like it was bile on his tongue.

"Only with you, babe." My legs began to shake. I needed to buy some time. I unbuttoned his shirt and slid it off. "Let's soak in the hot tub." I pecked his devil tat on the cheek.

He swept my hair over my shoulder and fingered the lacey straps of my negligee. "Is this how you will attract a lover while I am away?"

I took a step back. "Vladimir, please—"

The *pakhan* backhanded me across the face. The force of the blow knocked me down. I fought to stay on my feet, but my body crumbled. I skid across the concrete and shredded the skin off my elbow. My right eye throbbed where his ring landed. I lifted my hands to protect myself from another blow.

What am I supposed to do?

Act as if nothing happened?

Apologize?

Make a run for it?

He turned around and downed another shot. It was then I understood why he'd kept his tats covered. Immortalized on his back was an inked portrait of my sister's head. A blue-eyed devil held her by the hair, and blood dripped from her neck like flames.

He killed her. He killed Sophia.

It had to mean that. What else *could* it mean? I clambered back to my feet and checked around for something to club the bastard over the head with. Before I had a chance, Playboy padded up the back stairs. The *pakhan* glared at me as he spoke to his *patsani*. Playboy flashed me a menacing grin.

The boss held his hand out for me to come to him. Reluctantly, I did. What choice did I have? He lifted my hands and looked into my eyes as if it were our last goodbye. "I hope you learn your lesson, angel." He removed my engagement ring, kissed my battered cheek, went inside, and locked the door.

The *pakhan* had fed me to his wolf pack.

There were two doors that led inside—the one he locked opened to the living room, and the other went into the kitchen. Behind me, there was a set of stairs that led down to the tennis court. If I could make it to the kitchen, I could get the keys and charge the gate in the G-Wagon, but the odds of making it past Playboy to get inside were nil.

Plan B: I stepped backward as Playboy closed in.

I had to make a run for it through the woods. I was in way better shape than that chain-smoking bastard. If I got a head start, I could make it down the stairs, but I had next to nothing on—jeans over my lingerie. Even if I could outrun him, I would have to plow through the snow in my bare feet, scale the barbed wire fence, and somehow find my way to the main road before I succumbed to the elements. It was a terrible plan—but it was the only one I had.

Playboy removed his jacket and offered it to me.

I kicked off my heels.

A sadistic smile crept up on his face when he realized I wasn't going down without a fight. I took off in a sprint and made it to the bottom of the stairs, but when my feet sank into the snow, Playboy pounced on my back and tackled me face down in a hard, ice-covered snowdrift.

The impact knocked the wind out of me. He straddled me and secured my wrists behind my back with cable ties. I struggled to catch my breath, but my lungs would not inflate. I needed air—*breathe, breathe, breathe...*

54

OBSESSION

I woke up sprawled on a filthy blanket in the back of the murderer van. I figured that's what they would bury me in. I wondered if seeing how they would dispose of my body was part of my lesson. I tried to sit up, but Playboy shoved me back down with his foot.

Skinhead drove. Grimace rode shotgun. Playboy taunted me in Russian, probably explaining how the three of them were going to gang rape me before they strangled me, shot me in the face, or went at me old school and beat me to death.

Where was Boris in all this? I had the feeling he'd wanted to "teach me a lesson" a dozen times at least, but once Vladimir and I were engaged, I'd thought…

Shit. Vladimir was right. I am naïve. Boris didn't give a damn about me either.

Playboy lit a smoke and flicked the lighter at me, over and over. I prayed it would be quick. If Boris had been in charge of cleaning up the *pakhan's* mess, he would've popped me like it was another day at work, hacked me to pieces, dumped my remains in the Ohio River, gone home, and toasted "the little *shlyukha* deserved it" to the boss.

My heart raced when the van stopped, and Grimace opened the back door. We were parked in front of an XXX strip club. The *pakhan* was done with me for good. Instead of killing me right away, he was going to teach me a lesson by forcing me to be one of The Girls.

No way.

I would rather die.

Screw him.

The plan: as soon as my feet hit the ground, I'd run for the highway. Before I could take one step toward freedom, Playboy clamped down on my arm, cut the ties from my wrists, draped his coat around me, and escorted me inside. He licked my swollen cheek where the *pakhan* had backhanded me, then said something in Russian that made the other two goons laugh.

When the door opened, the stench of stale beer, cheap hairspray, and unscrupulous dirtballs hit me in the face. Inside, two topless girls were pole dancing on a stage in the middle of the bar. The music was loud, the girls were around my age, and the men stuffing cash in their panties turned to get a gander of the fresh meat ushered in by the Russian brigade.

Mr. Cusimano was there. He glanced my way, showing no signs of guilt or remorse, and went back to watching the show. *Did he realize what was happening?*

Playboy sat me on a stool and checked out my lingerie peeking out from under his coat. He unzipped me, whistled, and laughed with his comrades as he pointed to the stage.

I wouldn't let those losers yank my chain. I zipped it back up, crossed my arms over my chest, and sat unaffected by their stupidity. Playboy dismissed the other two with a flick of his wrist, and they settled in a few seats down to watch the show. Playboy flagged the bartender and held up two fingers.

"I'd like a Sierra Mist, please."

The bartender ignored me and set down two heavy pours of vodka.

No way. I could not handle alcohol. I hadn't had a bite to eat all day. My nerves and hormones were so out of sync that I felt like I might spontaneously combust. Playboy picked up one of the glasses and offered it to me. I didn't take it. That amount of alcohol, basically a double, would seriously compromise my ability to think clearly or defend myself.

If they tried to make me dance on that stage in an effort to put me to *work*, I wouldn't do it. Damn the consequences. Playboy stood, hooked his hand around my elbow, and whispered something creepy in my ear. Despite the language barrier, I knew a threat when I heard it. I reached for the drink before he could set it down.

"*Spasibo.*" I lifted it to my lips and took a sip. I lowered the glass, but he put his hand underneath it and guided it back to my mouth. I took a deep breath and downed it like a Russian.

Playboy pointed at one of the topless girls and offered his hand to lead me to the stage. Ironically, one of the songs from my House Party playlist was pumping as the strippers worked the pole. I shook my head. His smile faded. He downed his vodka and motioned to the bartender to refill our drinks. He held out his hand again, urging me toward the stage.

"*Nyet.*" I watched the bartender top off my glass with another long pour of vodka.

Playboy scooted the drink in front of me. Before the

alcohol completely consumed my clarity, I had to come up with a game plan. The Russians were leaving in the morning. I would walk away from this nightmare unscathed, or I'd be a corpse before the night was over. My life depended on outsmarting those dimwitted goons.

Play the game, play the game, play the game...

I wrapped my fingers around the shot glass, lifted my drink, and grinned at Playboy. He lifted his glass and smiled back. We clinked, cheered, and downed our shots. The boys laughed when I set down my glass and almost fell off my stool. I had to work quickly before the alcohol knocked me unconscious.

I needed to up my odds. I slapped the bar to get the bartender's attention. I held up two fingers over our shot glasses and then pointed two fingers at Grimace and Skinhead. They whistled and clapped their hands. As the guy poured our drinks, I leaned over to Playboy and placed my hands on top of his thighs. He liked wherever I was going with that idea. I patted around until I felt his phone in the front pocket of his jeans. I tapped it. "Boris."

His smile faded. "*Nyet.*"

I shook my shoulders to the beat of the song. "*Da.*" I pointed to the stage. "Boris."

The bartender set out our drinks. Grimace lurked over my shoulder, leaned forward, and sniffed my hair. I must have had a freaky expression on my face, because Playboy cracked up.

Win the game. I swiveled around in my chair and met my admirer's shallow eyes. I pointed to myself, then to the stage. "*Da*?"

He nodded.

I held an imaginary phone to my ear. "Boris."

As Grimace thought it over, Playboy jabbed him in the

ribs. Skinhead glared at me like he would rather gut me than watch me dance. I committed to my game plan. I put the imaginary phone to my ear again. "Boris." I pointed to myself and then to the stage. I opened my coat and rocked my shoulders to the beat to give him a sample of the goods. "*Da*?"

He stared at my chest and pulled out his phone. The other two yowled at him, prompting him to lumber outside. Playboy yanked my hair and swiveled my chair around to face him. He pointed in my face and barked. I only needed one of them to call Boris. From that point on, I had to burn some time off the clock and pray my keeper would come.

Playboy unzipped my jacket, and Skinhead yanked it off, leaving me in a strip club in lingerie I'd worn to turn on my lethal fiancé—the one who'd ordered his thugs to teach me a lesson. Playboy offered his hand to walk me up to the stage.

From a common-sense perspective, I should've done it. My goal was to buy time, and I was sure I could work the pole well enough to keep their interest until my keeper got there—but screw them! My vodka cup runneth over. I'd had my fill of Russian gangsters and their *Bratva* Code of Bullshit. "*Nyet*."

Playboy yanked me off the stool and dragged me down a dark hallway. I called out to Mr. Cusimano for help. He turned and looked right at me, but instead of coming to my rescue, he stuffed a bill into a bony brunette's G-string.

Skinhead snatched the vodka bottle and followed close behind. I had trouble keeping up on wobbly legs in pumps. I stumbled a few times, which prompted Skinhead to grab my other arm. I glanced behind and saw Grimace closing in.

They shoved me into a small room with a brass pole, a few chairs, and a red spotlight. Instead of the pop songs that blared in the bar area, the music in there was a dirty, bump-and-grind kind of instrumental beat. The only lyrics were moans and sex sounds coming from the next room.

Playboy shoved me toward the pole and yelled. When I didn't respond, he shook me violently, reprimanding me for not following orders. I tried to fight back, but I was so disoriented I didn't have the strength or courage to defend myself.

Tired of my resistance, he shoved me back into Skinhead's arms. He squeezed my waist and dragged me down to his lap. He said something creepy in my ear, and I felt a cool blade press against my throat. I screamed. He covered my mouth. Playboy held a fistful of my hair while Skinhead cut it off right next to my scalp—a memento for the *pakhan*, no doubt. He didn't give a damn about me; I was his obsession. Our love was nothing more than a game to him, and he'd won the moment I agreed to marry him.

That was when I lost faith. I'd been swinging so long I'd run out of courage—and hope. It was time to let go. I would spend the last moments of my life enduring beatings and spread apart while those filthy animals oozed between my legs.

As I lay in Skinhead's arms, in shock, Grimace pushed a bottle past my lips. I drank willingly. I would rather die of alcohol poisoning than at the tip of a knife. I tuned out their catcalls and whistles and tried to drain every drop of vodka from that bottle.

Grimace yanked it away before I could drink too much and stole me away from Skinhead. I coughed from the burn of the vodka, and he dragged me to the pole and motioned for me to get to it. When I didn't do what I was told, Playboy saddled up behind me, held my hands against the pole from behind, and grinded against my body as he howled a victory song.

When I refused to give them what they wanted, he barked a final warning in my ear. Frustrated by my rejection, he flung my hair aside and sank his teeth into the back of my neck. I screamed and wrestled to get free, but he jammed me against the pole. Paralyzed by the pain, I couldn't fight back. The final chapter of my life was about to unfold.

I'm sorry, Sophia, Dad, Kiki, Megan, God.

Playboy spun me around. My body dangled from his arms like a limp noodle. As I prepared for my final breath, a big hand lifted my chin.

"Have you learned your lesson yet, *lapsha*?"

55

GHOSTS

Boris got a motel room like the one we'd checked into the last time I needed an emergency clean-up. Being with him seemed the better of the two options, although I had no clue what the boss had ordered *him* to do to me.

He wrapped me up in his big black coat, guided me inside, and sat me on the edge of the bed. I blinked to reorient myself as he turned my head to assess the damage the *pakhan* had inflicted. I fought to stay strong in the spirit of fixing things: no crying, no whimpering, no whining. If Boris thought I'd go home and cry to my papa, I'd be in the ground before dawn.

I was rounding third and heading home. If I could get over this last hurdle, I would be okay. The boss was done with me. They were leaving in the morning. I would be free.

"It's nothing," I said.

"What happened?"

"Um, I hit myself with my racket defending a shot." I demonstrated the swinging motion.

"Looks like someone hit you." He lined the back of his

hand against my cheek. "Finger marks." He slid off his coat I was wearing and examined me to see what else had been done. He pushed my hair over my shoulder so he could see the bite mark on the back of my neck.

"Just that," I said.

He ran his fingers over my ribs.

I winced. "And maybe a couple cracked ribs—nothing else."

He picked up my arm to get a look at my skinned elbow.

"I just need some bandages."

"Did they touch you?"

I knew what he meant. I shook my head.

He studied my expression. "Good. Very good." He lowered his hand to his belt, unbuckled it, and slid it off. "Hold out your hands."

I curled my knees up, buried my face in my lap, and did as he said. He tightened the leather strap around my wrists, pushed me back on the bed, and looped it around the headboard. I kept my eyes closed as the reality set in that Boris would be my first, last, and only.

He stuffed a gag in my mouth and tied it tight behind my head. Then he tucked a pillow under my head and covered me with the tattered bedspread. I begged him to let me go, but the gag muffled my pleas.

"*Shush.* I have to go out and get you clothes and something to eat. You don't want the boys to come back to babysit, do you?"

I shook my head.

"I'm waiting for my orders." He blotted my face with the sheet. "I have to do my job, understand?" He leaned over and kissed me on the forehead. "Try to rest."

When the door closed behind him, I called out to the universe for Sophia. I wanted her with me at the end so we could be together. Not so she could lead me to the Pearly Gates. I had no interest in cloud-hopping or harp-strumming. I wanted revenge.

I told her my plan to ditch the tunnel to the other side so I could stay on earth as a ghost, follow my killers to Russia, and haunt them for the rest of their evil lives. I wouldn't rest in peace until I found a way to scrape that tattoo of Sophia off that monster's skin—preferably with my teeth—if such goals were attainable for pissed-off little ghosts.

After I worked out my plan for the afterlife with Sophia, I lost consciousness. I woke in a fog when Boris shook me back to life. When I came to, I spotted a large serrated knife with a shiny blade lying on the nightstand. Under the yellow light of the lamp, I could see crude notches engraved in the handle. The knife had kept track of how many victims it had killed, too.

I turned my head and focused on a still life of a flower vase in a picture frame on the wall. I didn't want my murderer's face or his weapon to be the last memory etched in my mind for eternity.

"Look at me." Boris tilted my head to meet his eyes.

I turned my focus back to the knife. Boris followed my gaze and picked it up.

"I'm going to cut off the gag. Hold still." He sliced the fabric, pulled it from my mouth, freed my wrists, and brought me upright.

I sat there, stunned, not trusting his nonchalant tone, but also perplexed as to why he was removing my restraints.

Has the boss forgiven me?

"How much did you drink?"

"A couple shots. I'm fine."

He checked my arms and legs for needle marks.

"I'm clean."

He led me into the bathroom, lowered the toilet lid, and sat me down. He pushed my hair aside and cleaned the bite on the back of my neck. He rubbed an alcohol swab over it. It stung, but I didn't flinch. He smoothed some cream on it and then covered it up with a bandage. Next, he wrapped athletic tape around my ribs, then wet a washcloth and wiped my face and cleaned up my elbow.

After he patted me dry, he pulled a small vial from his pocket, popped the top, and dabbed oil on his thumb. He spoke in Russian and smeared it on my forehead and each wrist. It smelled like essential oils. A blessing, I figured. He helped me get dressed, led me back into the room, and sat me at the small table. He cracked open a Coke, set out a container of white rice with a fork stuck in it, and unwrapped a sleeve of crackers.

I chugged the soda and noticed Boris had set his black notebook and phone on the table. How could he work at a time like this? As I drank, he tapped his finger on the phone, waiting for his orders. My body began to shake. I scooped up a bite of rice and lifted it to my mouth. Half of it made it. The rest tumbled down my shirt.

"Want me to help you eat?"

I shook my head and tried again with similar results. I gave up and nibbled on a cracker. "Which one of you killed my sister?"

Boris's expression turned murderous.

"Don't deny it. I saw the tattoo of her inked on Vladimir's back. That's how you brag about your crimes, right? I know that knife on your neck means you're a hitman. Does one of those links on your arm represent my sister?" I pointed to his blue snake tat.

"Your sister's death was a tragic accident."

"Bullshit."

"Not bullshit. Vladimir was in Siberia when your sister died. I never told him about the accident until after he was released. The news would've killed him."

That was what Vladimir had told me, too. Maybe it was true. "So you did it?"

"Think, *lapsha*. Why would I? Why would anyone in the *Bratva* hurt her? Vladimir is like a son to me. The accident was just an accident. She lost control of her car and crashed. Not my fault. Not Vladimir's fault. Not *your* fault either."

Tears dripped down my cheeks. "I don't believe you. I saw the tattoo. Her face, the flames, a blue devil—"

"Guilt, my dear. Vladimir feels responsible because if he hadn't gone to prison, they would've stayed together in New York. No wreck in Cincinnati."

I would never know if he was telling me the truth, but his facts did validate Vladimir's alibi, hence she didn't die by his hand. "When is he going to call?"

Tap, tap, tap, tap...

"What time is it?" I asked. When he ignored me, my gaze darted to the alarm clock by the bed. It was almost midnight. I looked down at my wrist, and at the shiny oil mark Boris had rubbed on me. It looked like an X. No. It was a cross.

Oh, God. Holy oil. Last rites.

I knew then he'd already made up his mind. It was two hours past my curfew. I wasn't going home. "How are you going to do it?"

Tap, tap, tap, tap...

"Are you going to make it hurt to get back at me for all the times—"

A loud boom hit the door. "Freeze!" Two officers stormed the room with guns drawn aimed at Boris. "Put your hands up."

I leapt out of my seat, hands high, totally confused by the uniformed man with his gun pointed at Boris and the bushy-haired officer next to him—

"Officer Montgomery?"

"Are you all right, Carter?" Officer Montgomery asked, her entire focus on Boris, her gun pointed at his chest.

Oh, God. I'm safe.

But Boris wasn't. If I squealed, the *pakhan* would have my whole family whacked. This was my chance to do the right thing for once.

"Don't shoot! He's the one who saved me."

56

DEAD SILENCE

With my hands up, I skittered around the table, sat on Boris's knee, and curled my arms around his neck like a human shield. Officer Montgomery's partner kept his gun aimed at Boris as she peeled me off his lap and sat me on the bed. "Are you hurt?"

I shook my head. "How did you find me?"

"Your dad called the station when you didn't come home. He was adamant that something was wrong. You never miss your curfew," she said. "After we talked about your *grandpa*, I put an APB out on the Cadillac." She stood up and put her hand on her gun, still tucked in the holster. "Trouble seems to follow you, Carter." She nodded at Boris.

"Please put down your gun," I said to the male officer. "I called him for help after I fought him off."

"Fought who?" Officer Montgomery asked. She stood Boris up, frisked him, and pulled his gun from its hiding place. "Why am I not surprised to find this?" She slapped handcuffs on him and read him his Miranda rights while the other officer kept his gun on Boris. I waited for the big guy to make a move.

"You're safe. You don't have to lie anymore," Officer Montgomery said.

"I'm not lying. I was with my sicko ex-boyfriend. I agreed to meet him so we could talk about getting back together." I sucked in a deep breath to buy some time while I constructed a story. "We had a few drinks, and he started talking smack about how much he missed me." I dropped my gaze to the floor. "We made out, then he put his hands all over me. I wanted to leave, but he wouldn't let me go. We got into an argument, and then—" I glanced over at Boris.

"Look at *me*," Officer Montgomery said. "Then what happened?"

My lips quivered. I lifted my hand and touched the throbbing finger marks on my cheek.

"Did he assault you?" she asked.

"He tried, but I fought him off. When he left, he took my clothes and told me not to leave. I didn't know what to do. I was naked, drunk, and stranded in this shitty place. I was afraid my dad would be angry—he told me never to see him again—so I called Boris."

The cops eyed each other.

I grabbed the shopping bag and snatched the receipt. "He bought me clothes and food and medical supplies—"

"Where else are you hurt?" the male officer asked.

I rolled up my sleeve and showed him my elbow. The officer pulled back the bandages and winced.

"Rug burn. I skidded across the carpet after he hit me."

Boris's phone vibrated on the table.

"Why didn't you call the police, sir?" the guy asked.

Boris threatened the officer with his villainous stare.

"I begged him not to until I could pull myself together before I called my dad. Please, can I answer *my* phone? It's

Dad. He must be worried sick." I snatched up Boris's phone and tapped the screen, but before I could speak, a voice spoke in Russian—the *pakhan*. I locked myself in the bathroom and waited for him to finish his order.

"Ouch. That sounds painful."

I waited for him to speak. He didn't.

"Miss, come out of the bathroom," the officer ordered.

"I'll be right out." I turned on the faucet to drown out my voice. "I've got bad news, boss. Your *patsani* are a bunch of fuck-ups."

The cop banged on the bathroom door. "Come out *now*."

"Boris is in handcuffs as we speak. Only I can save him. My family and friends stay safe, and in return, I leave you and Boris out of this mess. Agreed?"

Nothing.

"I need an answer. You let me go, and I let you off the hook, deal?"

Dead silence.

I REFUSED to get into the ambulance, so I rode up front in the patrol car with Officer Montgomery. Boris was in the back of the cruiser, cuffed. I had the sense to claim his black notebook—filled with illegal gambling notes—as my diary, so the cops couldn't confiscate it. I needed every weapon I could use against the Russians.

By the time we got to the police station, my dad was already there—with Vladimir. Not only did I have the *pakhan* to deal with, but I also had to face the Wrath of Dad, too.

I got out of the car and prepared for Dad to deliver the

first round of punishment. I decided to swing first. "Dad, I'm sorry I—"

"Oh, sweetie." Dad's eyes welled up when he saw the slap mark across my face. He wrapped his arms around me. "That bastard you were dating behind my back did this? You're going to the hospital. End of discussion."

I stepped back from Dad before I screeched from having a set of cracked ribs. "I'm fine, really. It's not that bad."

I had no way of knowing what the boss intended to do. "Thanks for coming, Mr. Ivanov. I'm glad I got to see you before you left." On shaky legs, I walked up to him and gave him a hug to find out if he was packing heat.

Da.

"We have a deal, right?" I whispered.

He kissed my forehead. "I wish we were meeting under more favorable circumstances, Miss Cook." His eyes were bloodshot, lips cold.

Dad shook his head, confused, and set his sights on Boris, still in the back of the cruiser. "Why did you call him instead of me?"

As I was about to spin my tale, the chief came out to the parking lot and let Boris out of the car. With trembling hands, the chief unlocked his cuffs. "This man is a hero. Treat him with respect," the chief warned his officer.

Vladimir had already sunk his hooks into the chief, but Officer Montgomery was wise to this messed-up truckload of bullshit. She shook her head, taken off guard by the whitewashed attitude of her superior. "Hold on, Chief." She turned to Dad. "Mr. Cook, do you have any knowledge of this *alleged* ex-boyfriend?"

All eyes zeroed in on Dad.

He pulled me away from the *pakhan* and put his arm

around me. "She broke up with him before Christmas. That asshole tried to pressure her to sleep with him, but—" Dad choked up.

"See? There you go," the chief said, eager to end the interrogation.

Officer Montgomery held her hand up. "One more question." She turned to Dad. "Mr. Cook, you believe your daughter would call *him* in a crisis instead of you?" She pointed to Boris, scowling like she'd gotten a whiff of dumpster trash.

Dad wrapped his arms around me in a full bear hug. He nodded against my shoulder. "I've been a terrible father lately. I'm sorry I've been so hard on you, pumpkin."

"No, Dad. Don't blame yourself. This is all my fault."

Dad pulled back, his eyes wide with astonishment. "Don't say that, Carter. How could you possibly believe—" He swallowed hard. "That asshole made you feel like getting smacked across the face was *your* fault? No matter what his excuse was, no matter what he said you did, no one has the right to hurt you. You didn't ask for it, you didn't deserve it, and *love* doesn't make a man hit a woman."

I glanced up at the *pakhan* and met his bloodshot eyes.

"Your daughter has been through enough tonight, Mr. Cook." The chief shifted his gaze between the Russians. "Take her home now."

Officer Montgomery opened her mouth to argue, but changed her mind after a scowl from her superior. "First, I'll need statements." She pointed her pen at Boris and me.

"Wait. Doesn't she need to go to the hospital for an examination?" Dad asked. "She's terrified. How do we know he didn't...*assault* her?"

Boris fired a warning over my dad's shoulder. A trip to

the hospital for an examination meant my history of abuse would be abundantly clear. I understood this had to be a one-time occurrence. I couldn't afford to punch holes in my story.

"I'm not going to the hospital." I took Boris's hand and led him toward the door. "Let's give our statements and go home."

Dad stood his ground. "Carter, you need to be seen by a doctor. End of discussion."

I turned, dropped Boris's hand, and laid into my father. No more silence. "Even if you drag me to the hospital, I won't consent to an exam."

Dad stared at me like I was a lunatic. "You're hurt, sweetie." He caressed my cheek. "They said he took your clothes and—" Dad couldn't finish his sentence.

"I already told the cops he didn't rape me. Now do you see why I called Boris when I needed help instead of you? After all I've been through this evening, you still treat me like *I'm* the criminal."

I'd officially shattered my father's heart. Eager to close the books, I tugged on Boris's arm and led him inside the station. Once I gave a statement and details of my pretend boyfriend, I hustled back to Dad to get the hell away from the Russians.

Before we left, I gave Boris a stomach-churning farewell hug. I slipped his phone and evidence-ridden black notebook into his hand and whispered, "We're even." Then, for everyone's ears, I said, "Have a safe trip."

Boris distracted my dad, filling him in on the bogus statement I'd given the cops, and I stepped up to the *pakhan* for our final goodbye.

He reached out to caress my battered face.

I blocked him. "Don't ever touch me again."

He held up his hands, mocking my defiance. Then he lifted a length of my stolen hair out of his pocket and wrapped it around his fist.

My heart raced, chest heaved.

He kissed my locks. “Until we meet again, angel.”

57

THE V CARD

Ten weeks later...

The last of the dirty gray snow had melted in front of our apartment, making room for the pink tulips to break free from their winter hiding place. Spring had arrived, and in one week I would be headed to Punta Cana with Kiki and a group of friends to bask in the sun, splash in the waves, and breathe in the salty, tropical air.

The trip was an early birthday present from Dad and Karen, and the perfect motivator to ditch my demons and stop living like a prisoner. Since the incident, I had moved out with Kiki on schedule and started my spring semester as planned. Dad was against the idea, but when I flashed the "I will not let one bad experience define me" card, he gave me his blessing.

On the outside, I was calm and confident. On the inside, I was a paranoid disaster. But every day I left my apartment and came back alive, I was stronger, braver, and more confident that I'd be okay.

The Russians were gone.

Vladimir was out of my life.

I had won.

On a perfectly sunny and unseasonably warm Saturday in mid-March, I felt brave enough to go for a run in the park off campus. It was stocked with moms and dads pushing strollers, skateboard kids, and dogs playing fetch with their families. I jogged past a group of guys playing a pickup game of soccer on the rec fields. One of the guys attempted a goal, but the defender blocked it. The ball bounced high and was headed straight for me.

"Watch out!" one of the players yelled.

I zeroed in on the ball, shuffled sideways to get underneath it, and popped back a header. The ball bounced back to the field, and the guys cheered.

"She's on my team," a cutie with sandy brown hair pulled into a messy man bun said.

I blushed and waved dismissively, embarrassed by my sporty nature.

The cutie jogged over to me. "Seriously, we need a fourth. You in?"

My experience with the Russians had taught me a valuable lesson: life is precious. Get over your bullshit.

"Okay," I said.

"Great. I'm Benji." He held out his hand. His wrist was loaded with braided nature-boy bracelets.

"Carter." We shook.

We played against his friends for an hour. Then he invited me to stay for a picnic lunch. In the weeks following my ordeal with the Russians, I'd been going through the motions: tennis, classes, work, study, repeat. I'd played it safe, not quite ready to jump back into my new Russian-free normal. Hanging out with someone new, reaching out, felt like life to me. Maybe I was finally coming back.

We joined the other two guys at a picnic table, and Benji

unpacked a stack of sandwiches, cold salads, chips, and natural cola.

"Turkey club or egg salad? Both organic," Benji said.

"Oh. I'm a vegetarian. I'll just have some chips."

"What kind of vegetarian? Vegan, ovo, lacto..."

"Lacto."

"I knew there was a reason I made my asiago and sun-dried tomato pasta salad." He opened a glass container, loaded up a plate, and handed it to me.

I took a bite of the pasta, chewed, and swallowed. "This is delicious. You made it?"

"One of my many talents." Benji smiled. "If you like that, you'll have to try my famous mushroom risotto." He peeked over at me and wiped his bangs out of his eyes. "If you want to hang out sometime, I'll make it for you."

I felt my cheeks flush.

Yes, yes, yes, Sophia said.

"Like, tonight?" Benji said. "My place is over there." He pointed to the apartments across the street. "We can swing by Whole Foods on the way back."

"Uh, tonight?" Paranoia set in. *Maybe he's trying to lure me to his house because the pakhan has come back, and he's there waiting for me. It'd be just like the Russians to use a hottie to trick me—wait. Is this the devil talking?*

"Or another time." Benji looked down, dejected.

His buddies chided him.

Sophia folded her wings across her body and hung her head in defeat.

Enough. This is my life. I'll make my own decisions. I vanquished the devil first. Mentally, I torched the forked-tongue bastard and watched him burn. Next, I let go of Sophia's angel voice of wisdom. She spread her silvery wings and ascended into the heavens, making room for my own thoughts and my own voice of reason that said: *Stop living in fear.*

Game plan change: "Tonight's good."

"Really?"

"But..."

"*But*?"

"Is it okay if we go out for coffee instead? Mushroom risotto is a big step for me."

LATER THAT AFTERNOON, I met Benji at a crowded indie coffeehouse around the corner from our apartment. We ordered our drinks and a big slice of vegan carrot cake with thick, creamy frosting to share. Two forks. Benji was a junior majoring in urban planning. He taught me about sky farming, and he sketched out a design on a napkin of a self-sustaining community he wanted to develop that could, ultimately, end world hunger.

He's passionate, ambitious—and hot.

Since we met, Benji came over to hang out after class. We had fun kicking around a soccer ball, making hemp bracelets out on the balcony of my apartment, and just being together.

On the eve of my trip to Punta Cana, Benji tied a special friendship bracelet around my wrist. "This is so you won't forget me."

"Aw, thanks. It's beautiful."

Benji shook his head. "Not the bracelet. This..." He lifted my chin and pressed his lips against mine. I melted when his beard scratched against my skin and his warm hand massaged the nape of my neck. I ran my fingers up his back and through his hair. His earthy scent of hot guy and patchouli lit my fire. I'd only known Benji for six days, but I invited him to spend the night. Kiki was staying with Toby, her lab partner she'd been lusting after for months, so we had the place to ourselves.

My bedroom was tiny, and I just had a twin bed. The idea of snuggling with Benji all night, crammed in that tiny space together, was exciting, but also nerve-wracking. I hadn't yet told him I was a virgin. I mean, we were in *college*. I didn't believe this gorgeous guy would stick around too long while I was still waving my V card.

But I was wrong.

When I broke the news, he honestly seemed impressed. And to put me at ease, he came up with a brilliant, less intimidating sleeping arrangement. We moved the living room furniture, tossed the cushions onto the floor, and made a fort out of sheets in front of the balcony. We kissed under the streetlights, touched, laughed, and did all the things lovers do—without going all the way.

This is what a healthy relationship feels like.

58

SPRING BREAK BOUND

It was dark when Kiki and I left for the airport. I felt a rush of paranoia when a black Cadillac got off the exit ramp behind us. I took a deep breath and talked myself out of a panic attack as Kiki parked the Mustang in the long-term parking lot. We rolled our suitcases over to a covered hut and waited for the airport shuttle to pick us up.

When the bus screeched to a halt, and the door opened, a big dude with a buzz cut and a guy as wide as a dumpster with a deep scar on his cheek came out to help us with our luggage. They were wearing gloves—at the end of March. Kiki thanked them, but neither of them said a word.

Oh, God. They looked like they'd just stepped off the prison yard. They had to be Russian. Why else wouldn't they talk to us? They didn't want us to detect their accents, and they were wearing gloves to hide their tats—or to avoid leaving fingerprints.

My hands began to shake.

"Are you all right?" Kiki asked. "What's wrong?"

I couldn't speak. I had to warn her. This was all my fault.

Kiki put her arm around me and rubbed my back, trying to rub out the crazy.

The buzz-cut guy eyed me like a drooling predator ready to eat me alive. "Sorry, miss. I know it's freezing in here. Crazy Cincinnati weather, huh?" No Russian accent. I was wrong. The guy held up his gloved hands to back his story. His innocent, Cincinnati-cold hands. "I hope it's warmer where you're going."

"Oh, yes. We're spring break bound. In a few hours, we'll be in our bikinis basking in the sun," Kiki replied.

I inhaled and let out a chuckle. I was a paranoid disaster, that was all. Clearly, I was so ready to say goodbye to Cincinnati and move on to paradise, where I could stop checking over my shoulder in search of the Russian boogeyman.

I glanced out the window and noticed the driver passed an old couple waiting in a hut for a ride. The bus was empty except for us. Buzz Cut grinned, as if he knew what I was thinking. The bus left the long-term parking area en route to the international terminal, a couple of miles away from where we'd parked.

As Kiki rambled about what outfits we should wear on our first night, the bus turned down a secluded side road and screeched to a stop. Buzz Cut got up, and the driver cruised over and stood next to him. Instead of facing the door, they towered over us.

"Is there a problem?" Kiki asked, looking out the window. "This isn't the airport."

Scar Face smiled at Kiki, then turned to me. "*Nyet.*"

I grabbed Kiki's arm and tried to shove her out the door. Scar Face intercepted and smothered Kiki with his big body. She kicked and screamed, and he dragged her to the back of the bus. I lunged forward to try to fight him off, but Buzz Cut tackled me in the aisle. I screamed for them to let Kiki go. Scar Face held a rag over her face. My dear friend stopped fighting and fell limp in his arms. "Don't hurt her. She doesn't know anything."

The goon injected a needle into her arm.

"No!"

While I was pinned on the ground, the door opened, and Boris climbed on board.

Oh, God.

Buzz Cut held my wrists behind my back and yanked me to my feet. I slumped forward. He wrapped his arms around my waist and forced me onto his lap. Boris sat next to me and twisted the cap off a bottle of vodka.

"Please let Kiki go. I'll do anything you say. Don't hurt her."

Buzz Cut covered my mouth with his gloved hand.

Boris lifted a small plastic bottle out of his pocket, tapped a couple of pills into his hand, then dropped them into the vodka. "Like old times." My assailant pushed down on my chin to spread my lips while Boris lifted the bottle to my mouth.

I shook my head, stomped down on the goon's foot, and tried to struggle out of his grasp. In retaliation, he squeezed his arms around my ribcage so tightly I felt like my body was being crushed inside a trash compactor.

"You never learn, do you, weasel?" Boris said something in Russian to Scar Face, and he responded by dropping my best friend to the ground. As she lay unconscious with her arms outstretched on the dirty floor, he drew his leg back, ready to kick her in the stomach.

"No!" I cried. "Boris, please."

Boris held up a hand to stop the guy. "Thirsty now?"

Live to fight another day. I drank.

"One more sip, dear."

"Why are you doing this? We're even." My vision blurred.

"You've caused some trouble for us back home."

"I never told a soul what happened." My words came out slurred.

"I know, dear. *Trouble* has come looking for you." He unfolded a sheet of paper. "The boss would like to cash in his wager now." He turned it around and showed me the picture I'd drawn—a winged heart with an arrow through it, the word *forever* scribbled across the center.

"Never make a bet you're not willing to lose."

I fought to stay conscious.

"And remember the bet you won? Use of the private jet, anywhere in the world. A Russian never goes back on a deal. Boss would like to fly you to his home for an extended vacation."

My head tipped to the side. The bottle went back between my lips. Vodka swished in my mouth.

"There's a war going on at home. Our rivals have put a bounty on *your* head to get to the boss. If they capture you, they'll force Vladimir to surrender—his life in exchange for yours. To protect the *pakhan*, I must protect *you*."

My body went limp.

"Living in our world is not so bad."

The goons bound my wrists and ankles.

"Our family is anxious to meet you."

The last thing I remembered was Boris's taunting words.

"Forever is a long time, *lapsha*."

A blindfold covered my eyes.

And then...*nothing.*

THE STORY CONTINUES IN RUSSIAN TATTOOS: PRISONER

I woke up with a silky blindfold wrapped around my head, a throbbing headache, and a sickening feeling in my gut. I tried to get out of bed, but my wrists were bound at my side.

Oh, God. The Russians.

Get your copy of Russian Tattoos: Prisoner on Amazon

PREVIEW OF RUSSIAN TATTOOS: PRISONER

Twisted

I woke up with a silky blindfold wrapped around my head, a throbbing headache, and a sickening feeling in my gut. I tried to get out of bed, but my wrists were bound at my side.

Oh, God. The Russians.

I stretched in my restraints to assess my situation. My legs were free, no gag. A feather pillow was tucked under my head, and a soft blanket that smelled new, like it had been unwrapped from plastic, covered my body.

I held my breath and listened for signs of life. "Kiki?" I whispered. Nothing.

My muscles felt shredded, as if a pack of wolves had each taken a limb and pulled me in four different directions, and with every breath a sharp pain needled in my side. No serious injuries or broken bones as far as I could tell. Then a new fear took over me. I scooted back and forth to determine if I still had on clothes. My feet were bare and my jeans off, but the lacy fabric of my underwear rubbed against my skin, my underwire bra poked my ribcage, and I felt like I had on a t-shirt or a dress covering my body. Having clothes on had to be a good sign.

The drugs had knocked me out cold, but I didn't feel like I'd been assaulted. My ex-fiancé was behind our abduction. Knowing Vladimir, he wouldn't take my virginity while I was unconscious. He was the *pakhan*, the boss, of their mafia family, and his ego would demand I remember every moment of our first time together.

"Kiki?" I whispered louder to wake her up.

I tried to piece together a timeline of how long I'd been out. The last place I remembered being was at the airport in Cincinnati, ready for a wild spring break trip to Punta Cana. Then two thugs grabbed us on the shuttle bus. One of them injected a needle into Kiki's arm. Vladimir's henchman Boris made me drink spiked vodka—then nothing. While we were unconscious, they'd probably transported us to their hometown of Ekaterinburg. In Russia.

The shock of waking up strapped to a bed was wearing off. Fear and panic had taken over. I yanked and pulled on my restraints. My heart raced. Sweat trickled down my back. At any moment, I would have to face Vladimir. *Will he hurt me?* If he was still angry with me, he would, or he'd have Boris do it. What would that monster do?

Screw whispering. "Kiki!"

Where was she? Did they kill her to keep her quiet?

"Kiki! Wake up! Kiki!"

I gasped for air. This was real. My best friend and I had been kidnapped by the Russian mafia.

"Help. Help me!"

Heavy footsteps pounded toward me. A lock clicked. A door squeaked open.

"No. *Nyet*. Stay away from me. Don't touch me." Unable to see who had entered the room, I thrashed my legs and snapped my teeth, ready to bite a hand or a face or whatever came near me. A male voice I didn't recognize scolded me in Russian, shoved a gag in my mouth, and cranked it tight behind my head.

A cool blade slid in between my left wrist and the straps

that secured my arms to the side rail. With a knife that close to my artery, it would've been in my best interest to relent and stop thrashing, but my survival instincts took over. The second he sliced that hand free, I went after him like a crazed animal, clawing at his face like the keys to my freedom were buried somewhere under his skin.

"*Nyet*, Carter," he chastised me in Russian, adding a *sh* and a *tsk* to compensate for the language barrier. He folded my arm across my chest, cut the strip that secured my other wrist, and dragged me out of the bed. *Head rush.* Unable to see, I couldn't tell if I was upside down or right side up. The guy held onto the base of my ponytail, latched onto my shoulder, and shoved me forward.

With the gag in my mouth, I couldn't catch my breath. I was going to suffocate. Disoriented and weak, I dropped to my knees. He scooped me up and cradled me in his strong arms. As he walked, the rocking motion made me seasick. If I vomited, I would choke to death. I tried to keep my head still. He stopped. A door creaked open. He pushed me down in a chair.

The thought of what the Russians were going to do to me made my stomach churn. I tried to slide down the chair to get away, but the guy grasped my shoulders and held me in place. I heard someone breathing a few feet in front of me and smelled the noxious odor of burning tobacco. The thug unraveled my blindfold, and a rush of bright fluorescent light cut across my face. As my vision came into focus, Boris's black eyes fixated on me from across the barren concrete room.

"Welcome to Russia, *lapsha*."

Boris. Sitting across from me. Vladimir's right-hand man with the power to punish me in every unspeakable way he could think of. I was trapped in a cold, cement cell with the monster who dominated my nightmares. Begging for mercy would only fuel his desire to watch me suffer a slow, agonizing death. My face burned. My body slumped forward. The guy behind me held my shoulders and brought me back to center. My chest heaved. I fought for air.

Boris spoke to my handler in Russian, which prompted him to remove the gag. I gasped and sucked in huge breaths of air in case it was taken from me again. Boris watched me struggle with the calculating eyes of a killer, enjoying my fruitless plight to stay alive. Once air filled my lungs and I caught my breath, I lashed out at my captor.

"Dad will report me missing. Everyone will know it was you."

The guy behind me, who I still hadn't seen, clicked his tongue, shoved the gag back in my mouth, and cranked it behind my head. I whimpered. The tough girl act wasn't fooling anyone, not even me.

"Evidence left at the scene of the crime tells a different story." Boris took a drag off his stogie. A ring of smoke hung above his head like a polluted halo. His lips curled into a sickening smile. "I warned you. I can make anyone disappear."

Through my tears, I caught a glimpse of my handler, a muscly brute around my age with bold green eyes like a panther. He had fresh bruises and scrapes on his milky-white face like he'd been in a fight. He was no doubt one of the low-ranking *patsani* for the Russian mob. A malicious young recruit with a passion to earn his way up the chain of command, willing to commit whatever sins necessary to appease the heartless *Bratva*.

To protest the gag, I pounded my palms on the armrest.

Boris leaned his humongous body back in the chair and scratched his bristly salt and pepper beard. I wished I had taken in more oxygen when I had the chance. I inhaled as much air as I could, but my nose was runny from all the crying. Every time I sucked in, mucus blocked my airway. I tried to tell them I couldn't breathe, but the gag muffled my words.

"You want Dmitri to remove the gag?"

I nodded.

"You will keep your mouth shut?"

I nodded again.

Boris snapped his fingers. The guy, apparently Dmitri, removed the gag. My lips trembled. I sucked in and out like a toddler calming down from a tantrum as the consequences of pissing off the Russian mob raced through my mind. Rape, torture, beatings...*Vladimir is going to make me suffer for my crimes against him.*

I had to focus on surviving and push away the thoughts of the unspeakable acts of terror they would inflict on me. They were holding me in some sort of creepy interrogation room. There was a blinding fluorescent light glowing above a metal table, Boris and I occupied the chairs on either side, and the only other thing in the room, besides buckets of testosterone and an ominous cloud of smoke, was a punching bag hanging from the ceiling in the corner.

As I caught my breath and staved off a panic attack, Boris cocked his head and clicked his fat gold rings on the table. "Better?" Without waiting for my response, he continued. "This can be easy, or this can be hard. How this plays out will be determined by how well you follow the rules."

"Where's Kiki? Why did you take—?"

"Rule number one: No questions," he said. "Do you understand, Carter?"

Dmitri wrapped his hand around the back of my neck and squeezed lightly, a subtle reminder that it was in my best interest to comply with the ruthless gangster sitting across from me. *Message received.* I eked out a nod.

"Rule number two: Do *exactly* as I say."

I nodded.

"Rule number three: Relax. This will all be over soon." Boris's jaw was tense, and he was beyond frustrated with having to deal with me. He served as a hit man for the mob, but when Vladimir wanted to get closer to me, he dragged Boris to America and charged him with tracking and reporting my every move. He followed me around campus, stalked me at the tennis club, and sent his goons to spy on me and keep me out of trouble while I was out with my friends.

The most twisted thing about my history with the Russians was that Boris and I had spent so much time together, we had bonded in an unholy, dysfunctional kind of way. Vladimir was still obsessed with me and had probably given Boris orders to drag me to Russia so he could torture me or turn me into a sex slave or keep me chained down here in this dungeon as some kind of pet or trophy or toy. *I'm never going to fucking relax.* The monster in front of me had no soul. I closed my eyes to make him disappear.

"Open your eyes." Boris slammed his heavy hand on the table between us.

Startled, I did what I was told. Boris stalked around the table and leaned into my face, so close I could smell the tobacco on his breath.

"Remember who you're dealing with, dear. You're in our world now. No papa, no police, no problems." He patted my cheek. "You know better than to fight me. Cooperate, and you'll not be hurt, understand?"

He was lying. *I'm going to die in this dungeon.* My survival skills kicked in when I got a good look at Boris's prison tats, namely the chain that wrapped around his arm like a long blue snake. Each link represented someone's life he had taken. I kept my mouth shut and nodded obediently.

Live to fight another day.

Continue reading Russian Tattoos: Prisoner now

ARE YOU OBSESSED?

A quick review makes a huge difference, and helps readers discover the series. Thank you for your support!

Amazon

Goodreads

BookBub

ACKNOWLEDGMENTS

I am endlessly grateful to my incredible family for supporting me on my writing journey. Thank you to my husband for encouraging me to do what I love and for never doubting my creative vision for this tumultuous love story.

A heavenly shout-out to my mom, Jo. She loved reading my early drafts and thankfully read every final version of the trilogy. Her artistic spirit lives on in this work. She designed the double-headed eagle logo, which makes this story even more meaningful to me.

Thank you to my tennis team, coaches, and club owners for their support and for helping me get the details right. And to my editor, Deborah, and to all of my early readers who helped shape this story.

Finally, I want to send virtual fist bumps and high-fives to every reader who picked up this book. There are millions of stories out there, and I'm truly grateful you chose mine. *Spasibo!*

ABOUT THE AUTHOR

K.M. Shehata's stories explore power, obsession, and relationships shaped by control, desire, and consequence. Known for blending emotional intensity with morally complex characters, she crafts narratives that pull readers in and refuse to let go.

Sign up for the Russian Tattoos Newsletter and be the first to know about new releases, author events, exclusive editions, merchandise, bonus content, and more.

K.M. Shehata's Official Website
https://www.kmshehata.com

ALSO BY K.M. SHEHATA

Russian Tattoos: Obsession

Russian Tattoos: Prisoner

Russian Tattoos: Criminal

Russian Tattoos: The Complete Trilogy

www.ingramcontent.com/pod-product-compliance
Lightning Source LLC
La Vergne TN
LVHW041108080826
845145LV00007B/1735

* 9 7 8 1 9 6 9 6 5 7 0 4 7 *